ROAD TO NOWHERE

ROAD TO NOWHERE

A Nowhere USA Story

NINIE HAMMON

STERLING & STONE

Chapter One

DAWSON MCCADE TRIED to make himself let go of the steering wheel, relax his fingers and take his hands off the thing before he broke it in two.

Breathe.

In.

Out.

Calm down.

But Cade's heart was not just pounding. Or even hammering. It had blown by pounding and hammering, had progressed to humming, a constant sound where you couldn't distinguish individual beats, like a sewing machine at a thousand stitches a minute.

He clenched his jaw, or would have if he weren't already clenching it so tight he was in danger of breaking off a molar or a bicuspid or whatever those teeth were his dentist kept telling him he would wear off to nubs if he didn't stop clenching his jaw.

Cade had *lost three hours.*

Who loses three hours? In what universe does a thing like that happen? Unless you're a drunk in a blackout and he hadn't had so much as a beer since the party on Saturday night — back there when the world was normal and his life wasn't lying in shattered pieces at his feet.

Calm.

Down.

He forced himself to ...

Let.

It.

Go.

To release the steering wheel, breathe, and stop grinding his teeth off to nothing. Most importantly, to think.

He had lost three hours.

He had lost three hours!

Repeating that thought over and over in his head was not helping. Back up.

He had been driving down the highway in the pickup he had stolen ... A burp of inappropriate laughter barked out of his throat. Stolen. Dawson McCade had stolen a pickup. Just like that. All those times his friends told him to stop leaving his keys in his car, that somebody was going to steal it one of these days. This must be some kind of twisted karma.

Focus.

Driving down the winding road on his way to Nower County, Kentucky, he was speeding, trying not to, but so frantic to get there that he couldn't keep his foot from pressing harder and harder on the accelerator. He was risking his life driving the speed he was driving in these mountains. Miss a curve and you'd go flying through the guardrail and off into *nothing at all*, with an abrupt stop at the bottom hundreds of feet below that would definitely leave a mark.

Cade had never been to the mountains. How was that

possible? He had lived his whole life in cities all around them — Cincinnati, Pittsburgh and most recently Louisville and never ventured one time into Eastern Kentucky, to the Cumberland Mountains, a region of superlatives — a place with the most beautiful scenery, the most horrendous poverty and the worst drug addiction problem in the state.

And he'd never been there. That was like those folks who lived their whole lives in Kentucky and never went at least once to the Kentucky Derby. It was surely as important as, and definitely more entertaining than, taking a pilgrimage once in a lifetime to Mecca.

Focus, Cade.

He looked around, really looked, not with his eyes in some jerky jerky motion trying to look at everything at the same time and consequently not actually looking at anything at all. He was parked beside the Beaufort County Jiffy Stop, a little convenience store/gas station. He didn't remember pulling into the lot. Didn't remember anything except driving down the road too fast into the mountains, running for his life.

Now he sat here in a stolen pickup with absolutely no idea how he'd spent the past three hours. How can a thing like that hap— His gaze found the reflection of his vehicle in the dirty glass window of the convenience store and he froze.

No.

No, no, no.

But denying it didn't make it go away, and unless he was losing his eyesight as well as his mind, it was right there for all to see. He gaped in stunned disbelief at the front of the pickup that was mashed in, *wrecked,* had obviously been in a fairly good-sized fender bender.

The pickup had not been wrecked when he stole it.

3

He was absolutely certain. While he couldn't seem to call the events of the last couple of hours to mind, what had happened before that was indelibly etched, carved into his psyche. Would undoubtedly join the parade of other demons that stalked the dark corridors of his nightmares. Ducking down between cars in the parking garage. And then popping his head up every so often like some stupid gopher for a quick look into a window, seeking … oh, please, let there be some other lamebrain besides himself who really did leave his keys dangling in the ignition.

And there it was. The fourth vehicle he looked into, a white Ford pickup that looked like it'd lost a mud fight, probably a '93. Keys in the ignition. He pulled the door open and leapt behind the wheel, started the motor and managed not to hit any other cars in the garage as he drove toward the exit, expecting any second to hear somebody running along behind him, yelling, "Hey, that's my truck. What are you doing in my truck?"

But there had been no pursuit. Well, no pursuit by the poor schmuck who'd lost his wheels because he'd been careless. Cade vowed right then and there if he ever got out of this, he would never leave his keys dangling in the ignition again.

No, he *would*. He would on purpose. If his keys-in-the-ignition idiocy could save somebody's life — literally *save their life*, they were welcome to his car with his blessing. In fact, Cade would leave an envelope in the glove box with a thousand dollars in used tens and twenties, non-sequential serial numbers—

Stop it!

His mind kept jerking away from impossible reality like a finger from a hot stove.

This pickup had a wrecked right front bumper, crumpled fender, broken headlight.

How had the pickup gotten wrecked?

He didn't know how, but a creeping suspicion kept crawling up the back of his neck that he did know *when*. It had happened in the past three hours.

The pickup was fine. And then it wasn't.

Just like he was driving too fast in abject terror at ten o'clock in the morning and now it was one in the afternoon and he had no idea what had become of the time in between.

Maybe he was losing his mind. He wanted to scoff at the suggestion. Losing his mind, yeah, ha-ha. But seriously ... maybe he *was*. His thoughts were ping-ponging around, water spiders flitting from here to there, each one moving so fast that there was no time to catch one of them and hold it still long enough to think it.

Recognizing the phenomena seemed to accelerate the speed of the thoughts, around and around, faster and faster — he had to stop them or the friction would catch his hair on fire. This time, the bleat of laughter actually made it out of his mouth, a bark that sounded more like a cry of pain than an expression of amusement, but it centered him, confirmed that he might be so stressed he couldn't think straight, but if he still had a sense of humor, even a sick one, he was not crazy. Which meant he was capable of figuring out what was going on. And he had to do that or he was toast.

He took in a breath, let it out. A long cleansing breath.

Then another.

Might have done a third but feared he might hyperventilate.

Start at the beginning.

Which beginning?

The beginning beginning?

Because if he let his mind travel all the way there he

might really blow a gasket, fry some synapses and get hauled off giggling and drooling to St. Somebody's Home for the Bewildered. Where he would live ... oh, maybe a couple of days, probably not that long ... until they caught up to him and put a bullet in the back of his head.

How about the beginning of his time as a car thief?

Fine, that.

He had stolen the pickup out of the parking garage on Market Street, between Fifth and Sixth Streets, in downtown Louisville. Where he had taken refuge after he decided somebody had dropped the ball big time, that this operation wasn't as safe as he'd been promised. And maybe he was wrong. But he'd figured he'd rather be dead wrong than just plain dead. So he had bailed. Convinced he was running for his life, he had hauled butt out the door before they even knew he'd left. He'd run down hallways, out into an alley, down the alley to a parking garage and into a pickup belonging to somebody whose initials were JP. The pickup keys were affixed to a chain that had a fob with those initials rendered in three-inch-tall calligraphy. There were also half a dozen other keys on the chain, various shapes and sizes. The guy might have to crawl in a window of his own house tonight, might have to break down the door of his storage building or take a hammer to his toolbox to get it open.

There'd been dirty white stuffed dice dangling from the rearview mirror, though he hadn't even noticed them at first. Hadn't noticed that a hole in the front seat had been patched with duct tape either. He'd just careened onto Market Street and turned north on Fifth, looking back over his shoulder as he passed Vincenzo's Pizza, still expecting the "that's-my-truck" guy to come running after him. West Main took him to the Interstate 64 East onramp and he just kept going.

In the beginning, he'd just been running *from*. But as he drove down the highway toward the white-fenced horse country around Lexington, he morphed into running *to* rather than *from*. Duh. The safe house! It wasn't that the safe house was compromised. At least not that he knew of and if that were the case all bets were off, he might as well put his hands in the air and surrender to the nearest thug with a Spanish accent and a .357 Magnum with a suppressor, a "silencer" — who'd been sent to silence him.

The house was still safe — the marshals hadn't even told Cade where it was! He only knew because he'd overheard a private conversation while he was in a toilet stall, holding his feet up so he couldn't be seen — because he was embarrassed that he'd ignored the sign on the door "For Official Use Only." Hey, when you gotta go, you gotta go. Nobody knew the location of the safe house, not even the FBI. Good Cop Holmes said he had only been told it was "so far off the beaten track the sun only shows up to shine there a couple of days a week." Cade could go there now and call Holmes, or even Bad Cop, Special Agent Jack Armstrong. He could explain why he'd run and suggest that the two of them might want to have a conversation about security with the U.S. Marshals they'd handed him off to — because it sucked. The more he'd thought about it, the more convinced he became that just showing up at the house in a dirty white pickup truck would draw a whole lot less attention from the locals than a convoy of those black unmarked cars everybody could tell were the law.

So he'd headed toward Nower County. Gratefully, he didn't pass a single law enforcement vehicle of any kind, county sheriff or Kentucky State Police, in his entire journey because he would have been convinced on sight that they were looking for the stolen pickup he was driving and would pull him over, refuse to listen to his explanation that, oh by the way, *he* was the victim here, hadn't asked for any of this. They'd haul him in, lock him up, serve him on a platter to El Carnicero, a man who could outsmart the U.S. Marshals Service, so a dim-bulb county sheriff wouldn't likely present much of a challenge.

Maybe. Cade didn't know the "outsmart the U.S. Marshals Service" part *for sure* ... though somewhere deep inside he was absolutely certain.

But he saw no cops. Cruised along, managed to relax a little ... a tiny bit, enough that he wasn't panting and hyperventilating, grinding his incisors off to nubs. He distinctly remembered looking at his watch when he saw the Welcome to Nower County sign on the road ahead.

Even smiled a little at what some enterprising graphic artist had done to the sign. Letters had been inserted — an H after the W and an E on the end of the word, making Nower County NowHerE County.

That was clever.

And after that ...

Yeah, after that ... what?

The next thing he knew he was driving down the highway *toward* Nower County, but hadn't reached the welcome sign yet! And he knew that it was maybe half a mile ahead on the right — even knew that it had red-painted letters on it, though the memories were fuzzy, with no sharp edges, images in a kind of mist. Still, how could he know a thing like that if he had never seen it? And then he'd looked at his watch, and it was one o'clock. Three hours later than it'd been when he checked it ... what? Five minutes ago?

That's when he'd had to pull over, when he realized that three hours had passed between the time he looked at his watch before he went into Nowhere County and right now, as he sat here panting, heart thrumming, grinding his teeth down to the gums, in a convenience store/gas station parking lot — a geographic location that was inside Beaufort County, before you even got to Nowhere County.

Three hours.

Where had three hours gone?

A woman walked out of the garage bay door of the gas station, noticed his pickup sitting there ... really noticed it. Almost like she was a little surprised to see it there. She looked at him. And he at her. For a moment *something* registered in his mind, then was gone in an eye-blink. She looked away, back to the front of the pickup. Not a casual glance. An interested look.

What possible interest could the smashed front end of his stolen pickup be to a total stranger?

Chapter Two

BRIANNA HAGGARTY TURNED from the mechanic using a crowbar and a mallet to pry open the crumpled trunk lid of her car, stepped to the bay door of the garage and there was Dawson McCade on the other side of the building, sitting in the little white pickup that'd smashed into the back of her car — which was why the trunk wouldn't open.

Of course, Cade didn't remember that.

She studied the crushed front bumper and grill on the pickup for a moment, hadn't really looked that closely at it after he'd hit her, and decided his pickup had definitely suffered the you-should-see-the-other-guy share of damage from their chance encounter trying to occupy the same piece of real estate at the same time in the driveway of Roberta Callison's Chicken Farm — Hens, Pullets, Fresh Eggs, Chicks — on Ferguson Road, a couple of miles from the never-thriving, but now completely dead community of Twig.

She looked up at the man behind the wheel of the car and for a brief moment, they made eye contact. He seemed to recognize her ... and surprise blossomed and then wilted when she realized he'd just been wondering why some woman was standing there looking inquisitively at his truck. So she turned away toward the convenience store. She had to go to the bathroom! But the bathroom was all the way in the back of the building and right beside the front door was ...

Fighting the battle, always fighting the battle.

She would never win it, would never achieve more than a tentative truce. At least that's what Sarge had told her, and Margo Adams had been right about every other thing she'd ever told Brianna, so there was no reason to suspect she'd screwed up on this one.

Bri wanted her to be wrong, of course, wanted to believe that it was just a matter of time. Oh, it was okay if it was a long time, Brianna was down with that. However long it took — weeks, months, years, decades — she was fine with any amount. She just wanted to be able to look out there beyond all those tomorrows stacked up one on top of the other and see eventual victory. See a day when it would be over, when she'd won. When she would stand with her boot on the neck of her oppressor and could rest easy for the remainder of her days on earth.

Sarge had shaken her head sadly when Bri had asked her the how-long question: How long will it be before I don't care anymore?

"You'll care when you're dying. You will care with your last breath. With the last thought you ever have on the earth, you will think about it and *want*. Just got to suck it up, buttercup, and keep on keeping on *one day at a time*."

There was no way to get to the bathroom without walking past the liquor display by the door.

Her knees suddenly felt weak. A wave of desire and naked need almost staggered her.

How was she supposed to withstand an onslaught like this in the face of the total insanity that had replaced the real world she was living in? She wasn't the only person on the planet fighting moment-by-moment battles with addiction. There must be thousands, hundreds of thousands, no — millions of others just like her. But Brianna Haggarty would bet Aunt Tillie's corset that not a single one of those fine folks was fighting in a world gone mad. Their battles were in normal reality. She, on the other hand — was fighting for survival in an ocean of craziness. Bri's world was right-out-of-The-Twilight-Zone nuts. How was she supposed to …?

The mantra kicked in to save her.

She repeated it, the calming words that were all that kept her sane, sober and alive.

I have to build a chicken house, one simple chicken house.

If she built a chicken house, she would survive. If she didn't, she would die. If she built a chicken house, she could save a beautiful little girl with bright green eyes. If she didn't, that little girl would be sucked into dark oblivion. Pretty simple equation when you got right down to it.

That was all that mattered. She didn't give a rip that the whole world had gone wonky, didn't care. That wouldn't stop her. She would let nothing stop her. The natural laws of the universe could all turn upside down, wrong side out, stand on a street corner whistling Dixie out their left nostrils and Brianna Haggarty would ignore it. She would do what she had to do *no matter what.*

And right now what she had to do was pee.

She felt her hands clenching into fists and the pressure on the bandage on the two fingers of her right hand shot a dagger of pain up her arm. *That* got her attention. That was sobering. Ten stitches, five on each finger just below the first joint, to close the slice across them. That was slowing her down. But she would persevere, one step at a time.

Right now, those steps led through the front door of the convenience store, holding her breath, hurrying in that way of women who need to go to the bathroom, a body language cue other women intuitively picked up on, so the woman at the cash register just nodded — *I get it* — when she hurried past and slammed the little white door closed behind her.

Getting back out of the store would be trickier, but the mechanic helped in that regard, was waiting just outside the doors for her as she stepped out into the beautiful June sunlight.

"Got her open, but it's all bent and the latch ain't gonna hold it shut."

"So you duct taped it?

"All I could do. It'll hold till you can get it to the dealership. Brand new car like that, the thing's still under warranty, ain't it?"

Brianna had no idea.

"Sure is. So what do I owe you?"

When she'd inquired earlier how much he would charge to get her crumpled trunk lid open, he merely shook his head, spit tobacco juice on the floor, and intoned solemnly, "Well, it'll run ya …"

She hadn't heard that phrase in twenty years.

Now, he was more specific.

"I figger ten'll cover it."

She reached into her purse to get her wallet, all hand motions made difficult by the bandaged fingers.

"Hurt yourself, did ya?"

"Hand saw — a sharp one."

He gave an empathetic cringe. "Ouch."

She opened her wallet, fished out the ten-dollar bill,

and as she handed it to him, she noticed two things, one right after the other.

Thing one was that Dawson McCade — *my friends call me Cade*, to which she'd called him Dawson, a grumpy response occasioned by the fact that he had just smashed into the back of her car — was no longer sitting in his pickup truck parked next to the convenience store. He had left. She knew where he was going, too, although he didn't. Knew what was going to happen to him when he got there, too, though he didn't have a clue about that, either. She sighed, and that's when she noticed the second thing.

Thing two was the front page of the *Lexington Herald Leader* in the newspaper rack by the front door of the store. There was a picture of a man's face on the front page above the fold, security footage of the owner of a liquor store as he looked into the eyes of the gunmen about to shoot him. Brianna didn't recognize the *man*, but she did recognize the *look*. His features were twisted with a combination of shock, surprise, denial and terror. She'd seen that same look earlier today — just a flash of it and then it was gone, and at the time she told herself she'd just imagined it. She hadn't. The look on the face of the man moments from death on the front page of the newspaper was the same look she'd seen on Dawson McCade's face when she'd asked him why he had come to Nowhere County.

Chapter Three

CADE WATCHED the woman turn away from her examination of the front of his car and go into the convenience store. He was just being paranoid, right? She wasn't really interested in his particular truck for some sinister reason having to do with the people who wanted to see him dead. She'd just been standing there and her eye wandered to his crumpled bumper.

And then to him, where she'd made eye contact.

He knew her.

Except he didn't.

For that brief moment of eye contact, he had recognized ... what?

Nothing.

He slumped back against the seat and had to fight an urge to burst into tears.

This was not happening. Absolutely was not happening, couldn't be. When he finally woke up from this nightmare, sweating in tangled sheets, he would marvel at how totally realistic it had seemed.

Except he wouldn't. It was real. He really was on the

run for his life and until … oh, say fifteen minutes ago, *that* had been his biggest problem. Not too shabby as far as life problems went.

Now it seemed his biggest problem was finding three lost hours out of his day.

He banged his palm against the steering wheel. This was already hard enough, the whole people-are-trying-to-kill-me thing was already enough of a load to carry without some other kind of craziness edging it off center stage.

Though right now, he wasn't sure where he ought to shine the spotlight. The lost hours. The crashed car. Or the woman he'd never met who seemed familiar, the one who was looking at the crashed front of his pickup like this wasn't the first time she'd seen it.

The mechanic had gone back into the garage, the woman into the store. A car pulled up in front of the store and the man who got out looked like a parody of a hillbilly, like maybe he'd dressed as a hillbilly for a Halloween party. But it was authentic, of course. A filthy wife-beater tee shirt under equally filthy overalls, that had only one shoulder strap fastened, the other one ended in frayed fabric. He was missing what Cade's dentist would consider to be key teeth in front, an observation made even more disgusting by the fact that their absence was pretty much concealed by the wad of brown tobacco that swelled out the side of his jaw. A John Deere cap that had surely been handed down father to son for generations. Work boots covered in mud. Behind him trailed a skinny blonde girl whose face had been taken over by acne to the point it was painful to look at her. She was wearing jeans, plastic flip-flops and a tee shirt with the picture of a country western singer Cade couldn't place.

The woman glanced his way, then seemed to pause, to really look at him.

Okay, this was certifiable. This level of paranoia really *was* crazy. Even if she knew him from somewhere — even if she'd been his prom date in high school — he wasn't on the run from the whole world, wasn't trying to hide from all of humanity. Just from one human, and in truth he wasn't a human at all. Being afraid somebody would see him, recognize him, and would somehow be magically connected to Juan Renaldo Santiago, would call the guy up and give him map coordinates where to find Cade — *that* was textbook paranoia.

But his skin still crawled.

Reaching out with a hand he was surprised to see wasn't shaking, he turned the key in the ignition, backed out of the parking space and headed back to the highway. He had no idea why he'd stopped there in the first place. He had been on his way to Nower County — *Nowhere County, why did he know that?* — and he wouldn't get there sitting in a parking lot, contemplating the conundrums in his life.

First things first. Get to the Butterfields' house. Call the FBI — he could trust *them* — from there.

Then ... then he could figure out how the trip had managed to take three hours longer than it should have.

He saw the welcome sign ... just where he knew it would be, around the sharp turn after the spot on the mountain where there'd been a small rockslide. Past where the river ran along the roadside. The sign where somebody had added letters to make Nower County into Nowhere County. The red paint of the added letters had run in drips off the bottom of the sign.

Just like it had looked the last time he saw it.

Which had actually been the *first* time he had seen it,

making this viewing the second time. He had all those thoughts one on top of the other as he blew by the sign. And as soon as he did, his mind was mugged, assaulted by images and memories and understanding — *he got it!* It was so staggering that the shock of it made him dizzy. And nauseous.

He barely managed to pull over to the side of the road and get his door open before he lost the remains of the cup of coffee and a McDonald's sausage egg McMuffin, hold the cheese, on the side of the road. He heaved and gagged, the retching coming from some deep place inside him. It was both a physical and psychological response. Physical in that it seemed like his stomach was trying to evacuate its contents with a force and determination he'd never before experienced. The term projectile vomiting had clarity now. And psychologically, because what his mind had experienced in the past thirty seconds or so was so shocking, stunning and disorienting, it would have made a stronger man than Dawson McCade lose his cookies.

He heaved and heaved long after there was anything to deposit on the roadside grass, then fell backward into the seat gasping, tears running down his cheeks. He had never, *never* been that sick in his whole life! That's when he spotted a car drive past the Welcome to Nowhere County sign, the Pontiac Grand Am that'd been at the garage a few minutes before, where the mechanic had been working to get the trunk open. Of course, now Cade knew what'd happened to the trunk. *He* had happened to the trunk, just as the Pontiac's trunk had happened to the front of his pickup truck. He remembered it now, all of it. The memories had downloaded into his mind like a load of coal tumbling down a chute.

But why now?

No, that was not the essential question. The real issue

wasn't why *now* but why *at all?* The real question wasn't about the remembering. It was about forgetting it in the first place. He had been in a wreck, had run into the back of the Grand Am in front of him, what ... half an hour ago.

Why had he forgotten all about it? And about everything else that had come before it?

And then he remembered the last thing the woman had said to him — when he made the suggestion that he would call Triple A for her from the nearest phone. She'd said, "No, you won't." She'd seemed so sure. And she'd been right.

The car continued down the road, blew past his pickup parked on the side of the road, didn't even slow down. And he realized he couldn't let her leave. She obviously knew what was going on here, or at least more than he did. He hurriedly closed the door on the stink from the pile of vomit he'd deposited next to it, and took off after the Pontiac. He caught up to her about half a mile away, pulled up behind her, flicked his lights and honked his horn. She couldn't have missed him, but apparently intended to ignore him at first. Then, she must have thought better of it, pulled over to the shoulder of the road and stopped. He got out of his car and walked to hers. She rolled down her window, then just looked at him.

He must have looked exceedingly miserable and confused because what seemed to be a compassionate smile washed over her face.

"Deja vu all over again, huh," she said.

He couldn't have agreed more.

Chapter Four

As Cade drove along the winding mountain roads, following the Grand Am with a bashed-in trunk, he marveled at the wealth of memories that had downloaded into his mind in an instant. It was all clear now. It was crazier than a nuclear waste dump rat, but it was clear. He remembered it all, from the moment he first set "tire" in Nowhere County — *the first time.*

Cade is beginning to think he's taken the wrong road, that he's been too freaked out to watch where he's going, took a wrong turn somewhere, will never find Nower County at this rate, will have to backtrack, maybe go all the way back to Interstate 75 South—

Then he rounds a corner and sees the sign. Welcome to Nower County. He smiles then. U.S. Marshal Henry Shaffer, the one with the port wine-colored birthmark on half his face, had talked about that.

"Actually says 'Welcome to Nowhere *County.'" Shaffer had turned on the water in the sink then and Cade missed some of the next*

part. "... teenagers or somebody with a sense of humor added letters, an H after the W, and an E on the end of the word, making the word Nower into Nowhere."

He blows by the sign, trying to call to mind every detail he'd over-heard of the conversation between Shaffer and U.S. Marshal Phil Webster, the one who looked like an accountant, actually had a pocket protector.

"We'll come in on County Road 268 from Lexington — enjoy the road — it's the only good one in the county. It comes to a stop sign in the middle of nowhere."

"Funny."

"Not making a funny. True fact."

"The Middle of Nowhere is a place?"

"Yep."

Maybe Shaffer had raised his hand in a Boy Scout salute at that point because he said, "Scout's honor." Cade couldn't see a whole lot between the stall door and the jamb.

"It's actually the intersection of the two main roads and it's supposed to be the geographic center of the county."

"Ah ...the Middle of Nowhere."

"There's a little strip mall at the crossroads, a veterinary clinic, a Dollar General Store and a bus shelter, but I doubt a bus has stopped there since the Cuban Missile Crisis."

Who dates things from the Cuban Missile Crisis?

"Somebody put up a sign, though — not hand-lettered, a real sign — on the light pole: 'Middle of Nowhere.'"

"And the safe house is there because the middle of nowhere sounded like a good place to hide?"

"When you get there, you'll see why it's a good place to hide."

Then he'd described the charming names of the roads leading to the house. Cade is sure he remembers them. Five minutes after he turns off the main road, he discovers there are no road signs!

Okay, that's not accurate, there are some road signs. In the space *of half an hour, Cade sees three of them. Two of the three are so riddled with bullet holes they are unreadable. The third is only half a sign, but it's enough for him to figure out that he is on Something Stump Road, and there was nothing about a stump road in the directions he overheard so he turns off it the first chance he gets.*

After that, all bets are off.

Within minutes, he is hopelessly lost.

Apparently, the people who live here don't need signs to tell them where they're going and if the stories he'd heard about the Eastern Kentucky mountains were true, they wanted nothing to do with outsiders. Taking down all the road signs is a good way to deter the incursion of strangers, but he can tell the signs were the victims of vandalism, not intent and purpose. They'd been put up, and then vandals either stole them off the poles or shot at them as they passed by. After that, the locals never bothered to replace them.

Now what?

And so he wanders.

The roads wind and twist around through the steep valleys created by towering green mountains, wandering aimlessly, in no hurry to take anybody anywhere. Some small part of him notes that this is, indeed, one of the most beautiful places he's ever seen — lush mountains offering majestic views of valleys, meadows with colorful wildflowers, sparkling streams — and wildlife. Deer. He sees two of them in the space of half a mile. But the beauty is blighted by buildings more shack than house, trailer houses affixed to the mountainsides by black satellite-dish stickpins, yards bestrewn with dead appliances, cars up on concrete blocks and the accumulated flotsam and jetsam of generations in poverty.

He quickly becomes desperate enough that he would stop and ask for directions — even if a hillbilly with a shotgun threatens him with bodily harm. But he sees no one. The yards with broken tricycles and Big Wheels and tire swings on frayed ropes offer no children playing. There are no grownups on the porches. In fact, he realizes he hasn't even passed a pickup since he drove into the county.

The marshals were right. This is a perfect place to hide — as yet, not a single living soul knows he's here. But he will never find his little — what was it Webster called it? — a little hidey hole — if he can't find somebody to ask directions.

Half an hour passes. Forty-five minutes. An hour. An hour and a half. He's fighting a losing battle with the panic rising in his chest, but then he rounds a corner and the road he's traveling dead-ends into another road. Like a real road, with white stripes and everything. And at the stop sign — there's a stop sign! — there is also a sign that lets him know he's been driving on Gallagher Station Road. Which means this for-real road must be Route 15. And that means the road he's looking for, Little Knob Road, is just ahead and he's to turn right on it and follow it to the first left turn, which is Big Knob Road — that's why he'd remembered it, big knob and little knob. He'd remembered Gallagher because he'd loved the bald comedian who smashed watermelons with a sledgehammer and Route 15 because his first love in high school had lived on Route 15.

"Their names are Butterfield, Maude and Hurl," Marshal Shaffer had said.

"Who names their baby boy Hurl?"

"Mama Butterfield, apparently. They're good people, not the sharpest knives in the drawer, but it's only for a few days."

A few days. Thirteen, to be exact. Cade has counted. And re-counted. That's how long it is until he gets his life back. They'll bring him back to Louisville from the safe house on Wednesday night for the hearing the next morning. Today is Thursday, June 9, 1995. The hearing will be held in the federal courthouse in Louisville bright and early on Thursday, June 22.

The hearing.

He doesn't want to spoil the semi-joy of finding the right road by thinking about the hearing.

And there's the house! The first one on the right, name's on the mailbox.

He pulls into the driveway, gets out and crosses the kinda-sorta grass lawn to the sidewalk and up the steps to the porch. He knocks on the screen door. Silence. Knocks again. More silence. He opens the screen to knock on the door behind it and when he does he sees that the door is ajar.

He calls through the crack. "Mrs. Butterfield ... is anybody home?"

Silence. The kind of silence that indicates there is, indeed, nobody home. An empty, hollow kind of silence. He opens the door then, steps halfway in, opens his mouth to call out again, but then stops.

The doorway opens directly into the living room. And the room is empty. Not just no people. No nothing. No furniture, no rugs — bone empty. He feels a chill then. For all his self-congratulation, he has obviously come to the wrong ...

No, the name on the mailbox said Butterfield. He's in the right place. Though, of course, he can't be. Calling out "hello" as he walks, he makes a circuit of the house and his gut ties in such a knot it's hard to breathe. The rest of the house is as empty as the front room. No beds, no tables, no chairs. No clothes in the closets, food in the pantry, dishes in the cabinets.

Nobody lives here.

And when they left, they did a really good job of cleaning up after themselves. There's not so much as a gum wrapper on the floor to indicate anybody ever lived here.

His heart is hammering in his chest now so hard, he's having trouble controlling the trembling in his hands. Going out to the building that sits at the end of the driveway, he opens the unlocked door and enters the garage. No vehicle. There's a door on the right. It opens on stairs that lead to a two-bedroom apartment where he's sure he and marshals Birthmark and Pocket Protector were supposed to stay tonight. The apartment is nothing but bare floor and walls. Not a stick of furniture. Not even a rug on the floor.

Cade goes back to his pickup — not his pickup, the pickup he stole that belongs to somebody whose initials are J.P. — and gets behind the wheel. And sits there, wondering what to do. As he sits, he considers that he hasn't seen anybody since he drove past the *Nower/Nowhere County* sign. *Nobody in a driveway or on a tractor, or in a field, or driving down the road. No little kids playing in a yard. Nobody at all.*

At some point in the next half hour or so, Cade loses it. He makes it through four neighbors' houses — random houses, he just pulls up in the driveway and goes to the door. He knocks. He calls out. He intends to ask them if they could tell him, please, where the Butterfields might have gone. Did they see a moving van, because there had to have been a reasonable-sized truck to haul off a whole household — every piece of furniture, every spoon, fork, knife and frying pan, the vacuum cleaner, the toilet bowl brush, the dirty laundry, everything except the pictures and mirrors on the walls. One of those trucks with the little kid drawing on the side that's supposed to be two men and a truck — did they see anything like that? He never gets to ask the question, though. In the first two houses after the Butterfields', the doors are unlocked and he just walks right in. In the third house the front door is locked but the kitchen door isn't.

There is absolutely nothing in any of the three houses. It looks like the whole house had been cleaned out so it could be repainted — and none of the houses he goes in are the kinds of places anybody would waste a coat of paint on — then the furniture was never moved back in.

He loses track after a while of how many places he stops. He no longer knocks politely. He just leaves his pickup in the driveway with the engine running and the door open, and runs across the yard and barges right in.

Nothing.

Nothing.

Nothing.

He can't find a single live human being anywhere. He can't find the slightest indication that anybody was ever inside the houses he searches.

Everyone has vanished.

Then he pulls off the road at a sign advertising Roberta Calli-son's Chicken Farm. Bushes obscure the driveway and he's going too fast to stop when he sees the car that's parked there. It's a Pontiac Grand Am and he plows into the back of it. The driver is a woman named Brianna Haggarty.

Chapter Five

"Tell me, Ms. Haggarty," intoned her I.I.O., Internal Interrogation Officer, "if your grandfather was a falling-down drunk, and your father was a falling-down drunk, and your brother — the one and only time you ever saw him — was a falling-down drunk, why didn't it occur to you, oh by the way, that might be you'd ought to stick to ginger ale?"

"Because I'm an idiot," she always replied, "a gold-plated, fourteen-carat-or-whatever-is-the-purest-form-of-gold idiot."

And that was true, but that wasn't all of it. Maybe not even the biggest part of it. Ever since she got sober she has been coming around to the belief that it had been in the back of her head the first time she ever knocked back a shot of bourbon — Maker's Mark, in a bottle with a red wax seal, Kentucky's finest. She suspected she had walked quietly into that good night, had not uttered a single peep against the dying of the light, precisely *because* she knew what the end looked like. And she had sentenced herself to that end, knew its ugliness was exactly what she deserved.

She'd been trying to shake free of such thoughts, but they dogged her like hounds on the scent of a coon, whenever she allowed herself to be in close proximity to any kind of alcoholic beverage. All she could do was grit her teeth and bear it.

Go on, she told her I.I.O, *take your best shot. That booze isn't even visible in my rearview mirror and it's getting farther and farther behind me every second, so shaming isn't a viable tactic right now.*

The gas station/convenience store might be getting farther and farther behind, but the county line of Nowhere County, Kentucky, was looming on the horizon and she gritted her teeth at that prospect, too.

Gritting her teeth was getting to be her go-to coping mechanism. But she wasn't the only one. She'd noticed that Dawson McCade had been doing the same thing when he'd "bumped into her" in the chicken farm driveway. He was a teeth grinder as well.

TGA. Teeth Grinders Anonymous.

Not funny.

There was a time when she'd seen it as a blessing, but the older she got the more she realized that it was a curse to be such a keen observer of humanity. In grade school, she'd thought everybody'd noticed how Danny Holliday had looked, that crease between his eyebrows and the pallor of his skin — a clear "get out of my way" sign if she'd ever seen one and she'd stepped back quick. Didn't even get any on her shoes when he upchucked the lunchtime hot dogs all over the floor of the school bus.

In high school, she sailed right past most of the trauma and drama of teenage-dom. It was all smoke and mirrors — who couldn't see that? Carla Jean didn't give a rip about Willie Cunningham. You could tell by the way she looked at him, how she cringed just a little bit when he put his arm around her shoulders. She was just using him to make

Matt Bayless jealous. How hard was that to figure out? Obviously, harder than she'd thought at the time.

It wasn't like she was clairvoyant or anything like that, for heaven's sake. But for some reason, she didn't just look at the people around her, she *saw* them. Most people didn't, but she couldn't help herself. And when you saw, you ... well, *saw*. Saw that people were hurting even though they smile, smile, smiled. That her roommate's boyfriend was angry — he was easy, a fellow sufferer in need of TGA — even though he told Shelly he believed she'd been faithful. He was angry, and he'd get violent. But by that time she had long since given up warning people when she saw things like that that seemed so obvious to her. People rarely listened. And even when they did, her observation, or advice or warning rarely made any difference in the eventual outcome.

She'd watched Cade grinding his teeth as he babbled out his story to her, sandwiched between "I'm-sorry's," and "I didn't see you's" and "I'll bet that trunk can be fixed's" as they stood beside the two dented vehicles in the driveway.

Nobody's there!

Everybody's gone!

The houses are empty!

She just let him babble, he needed to vent. It wasn't like he was telling her anything she didn't already know.

Then she'd asked him a simple question, just making conversation. "Why'd you come to Nowhere County?"

And that look had washed across his face. The look she'd seen a little while ago on the face of the soon-to-be-dead liquor store owner. The all-inclusive surprise/shock/terror look. Real. Genuine. A look that bared his soul, however briefly, and Dawson McCade's was a tormented soul.

29

She knew she'd find him parked by the side of the road as soon as she crossed the county line. He'd be sick. Maybe not horribly sick. It was only his first time. Usually took several trips before it got really bad. Or so she'd heard. Gratefully, she hadn't had any up-close-and-personal experiences with Away-From-Heres crossing over.

She smiled just a little. Away-From-Heres. People who were not born in Nowhere County were from Away From Here, weren't they? So that's what locals called them. It was all coming back to her. Every day that she spent in Kentucky, here, *home*, she settled more into the person she had once been. No, not the person she'd been. She wasn't that, not that, not anymore. She couldn't be that. But the *kind* of person she'd been — a type, a Southerner to the bone, a hillbilly by birth who didn't even realize she spoke with such a profound accent until she'd tried to get rid of it.

But she'd heard the others describe it that day in the Waffle House — the day she'd gone back to her motel room and had a come-to-Jesus discussion with her reflection in the mirror. And the others had not painted a pretty picture.

THE ROOM SMELLS of bacon and coffee and maple syrup, and a half dozen other good-food smells Brianna would have recognized if she were paying attention. She isn't, of course. She's almost forgotten what hunger feels like and she didn't come in here to eat. She had come in here to sit down with people around, so she wouldn't do something stupid like start bawling or screaming, or fall down on the floor and kick her feet and have a tantrum like a four-year-old.

She is close.

Oh, so terribly, perilously close.

She picks up the cup of black coffee off the saucer with both hands because the trembling on one side of the cup cancels out the trembling on the other side and the coffee doesn't splash so bad.

It's a Waffle House with the interior arranged in typical Waffle House arrangement. There's a bar where single patrons can sit on stools. Down from the bar are the small four-person booths, two-on-two across from each other, separated from the bar by a partition. She'd have sat down in one of those, so she could have leaned against the back of the booth, except polite signs asked guests to "Please reserve booths for two or more patrons."

Behind the row of stools where she sits is an open area with tables, currently occupied by a couple of families with loud-mouthed kids who are creating a general din of background noise that blocks out all the sounds except those close by.

"Sure you don't want something to eat, honey?" the gum-smacking waitress asks her. In typical alcoholic paranoia, Bri assumes the woman knows that Brianna is hanging on by her fingernails, why, goodness knows she's seen more than her share of those pass through her Waffle House over the years, hasn't she, and none of them ever wanted to eat though all of them looked like they hadn't had a meal a week.

"Sure," Bri lies. "How about an order of toast." When she reads the look on the waitress's face as, "That's all?" she adds, " With lots of butter and jelly."

"Jelly, jam or preserves?"

"Jelly."

Please go away. Go wait on somebody else and leave me alone to think. I have to think.

"We got peach, blackberry, raspberry, strawberry and cherry."

"Peach."

"Sure you wouldn't rather have apple butter?"

"Apple butter, then. I love apple butter."

The other waitress is hollering through the opening between the counter and the kitchen that she needs "three over-easy, hash browns scattered, smothered and covered and wheat toast." The gum-smacker goes to the window to turn in Brianna's order, leaving her blessedly alone. At least as alone as it is possible to be perched on the last stool next to double rows of occupied booths on the other side of the partition.

And in that heartbeat of silence, the gruff voice of the man seated in the booth with his back to her is as clear as if he'd spoken into her ear.

"They said they'd do something, said they'd send in the National Guard or—"

"But they never," the man next to him finishes for him. "Just filled out they forms, looking all sympathetic and such, then they—"

"Went away and never come back. Same's all them people in Nowhere County, 'cept the law was still up walkin' around and them other people's gone."

Brianna stops breathing.

"The state police was better'n the Beaufort County sheriff," says the man seated on the other side of the booth. "Time I got there, he'd already heared the story umpteen times and didn't hardly let me get my name out 'fore he showed me the door."

"Know a fella named Cotton Jackson?" the man behind her asks.

Cotton Jackson! There couldn't be more than one Cotton Jackson. Mr. Jackson had been Brianna's math teacher in high school, had put her and Jolene Rutherford in detention for talking. His wife, Thelma, taught ... history, maybe? Brianna hadn't been in her class.

"I musta showed up at the state police post in Richmond five minutes after Cotton left, 'cause they were still laughing about it when I walked up to the desk, carrying on about how this crazy old man'd said everybody in the whole county had vanished."

"Thought it was right funny, didn't they."

Brianna would have gotten down off her stool and stepped over to the table, would have introduced herself, told them she'd overheard their conversation, and said she had her own story just like it to tell. She probably would have recognized some of them and they might have recognized her.

She'd have done that ... except her knees feel like bags of water and she's certain if she tries to stand up on them they will collapse out from under her and dump her on the Waffle House floor.

"Truman Pettigrew got throwed in jail is what I heard," says the first man. She had seen him when she sat down at the bar and didn't know him. He was a big bear of a man with a flat brow and a lone black eyebrow extending over both eyes.

"So'd Barney Caswell."

"Barney's brother, Roger, did, too — the way I heard it."

"I come this close to getting jailed my own self."

And Brianna thinks in fervent agreement, So did I!

She remembers the angry words, the dismissive tone: "Ms. Haggarty, if you come back in here one more time with some hare-brained story about missing people, I'm gonna have to lock you up." And if she gets locked up, all is lost.

"Do they think them folks from Wisconsin they hauled off in ambulances was just making stuff up?"

His voice has risen, banked anger behind it, but the other men calm him down.

"Ain't nothing for it right now but to suck it up, Harry. It can't last forever. And eventually they's gonna be enough stink raised over it that something'll get done."

"Kicking up dirt don't 'complish nothin' but getting your own butt in a crack."

"The law can't help it that they forget. All the away-from-heres do. And what if the law did keep coming back like they promise they will? They'd get just as sick as them Wisconsin folks."

"How many times you think they come back?"

Nobody seems to know.

"I got a friend knows the EMT who was on the ambulance that took the man — name of Benjamin, I b'lieve. I'm thinking his daddy musta been Sarah Throckmorton's oldest. Accordin' to the EMT, him and his wife both was half dead — unconscious, bleeding out they ears and noses."

Sarah Throckmorton! The crazy cat woman. She lived on Elkhorn Road, or used to, had had a whole bunch of children, like six or seven, and then started taking in stray cats. Everybody knew Sarah, a sweet little old lady, white hair in a bun and granny glasses perched on her nose — she'd always reminded Brianna of Tweety Bird's grandmother.

"They mighta been looking for they granny when they showed up the first time, but by the end of it they couldn't a'told you Sarah's name. Got into some kinda loop, they did — that's what happens to all them people. They leave. They forget they was ever here, so they … I guess they minds reset, go back to whatever they last remember — that they'd purposed to go to Nowhere County."

"That's the difference t'ween them and the law — doncha think? The law didn't never want to go there in the first place, not their own selves, just got talked into it by somebody who told them a story they didn't b'lieve nohow."

"Sarah's kin wanted to, come all the way from Wisconsin, so they's determined! The last thing they remembered was they was on such and such a road going into Nowhere County, so they went back to that road and tried again."

"And again, and again—"

The waitress comes with her order of toast. Brianna looks at it like she doesn't know what it is, can tell the waitress picked up on the look. Soon as the woman's back is turned, Brianna slips the two slices of bread down into her purse so the woman won't know she didn't eat them.

The men keep talking. Brianna keeps listening. They argue about the freak storm that had blown through Nowhere County on Friday night. It'd been so queer, out of nowhere, not a cloud in the sky, then a wind strong enough to rip trees right outta the ground.

"That's what caused the Jabberwock," one man says.

"The Jabberwock? What — you named it, like it was a new puppy!" *The voice is incredulous.*

"I didn't do no such a thing. That's what Shep Clayton called it, said that was its name."

"Shep Clayton's wife disappeared and he went nuts. You can't b'lieve nothin' he says. This here ain't no live thing. It's some 'gubmint' experiment gone wrong and they's trying to hush it up."

No, it was caused by sunspots.

A meteor.

Swamp gas.

"Whatever it was killed off the dinosaurs, that's what happened to the people in Nowhere County," says a voice speaking for the first time. It's Milt Greenleaf, whose wife Wilma is the dispatcher at the sheriff's department. He's had throat cancer, speaks through an artificial voice box.

After a while, something inside Brianna settles. Discovering you're not crazy does wonders for your equilibrium. She'd have shared her story with them, but knows she will break down into sobbing if she tries. Besides, hearing her story would not be as life-altering for them as hearing their stories has been for her.

She pays for her meal. Leaves a ten-dollar tip, which is more than the check, but it's the smallest bill she has and she can't negotiate any more interactions with people right now. Even something as simple as "you got change for a ten?" seems like much, much more than she can bear.

She exits out the door beside the restrooms, doesn't want to walk past the men in the booth, is sure she'll recognize one of them or they her. Her motel is way out on the interstate, and she has no memory of driving there. She only knows when she closes the motel room door behind her, she slides down it to the floor and lets herself cry.

She cries for hours.

Chapter Six

BY THE TIME Brianna got to Baxter Trace, the road that lead to her grandmother's house in a meadow on the mountainside — with the little white Ford riding her tail like a baby possum — she had stopped kicking herself for stopping. What was she supposed to do? It wasn't like the man was going to give up if she ignored his honking and light flashing. Not like he'd just say, oh, never mind, I didn't really need to talk to you all that bad anyway.

The man would have followed her to the ends of the earth. She'd have to give him what he wanted — which was an explanation. An explanation he wouldn't remember a word of the instant he crossed the Nowhere County line.

And then he'd be back. Maybe. Who knew? Maybe again and again.

And he'd get sick and—

She was sorry about that, she really was. But there was nothing she could do.

You couldn't save every puppy in the pound. And even if you could, it might not be a bad plan to start with the one that had rammed into the back of your car.

She would do what she could do, offer the little bit of help she could offer. It was the kind thing to do, and in the twelfth step she had promised to "practice these principles in all her affairs." Her help would do zero good in the end, but she was not responsible for the result, only for her own effort.

Granny Haggarty's house was snuggled in the far end of Freeman Hollow, on the east slope of Shagbark Mountain, which was in Beaufort County. A single ridge of the mountain edged into Nowhere County, though. If Granny'd lived another half mile west, she'd have been waiting on her porch when Brianna drove up the driveway, wouldn't have fallen victim to the mass vanishing that stopped at the Nowhere County line.

As Brianna drove the winding road through the trees up the mountainside, she allowed the memories and their associated emotions to roll over her. How many times had she come up this road — in the springtime with the smell of honeysuckle in the air, the summer with the buzz of cicadas, autumn with the impossibly staggering beauty of color, and winter ... when she didn't come up it at all and neither did anybody else because it wasn't a route on which state road crews wasted a snowplow. She slowed automatically on the hairpin turn that opened onto Antler Creek bridge, where a broken guardrail was all that stood between her car and a ninety-foot drop to the rain-swollen creek below.

How had she not noticed all the things she noticed now, the green of the spruce, the tall pines with carpets of needles pebbled with fragrant cones beneath, miles and miles of them, and then the picturesque sight of her grandmother's small house set at the end of the wrap-around driveway? Not a shack, as so many were. Or a trailer house! Grampa had been a veteran and state meat inspector with a pension, Granny drew federal disability, so she had more of an income than the average mountain person dependent on basic *gubmint* welfare checks for support. The house was painted white every spring until her grandmother was so old she had to hire somebody to do it. Then it became every other spring, but that was enough. There was the semblance of a yard. Once there had been grass and a stone walkway up to the front porch, with its obligatory duet of rocking chairs and a porch swing to sing its equally obligatory eech-eech in harmony with the sounds of crickets and tree frogs in the evenings.

Here was the essence of taking a thing for granted. She'd lived here with her grandmother after her mother ran off with whoever it was she'd run off with and her father started drinking, lost his job and the house and eventually— What was it Sarge said? *Booze takes everything you have and then it kills you.* True that. When she pulled around the last bend, her granny's house came into view and the stab of longing punctured her heart. Though Granny was the very essence of crotchety and cantankerous, Brianna had envisioned long talks with the old woman, sitting on the porch, tasting her grandmother's legendary lemon meringue pie and hearing her sing off-key hymns in the thick mountain dialect Brianna'd been so desperate to shed when she left.

None of that happened, of course.

She pulled up to the motorhome that she had parked behind the house, in what had once been Granny's back yard. There wasn't an over-abundance of flat land available to fit in such a behemoth vehicle — the drive out front, the back yard — because in the remainder of the area beside the house was where she intended to build the chicken house.

Dawson McCade pulled his limping white Ford up

beside hers, got out, and looked at the motorhome, which was a 1994 Fleetwood Bounder, thirty-two-foot Class A motorhome.

He let out a low whistle.

"Now that's a motorhome!"

"Had to have somewhere to live," she said and headed toward the door. "Come on in and I'll make coffee and we can talk."

"Coffee's fine, but given the circumstances, what I could really use is a drink — one strong enough to dissolve the swizzle stick!"

"You want booze, you're in the wrong place! You can get right back in that pickup and drive out of Nowhere County to the convenience store where you were parked before. I happen to know they've got a big display right by the front door."

He held up his hands in a "don't bite my head off" gesture that was massively annoying. Like somebody telling you to "calm down" when you're upset. As if words and gestures like that weren't pouring gasoline on a bonfire.

"Coffee's fine," he said meekly.

She opened the door and stepped inside, told him to come in and have a seat. She went to the galley kitchen and started making coffee.

Get him coffee, have a conversation he won't remember and tell him to have a nice day.

"What's going on?" He said the words softly from behind her. She turned and faced him. That was as good a place to start as any.

Chapter Seven

CADE HAD BEEN SURPRISED by just about everything about the mountains. He hadn't imagined they were so beautiful, or that the clichés about houses with cars up on concrete blocks and non-functioning appliances in the yard had been true, or that every now and then he'd come upon a house that looked like it'd come right out of a fairy tale. The Butterfields' house hadn't been like that, but one of their neighbors' houses — to which he'd run frantically seeking a single specimen of live humanity — had been. The one that came into view after he'd snaked up the mountainside behind Brianna Haggarty was one.

But the behemoth motorhome parked in the back yard more or less ruined the whole effect.

His thoughts had settled somewhat as he followed the woman with a bashed-in trunk — held shut with a couple of strips of duct tape — along the winding roads leading he had no idea where.

He thought he understood the nature of reality as it now stood. He didn't understand the reality, but there was apparently some logic to it and he was grateful he had "run into" Brianna Haggarty so perhaps she could shine some light on the subject. She was the only person he'd seen in Nower County, and he was rapidly coming to believe that if he hadn't met her, he would have been totally alone here.

As he pulled around behind the tidy little fairytale house, he realized the huge motorhome was even bigger than he'd thought. It was enormous, maybe the largest one he had ever seen. The price tag had set somebody back a small fortune.

So how had whoever lived in the little house, that he was sure was as empty as the Cowardly Lion's chest cavity right now, scraped together the money to purchase it? And why?

Brianna offered him coffee, snapped at him when he offered lame humor in exchange. Now, he stood in the incredible interior of an expensive motorhome parked on a mountainside and wanted nothing else in life as much as he wanted to understand what was going on. Okay, he wanted to live until Christmas more, but survival was the only thing that nudged understanding out of first place.

She unhooked something on the wall, and a table dropped down in front of the small couch where he sat. She set a cup of coffee on the table.

"Cream?" She indicated packets in a little bowl. "Well, cream-*er*?"

"A little milk, if you have it. Don't go to any trouble. No sugar."

She stepped to the refrigerator, got out a plastic quart bottle of milk and set it on the table, then sat down opposite him with her own cup.

"So tell me your story," she said.

He'd been anticipating the question and had concocted one as he drove.

"I came here from Louisville to visit some friends, the Butterfields, who live on Big Knob Road. And when I got to their house ... you know what I found — nothing. I started looking for people, and that's when I bumped into you in a driveway — but we already had this part of the conversation ... I mean, we did, didn't we?"

She was giving him an appraising look that was unnerving.

"We did. That's what really happened, even if for a few hours this afternoon, you didn't remember it. That really did happen."

"So you remember it, too?" He hated the desperation he could hear in his own voice. "And we talked—"

"You said you were sorry for slamming into the back of my car. And when I said I wasn't interested in calling the police, you were all over *that*, and there was a ton more damage done to your truck than the dent in the trunk of my car."

"Like I told you at the time, I didn't want the points on my driver's license. And insurance rates for both of us would have ... I was glad you wanted to just walk away, call it even."

He remembered it all now, in vivid detail. How he'd unloaded on her about the ... craziness. How could everybody be gone? And she hadn't been surprised, told him she knew that, but didn't know any more about it than he did.

At the time, he had been so freaked by the disappearing he hadn't been thinking straight. Was in pure fight-or-flight mode and he'd picked door number two. He was scared of ... what was going on here? And he'd panicked, pure and simple. Just like he'd gone running away from Louisville in terror, he'd turned tail and run away from what he'd seen at the Butterfields' house and the other houses he went to. It was the most incredible thing he had ever experienced in his life and all he wanted was to get away from it.

At least, it had been at the time. But that was before he left, forgot he'd been here, came back and remembered it all again. Among all those impossibilities, he had no idea anymore which one was the most incredible.

All he did know was that he couldn't just bail out of here in mad flight a second time until he understood what was happening.

"You just wanted to leave, get out of here. But you did politely tell me you'd call Triple A for me as soon as you could get to a phone. "

"And you said, 'No, you won't.' You knew I wouldn't remember, didn't you?"

"I knew."

"Why didn't you tell me?"

"Would you have believed me?"

She had him there.

"Yes, I knew you'd forget and I knew you'd come back — would *probably* come back — if you had a really good reason to come here in the first place."

"You knew I'd remember it all as soon as … as what? Why did I suddenly remember …"

"The county line. That seems to be the bugaboo, the trigger. When you cross it leaving, you forget about being here. And when you cross it coming back, you remember everything. And you're sick."

He remembered being sick, oh so unutterably sick.

"So what is it? What's going on? Is this some … what, government experiment? Or … or?

"Alien invasion? Trap door into the Twilight Zone?"

"Well, is it?"

"Maybe the trap door into the Twilight Zone part. I don't know." She let out a breath in a long sigh. "Okay, here's what I know. And it's all I know. I'm not an expert ... I just came here, same as you, to visit my grandmother. She wasn't here, neither was anybody else. I freaked out just like you did."

"Then why didn't you ... report it? Call the police ... something?"

"I did. So did a lot of other people, a whole lot of other people."

"Then why didn't the police do something?"

She lost patience then.

"Why? You *know* why — because whenever somebody came to investigate the mass-vanishing, they saw that it was real, true, everybody really was gone. So the investigators leapt on their horses and rode madly off to get reinforcements ... crossed the county line and forgot everything they'd seen here."

Cade was so staggered, he didn't know how to think.

"But ...?" That was all he had.

Then she told him the story of her own efforts to report the phenomena, about what had happened to other people who also tried to report it. And about what happened to people who kept trying — who kept coming back again and again.

Then he slammed into it.

"Wait a minute. You left and you remembered. You reported it. Other people left and they remembered and they reported it. Why—?"

"I think it's about being born here, being a native. You saw it yourself — everybody in Nowhere County is gone, vanished, I don't know where. But other people who are *from* Nowhere County, like me, people who were somewhere else when ... whatever happened happened — we don't forget. Only outsiders lose their memories when they leave."

"But why would being born here——?"

"I don't know! I'm only telling you what I do know, what I've seen and heard. I don't know any of this for sure. It's not like the Jabberwock left a set of operating instructions."

"Jabberwock? Like the poem?"

"I heard some guys at Waffle House ... a fellow who lives in Poorfolk Hollow, his name's Shepherd Clayton, he said that's its name."

Cade shook his head, repeated the words "Shepherd Clayton says that's its name" like a zombie.

"Shep's older brother, Davey Ray, and I went to high school together."

Like that should authenticate everything Shepherd Clayton said? This couldn't be happening, absolutely could *not* be happening.

"... so the Jabberwock is ...?"

"Whatever it is that made everybody vanish. Or took everybody. The 'it' that makes outsiders forget. Makes their memories ... *vanish*. See a common thread here?"

"So you're telling me that if I go out there and get in my truck" — he flinched a little at the *my truck* part — "get in and drive away, I'll forget I was ever here?"

"You don't have to take my word for it. I'm not trying to jam some explanation down your throat. I'm just telling you what I have seen, one beggar telling another beggar where to find bread. What you decide to do with the information is none of my concern."

She paused, and added, "But from what I have heard, what I know about it, every time you try to leave and come back, you get sicker. They had to haul some people off in an ambulance. Didn't even know their names."

"So every outsider who comes here is *trapped* here? If

they leave, they can't help coming back over and over again until … what? They die?"

He couldn't keep the demanding tone out of his voice and he could tell it was definitely rubbing the woman the wrong way.

"I told you I don't know! I am not the repository of all information about the mysterious vanishing phenomena. But the 'compelled-to-return' part — it seems like that only happens if you wanted to come here really bad in the first place. Not like some police officer, investigating a story he doesn't believe. But I'm no expert."

She paused.

"Maybe you haven't noticed, but Nowhere County, Kentucky isn't exactly a tour bus destination. I bet there aren't half a dozen outsiders come here in a month. I got here Sunday — five days ago — and you're the first one I've seen. I don't have any idea what happened to other people like you. I've heard about a couple of them, but the rest … Maybe they gave up, changed their minds … were too sick to come back, had massive brain hemorrhages and died, or remembered enough that they … I flat out don't know."

He was sure the look on his face was totally blank. Just like his mind.

"This is just a suggestion, but before you drive out of here, write yourself a letter. Tell yourself that you don't really need to visit the Butterfields, that it's not that important, that you had a bad experience there … *something.* Just be convincing enough to talk yourself out of trying to come back. Whatever your reason for wanting to visit the Butterfields, it can't be important enough to risk your life over."

Chapter Eight

BRIANNA SET HER COFFEE DOWN. She was done. She'd been the Good Samaritan and all that, now she had other things to do besides hold this man's hand.

It struck her then that she didn't like him. He was cocky, arrogant and smooth, and if there was anything that made Brianna's skin crawl it was smooth.

And he was a terrible liar. She knew the Butterfields — well, at least had seen them around, talked to them maybe a time or two. And Brianna was here to report that Maude and Hurl Butterfield were the last people on the planet a man like this would have walked across the street, let alone drive all the way from Louisville — there were Jefferson County plates on the pickup — to visit. And if he had come for the weekend, well, he was planning on washing out his underwear in the sink every night because there was no suitcase in that truck.

He was as phony as a three-dollar bill. What was a man like him doing in a mud-splattered pickup truck with a duct-taped front seat? Seriously? Once she got a good look at him, she could see that the Italian shoes he was wearing cost more than what he was driving. He had manicured fingernails. His hair was "styled," not just cut.

She'd been rubbing elbows with the likes of Dawson McCade for more than a decade. He had the air of confidence that only a large bank account granted. A large bank account and the hour-in-the-gym-every-day fitness that kept his belly flat and his suit-coats just a little tight in the shoulders.

And handsome — good looks never hurt anybody. Brown hair, cut so the widow's peak was prominent, warm brown eyes in a tiny web of smile wrinkles, and the kind of smile afforded only by those with a lifetime of good dental care.

Regardless of what he said, two things about him were undeniable. He had money. And he was scared spit-less. Beneath the facade was a frightened man. She could practically smell the fear.

She didn't know what his story was and didn't care.

"I'll get you a pen and some paper," she said, got up and put her cup in the sink. It was as clear a how-about-you-leave-now gesture as she could have given him, but he didn't get up, looked at her uncomprehending. She pulled a notepad and a pen out of a drawer and set it in front of him on the table.

"Write yourself a letter, try to keep yourself from going back and forth across the county line until your mind's oatmeal."

When he made no effort to pick up the pen and paper, she shrugged.

"If you think you'll remember this time, I hope you're right. I hope you recall every detail you saw here, and have the good judgement to stay out of Nowhere County for a while.

"A while."

"You know, until … I don't know." She leaned back against the sink. "I don't have any idea what this is all about, but I can't imagine that it's *permanent*. I mean … can you? Some freak *something* … storm, sunspot, E.T.'s buddies — something caused it to happen and I think eventually it's going to 'un-happen.' Reset. And I bet when it does, the outsiders who show up trying to figure out what on earth happened will be so thick you couldn't stir them with a jon boat paddle." She made eye contact. "But until then, I would strongly advise against reporting what you saw here to the 'authorities'— if you remember, that is. You won't get anywhere except in trouble."

Still, he just sat.

Well, it looked like she was going to have to be rude.

"I don't mean to give you the bum's rush or anything, but I'm not ordinarily the most hospitable bird in the flock and I've just about run out of cordial small talk. I have work to do."

"Work?"

"Yeah, I have a … construction project." She looked at the bandage around her cut fingers and winced. "And it's going to be a whole lot harder now than it was twenty-four hours ago."

"Construction project?"

"Is there an echo in here? Yes, a construction project. That's why I came here."

"I thought you came to visit your grandmother."

"I did. I'm building something for her."

"Why?"

Because if I do, I will survive.

Now, she was annoyed.

"What do you care why? You slammed into my car at Roberta Callison's Chicken Farm. I'd gone there to get a look at theirs." She gestured to the pile of books on the

49

floor. "I'm sure it's easier to build a widget when you've seen one recently."

She stood, waited. Let the silence get uncomfortable.

Some of his facade broke.

"I don't get it. You seem to be totally okay with all this. A whole county full of people — how many? How many people live here?"

She shrugged. "It's a nowhere place. I don't think anybody knows ... or cares."

"Let's say two thousand — a thousand, whatever — all those people vanish in a puff of smoke and you don't appear to care. Oh, everybody's gone, and oh, by the way, outsiders who see the vanishing phenomena forget all about it when they leave ... have a nice day. Why aren't you upset about it?

"I *was* upset. I got over it."

AT SOME POINT she got up off the floor in front of the motel room door and sat down on the bed. She doesn't remember doing it. She only knows that her nose is either running — she hopes that's it — or bleeding down her lip and her diaphragm aches from sobbing.

Waves of emotions flow over her like sitting on the beach and the tide's coming in. Different emotions.

Anger — she had enough problems in her life, thank you very much, even before some kind of ... of ... supernatural thingy screwed up her world. Not now! Go away!

Fear — is she crazy? Did the alcohol kill off too many brain cells and now she is a nutcase? Now, she's imagining ... an absurdity. A ridiculously impossible reality.

Despair — she is totally going to lose it over this. Even a normal person would crawl down into the bottom of a tequila bottle and cuddle up with the worm if they went home ... home ... and found everybody gone. Missing. She won't be able to hold it together now. It's over.

She lifts up the corner of the bedspread and uses it to wipe off her face, grateful it's not blood on her upper lip. She should call her sponsor. That's what alkies do when they're teetering on the brink of the abyss. They call their sponsors to talk them off the ledge.

"Hello, Sarge, it's me, Brianna, and I'm about thirty seconds away from drinking a whole bottle of Maker's Mark in one swallow because … you see, I went home to do what we talked about, but my grandmother wasn't there. Neither was anybody else. All however-many thousand people in the whole county are missing. Can you help me?"

Of course, Sarge will assume she's already *downed the whole bottle of Maker's Mark in one swallow.*

No one will believe her. She came here to do the most important thing in her life and now she can't because everybody's vanished.

What difference does that make?

She looks up and there's a dresser across from the bed. The person who asked the question is in the mirror there.

"You weren't planning on getting anybody to help you build it, were you?"

"No."

"Then build it anyway."

I'm having a conversation with my reflection in a mirror. It's over.

"But …"

"Repeat after me: 'I have to build a chicken house, one simple chicken house.'"

Brianna stares at her reflection.

"Come on, say it. 'I have to build a chicken house, one simple chicken house.'"

Brianna repeats the mantra and feels stronger. She says it again. And again.

One. Simple. Chicken. House.

. . .

Brianna looked at Cade, felt again a little of her initial sympathy. But not much.

"I have to build a chicken house. One simple chicken house. It's getting late, so if you'll excuse me now, I have work to do."

Chapter Nine

CADE'S MIND was spinning again. Water-spider thoughts pirouetting out of his grasp before he could think them. He had to bite his tongue to keep from arguing with her, trying to convince her that what she was saying couldn't possibly be true, that she was mistaken ...

As if convincing her she was wrong would change the reality of it.

As if arguing her out of her unreasonable, impossible conclusions would make it all not so.

As if getting her to admit that what the two of them had seen with their own eyes was not, after all, the way the world was — would change the world.

She was as much a victim of the — what had she called it? The Jabberwock — as he was. But that's as far as the similarity went. She could leave and remember she had been here. He couldn't. She could cross back into Nowhere County and not get hammered by returning memories and vomit up her breakfast. He couldn't.

"I need to think," he stammered. "I have to ..."

"I get it. You're confused and upset — a normal

response to being confronted with the impossible." She picked up the pen and notepad she had put on the table and held them out to him. "Take these out to your truck with you while you think. You might decide you need them."

Clearly, she wanted him gone. He'd worn out his welcome and needed to leave and go—

Yeah, go *where?*

What could he do?

When he'd left here the first time, he'd been running in a panic from the discovery that a whole county full of people had gone poof in a puff of smoke. He hadn't been *thinking*, he'd been responding. Fight or flight and all that. He hadn't had a plan, some destination in mind. He'd just been running, like a little kid who finds the boogeyman in the closet.

He wasn't panicked anymore. Oh, he was still scared, all right. He was laboring under so many different layers of fear now that he could barely stand up under the load. He was more totally freaked out than he had ever been by anything in his life. But he was not panicked. This time, he had to think it through, plan out what—

"... ahem." She cleared her throat and he realized he was just sitting there, staring at the notepad of paper in her hand as if he had never seen one before.

"I ... I can't leave," he stammered, voicing the thoughts as they formed in his mind.

He couldn't leave.

For starters, he had nowhere to go.

He had come here to a safe house to hide for thirteen days until he could testify and get his life back! Say the Butterfields just hadn't been home, or their house burned down — something normal. What would he have done then? Where else could he have gone to hide?

He remembered his headlong flight out of Louisville — he'd stolen a truck, for crying out loud. Where else did he have to go?

"I get it that you don't want to live through seesawing back and forth. I don't blame you." She gestured again with the notepad. "Just do a reeeeeeally good job of convincing yourself that you don't want to be here, that you can't come back."

"No, that's not ... I don't have anywhere else to go."

That was a conversation stopper. She looked at him, too surprised to say anything.

Crossroads. Crisis of faith here. Did he tell her what the deal was, the real deal? Or did he make up some kind of plausible story? If he told her the truth, if she knew that he was hiding from ... no, he had to come up with—

"What do you mean nowhere to go?"

"The Butterfields, they were going to put me up for a couple of weeks. I was counting on that, and I don't have anywhere else to go."

"How about the Motel 6 out on the interstate? Tom Bodette will leave the light on for you."

"I wasn't just ... visiting." Think of something. "I was planning to hide out there."

Exactly the response he figured he'd get. She drew back. He watched all her emotional doors slam shut, could almost hear the banging, windows down, curtains drawn, locked up tight. She would not be sympathetic to the truth.

Come up with a good lie, quick.

"From the bank. Several banks. I'm running from my creditors."

He stumbled, bumbled and kept going.

"I'm a businessman." He drew himself up and tried to look like one, not a simple task with barf stains on his tie. "Got a lot of financial plates spinning at the same time.

Real estate, stocks, bonds ... other endeavors. Particularly, a shopping center complex that I'm financing ... and ... let's just say I had to cook the books to make it all look legitimate."

"Some kind of Ponzi scheme?" The contempt in her voice was thick enough to spread on toast.

"I like to think of it as ... creative financing."

"And they're after you ... as in *chasing* you?"

"Oh, no, nothing that dramatic." He spread his hands out in front of him, palms up. "I just have to stay out of sight until the big closing on June 22. So almost two weeks. If they can't locate me, they can't serve the papers on me. If they can't serve the papers ... The money's not there now, I'd be screwed if I had to cough it up today, but a couple of deals will come through by the twenty-second. There won't be any missing financing then, and all will be well."

"You're hiding from your creditors."

"John D. Rockefeller once stayed on the run from process-servers for months. History, look it up. Things like this happen in business."

He let out a breath. He had to make this fly and he was improvising as he went along.

"I bailed out of a meeting in Louisville. Happened to look out the window and saw them coming. And I jumped into this pickup truck in the parking garage."

"You *stole* the truck?"

"No, no. I didn't steal it. I just ... *borrowed* it." She was backing up and he was scrambling. "I know the owner. He works for me. His name is" — the briefest of pauses — "Jim Bob. Biggerstaff." Where did *Biggerstaff* come from? "I knew he always leaves his keys in the truck so I just ... borrowed it. I was planning to make everything right, planning to come here, call Jim Bob on the phone from the

Butterfields' house. He wouldn't even have missed it by the time he found out I took it. He'll be fine with that. Everything would have worked out except ... I got here and the Butterfields weren't home."

"How ... why the Butterfields?"

Oh, boy. Come on, you're on a roll.

"They're ... the guy I borrowed the truck from, Jim Bob — they're his aunt and uncle."

He was skidding out there toward the bounds of believability so he corrected, hoped he didn't over-correct.

"He ... Jim Bob had a drinking problem." Cade saw her physically flinch. Either she knew somebody who was an alcoholic and that person had screwed her over and she hated all worthless drunks, or she knew somebody with a drinking problem and she felt sorry for him. The "drunk" part would either earn him sympathy or kill the deal. He had to gamble.

"Look, Jim Bob's a good guy. A really good guy. He just had a problem with alcohol. And consequently he had trouble keeping a job. I tried to help. Came and bailed him out of jail a time or two. Let him sleep it off in the basement of the building. Things like that. Even put him in rehab once, paid for it out of my own pocket. That's how I know the Butterfields. They came to visit him one day when I was there." He shrugged, tried to look mildly chagrined. "It was kinda socially awkward — I got trapped with them being grateful and all, and the next thing I knew they were telling me their life stories, where they lived ... directions here." He went bone honest then. "I almost didn't find the place. There are no signs on any of these roads!"

She was still processing. He had no idea where she was going to come down on this. But he'd painted a picture, so he'd go with what he'd drawn.

"Look, I'm not saying I haven't played fast and loose with finances for years. I have made and lost millions. But I'm not a bad man, a bad person." He went palms up. "I don't know how to be anybody else but who I am. And to keep from losing everything I own — *again* — I have to vanish, as in no paper trail. I went bailing out the back door with exactly forty dollars in my wallet and a handful of plastic. If I use the cards, if I buy gasoline, or check into a Motel 6 … that's trackable. I had intended to crawl into a little 'hidey-hole' with the Butterfields and pull the dirt in after me. Then I'd reappear in thirteen days and make all the problems go away."

He stopped, spoke softly.

"Then I got bitten by … what'd you call it? The Jabberwock."

She still didn't say anything.

"I have nowhere to run to if I leave Nowhere County. And apparently, if I even try to leave, I'll keep coming back again and again — because I wanted to come here really, really bad."

He paused. "I need help." Then he went for broke. "And so do you." He gestured at the bandage on her fingers. "How do you plan to build a chicken house when you can't use your right hand?"

Silence. He was running out of steam.

"Either I take a chance on my own eloquence," he gestured at the pen and paper, "bet my life that I'll be able to talk myself out of coming back, or I stay in Nowhere County *somewhere*, camp out in some empty house, figure out a way to survive on wild nuts and berries for two weeks." He paused for a beat. "Or I stay here—"

She drew back.

"I don't mean *here* here!" he said, gesturing at the motorhome. "I mean stay somewhere nearby. You keep me from dying of starvation and I'll help you build your chicken house."

He nodded toward the pile of books that he'd noticed were "construction for dummies" books. "I don't need instructions. I've spent enough time on my construction sites — hotels, strip malls — to know my way around a hammer and nail."

He absolutely could not read her face. She was missing a real career opportunity as a professional gambler.

"I don't know if you have any kind of ticking clock on this project, but I definitely do. I'll guarantee completion by June 21."

She stood there, looking at him.

Chapter Ten

Dawson McCade was a crook! She knew it! She hadn't liked him from the git-go, too slick and shiny and definitely hiding something. She'd seen it in the very beginning — that look on his face, how scared he was. Understandable if you're about to get caught with your hand in the cookie jar.

She hated crooks.

But he'd helped Jim Bob.

That shouldn't matter as much as it did. She knew she had a blind spot. It was just that ... all the times she'd needed somebody to give her a break, cover for her, help her out. Nobody did. She had run into nothing but the ruthless, I'm-in-life-for-what-I-can-get-out-of-it types, people who looked right through you. She hated that look. When some "upright citizen" looked at you in ... less than your ideal state, and didn't even see you at all.

This guy, whatever level of financial slimeball he might be, he'd helped a fellow alkie. He'd been a good guy in that one small way and that ought to count for something.

She absolutely understood how running into a

phenomenon this mind-altering could ruin your whole day. He'd had a plan and *bam*, the impossible happened. She could relate. How did you come up with Plan B, when Plan A had been derailed by thousands of missing people, involuntary amnesia and death-by-puking?

But what should *she* do about? What *could* she do?

She could send him on his merry way — and she was absolutely leaning toward that choice, but for two inescapable realities. One, he could not survive in Nowhere County on his own — without a speck of anything to eat in any pantry between Beaufort and Drayton counties. And two, the "write-yourself-a-letter" advice was nothing but smoke and mirrors. It couldn't possibly work. If he'd desperately wanted to come here, he'd be *back*, would become a continuously cleaning oven, the gift that keeps on giving, in possession of fewer marbles every time she saw him. And if that was the case, then she'd rather be stuck with the guy before he started babbling and drooling.

Like it or not, he did make a point, one she had been trying not to think about ever since she sliced into her fingers. She'd gone to the emergency room at the Beaufort County Hospital to get the wound sewn up, and she'd hated it that her experience at the emergency room proved that all the bad things she'd heard were true. The ER doctor literally shoved drugs at her, powerful Oxycontin, warning that she'd have trouble sleeping when the feeling returned to her fingers if she didn't take them. She couldn't have refused without making a scene, and Brianna Haggarty was all about not making scenes. The doctor was some kind of pusher or in cahoots with one, got garden-variety people with cut fingers hooked on painkillers and then a buddy would crawl out from under a rock somewhere and became their drug dealer. Nice little racket.

Pill-pushing physicians notwithstanding, she still had a

job to do without the use of her right hand. And the truth still in the husk was that even without the injury, the Jabberwock had pretty much screwed her to a tree. She'd *planned* to come home, talk to Granny, plan out with her what kind of a chicken house the old woman would like for her to build. Get her direction ... maybe even her help.

Except there was no Granny to give instructions or help. Brianna was on her own. And building the thing all by herself from a plan in some book would have been hard enough — all right, borderline impossible — even with two functioning hands, eight cooperating fingers and two opposable thumbs.

Well, there was no sense in whining about what wasn't. She needed to concentrate on what was. She had to decide what to do about Mr. Dawson McCade. Though in truth she didn't really have a choice. Getting him to help her while he was still a functioning human being seemed preferable to him showing up on her doorstep in varying degrees of degeneration until he was dead.

And there was that, too.

The man was a crook, dishonest, a royal sleaze-ball ... but last time she checked, none of those "crimes against humanity" carried the death penalty. Wasn't his fault he'd fallen into this, and he didn't deserve to die because he had.

"Fine, you can stay." She hated the look of relief she saw wash over his face. "You'll have to sleep in your truck ... Jim Bob's truck ... tonight. Tomorrow I can go back to the storage building in Beaufort County where this thing was sitting and retrieve some of the camping gear that's also stored there."

She didn't need to explain, but she did. "I ... had more money than good sense and Granny was the only kin I

had, so I ... she'd always said she wanted to travel so I ..."
She let it go. "You can camp out in Granny's house."

"I don't know what to say, how to thank—"

"Don't! I absolutely do *not* want gushy gratitude. I don't
like what I'm doing. If I could figure out any way out of
doing it, I would and you would be out on your can. But
right now ... Just don't ... don't act like this is ... that we're
going to join hands around the campfire and sing
Kumbaya. Now ... just go away. Sit in your pickup. Take a
walk. Baste a duck. Something. Just get out of here."

She turned to a cabinet, opened it and took out a jar of
peanut butter and a loaf of bread. She grabbed a canned
soft drink out of another cabinet, then looked around in
the bowl on the counter for one of those packages of
plastic utensils they give you at Long John Silver's — a
fork, a spoon, a napkin, and a hand wash thingy to get
some of the grease off your fingers. She put them all in a
Kroger sack and handed it to him. "We start to work at
nine — and no, I don't keep banker's hours. The sun
doesn't make it over the top of Bishop Mountain until ten,
but you can see well enough to work by nine."

He was still shell-shocked, of course, just stood looking
at her, so she made brushing motions in the air with her
fingers. "Shooo, out. Go."

He started to say something, thought better of it, and
went down the three steps to the door, opened it and
stepped out.

"Mr. McCade" — she made her voice as cold as she
felt — "this motorhome has the biggest, baddest, meanest,
most expensive anti-theft system known to man. When I
lock the doors, any attempt to unlock—"

He held his hands up, almost in supplication.

"I get it. I may not be your definition of a guy in a
white hat, but I'm not dangerous. I'll ... leave you alone."

And he kept that promise. At least until she started screaming in the middle of the night.

Chapter Eleven

THE MOVEMENT JARS HER AWAKE. Or back to consciousness. She could have been asleep or passed out. It's impossible to tell which at this stage. The world is spinning, and Brianna doesn't know if there really is movement, or if the sensation is just a part of the general spinning of the universe around her that never stops. It never holds still. The street she walks on, the floor she sleeps on, the ground she falls down on, it's always spinning and turning. And it might possibly be true that if it ever stops, if the world ever stands still, she will fall right dead off the edge of it into eternity.

Another jolt accompanied by a sound this time. A grinding noise and then a hydraulic sound, a little like the air brakes on a bus.

She opens her eyes, watches her world spin, and does pause to notice that not only is it spinning, but the individual pieces of it are moving on their own. Tumbling. Falling.

The stench is the reek of decay, of rancid cheese and three-day-old marinara sauce, of bad meat and something else, vomit maybe, all mixed together and served up for her olfactory enjoyment.

Thump!

It's a big sound. A booming sound, like it has come from inside an oil drum.

She's becoming more aware and alert by the moment, trying to figure out where she is. She doesn't bother trying to process how she'd gotten to wherever she is because that's an exercise in following one piece of spaghetti through the whole pile. She concentrates on the simpler question: where is she right now?

What she can see are shafts of light, like streaming through a window with the curtains drawn, except the angle is all wrong for a window. And there is nothing fabric-like about—

Thunk!

And then the whining sound again, the hydraulic sound.

The sound is sinister somehow, in a way Brianna doesn't try to interpret, just goes with the gut knowing of it. Something bad is happening, but she doesn't know what, and doesn't know what it is she ought to do to avoid the bad.

Then she's thrown violently to the side and slams into something metal, dirty stinky metal, and things are falling all around her, pieces of things, trash-like, boxes and pieces of cardboard, disgusting gunk. Suddenly a black garbage bag crashes down on top of her and she figures out where she must be, a place where somebody might toss a trash bag on top of her. Duh. But that doesn't compute with what's happening.

The whole world suddenly turns upside down and she's falling, falling, screaming, falling down into a pile of trash, garbage bags and filth, all of it moving as she's moving, and that grinding sound gets louder and louder.

The hydraulic sound rings out again and she looks up into light, as something is lifted away, like a lid, off the top of—

What is it?

A green dumpster.

But it's upside down, moving away from the square of light above her that begins to close, a door closing, from both sides.

The hydraulic sound again and the grinding.

And then she knows.

Dear holy mother of God, she's in a garbage truck. The back of a garbage truck.

Suddenly, the world begins to squeeze in on her, to get smaller and smaller and she can't move, tries to move, like swimming upward through the bags and trash. She's screaming, shrieking in inarticulate terror because she gets it now. She gets it.

Then a pain unlike anything in the whole of her existence races up her leg to her hip, a pain so horrifyingly intense that it makes her want to vomit. But she's so frightened, the pain recedes as secondary. Blind terror.

Squeezing. She can't breathe.

Help! she cries out at the top of her lungs, but the word seems to hang out there in front of her and go nowhere. Just hangs there.

And the crushing, squeezing gets stronger, more suffocating.

"Help!"

Something bangs into the side of her head. And after that, the person doing the screaming is next to her, and she can see the person screaming, can watch the life being crushed out of that person. But Brianna is no longer that person. She's just an observer. Just watching the garbage truck crush the garbage, crush the woman who is just another piece of garbage. She watches the machine crush the life out of her until all is dark and quiet.

Dark and quiet.

Beep. Beep. Beep.

A sound, a beeping sound.

The sound of the truck, the garbage truck. The backing-up sound.

She screams, "Noooo, get me out, help, help!"

The beeping continues. Ceiling tiles above her. White below. Blurred faces. Elongated words.

"Alllll riiiiiight noooow. Saaaaafe noooow."

But she keeps screaming, until she feels warmth spread out all over her and the world goes dark again.

There is light beyond her closed eyelids but she doesn't open her eyes. She's terrified to open her eyes because she knows she is dead.

Brianna Haggarty is dead and that means she is in hell. Of course, she is in hell. Mothers who kill their own children go to hell.

As soon as she opens her eyes, sees it, sees hell, that's when eternity there starts. That's when the eternity of never, never, never-ending torment begins. She can put it off, a second or two, until somebody in charge figures out she's really awake, just faking sleep. A few seconds.

A precious few.

"Brianna."

It's over. She shudders out the last breath she will ever release on this side of forever. She opens her eyes and what she sees is a man in a white coat. Standing beside ... a bed. She's in a bed. She closes her eyes again, trying to process.

"Brianna, can you hear me? Open your eyes."

"Busted," she mumbles.

"What did you say?"

"Caught me."

"Caught you?"

She is about to explain, but when she opens her eyes then, looks around, really looks around, she has nothing to say. She turns her—

The tiny movement shoots lightning bolts of pain up from her leg into her groin so powerful she can only gasp, wants to scream, but it's too ... hurts too bad to ...

She screams. The warmth again.

Dark.

And then she senses movement. She's somewhere that is dark and smells of filth and that somehow is moving, is lifting, is dropping her and so she screams.

Screams with every ounce of her strength. Screams out the unutterable terror of being crushed alive, the unimaginable pain of that crushing—

BAM, bam, bam, bam!

Brianna sat up in sweat-drenched sheets, a scream on

her lips that she was sure wasn't the first one because her throat was raw.

"Brianna — are you alright in there?"

She scoots up to the head of the bed, gasping, looking around, trying to make the reality of where she is more real than the place in her head where she has been.

Nightmare.

Flashback.

She wasn't sure she knew the difference. She *was* sure that when it was happening, she couldn't tell one from the other and was even more certain that it didn't matter.

"Brianna!"

Oh, goody. She'd awakened the man who was asleep in his pickup truck — correction, somebody else's pickup truck — on the other side of the house.

"What's wrong?" Cade called out and then she heard him try the front door handle.

"Nothing's wrong!" The words come out like a frog croak from her raw throat. "I'm fine. Go away."

"You were screaming like—"

"Like I was having a nightmare. People do that, you know. Have nightmares. It's very entertaining, you should try it sometime. Now, go back to your truck and leave me alone."

She listened. He didn't try the door again and said nothing else, so he must have left.

It wasn't surprising that he'd heard her, even parked out there in front of the house. If previous reports were to be believed, Brianna's screaming during flashbacks would wake the dead. Sarge told her that, after Brianna moved in with Sarge when Bri was released from the hospital.

After the trash compactor crushed Brianna's leg and almost killed her.

After a garbage truck saved her life.

Chapter Twelve

CADE'S HEART was still racing as he walked back around the empty house from the motorhome parked in the back yard. The terror and anguish in those cries — sounded like the woman was being attacked by an ax murderer.

"A nightmare," she'd said, right before she'd demanded that he *leave her alone*.

Message received.

It'd been his life experience that *those* kinds of nightmares were little chunks of some previous reality. Wasn't just a guess on his part. Waking up in sweaty sheets — yeah, been there, done that. Maybe he'd been screaming, too. He'd certainly felt like screaming.

A ticket on the train to a place like that wasn't free. You had to purchase it and it wasn't cheap. Couldn't buy one just anywhere, either. Only available in dark, ugly realms where really bad things happened. Understanding that the woman who'd been shrieking like a banshee had obviously spent considerable time where the wild things are helped explain why she was such a wrapped-tight bi—

Hey, not fair. She had helped. *Clearly* hadn't wanted to

help, but she had. And if it weren't for Brianna Haggarty, where would Cade be now?

He crossed the dark front yard of the empty house to his bedroom for the night — the front seat of a stolen pickup truck. It wasn't like the screaming from the motorhome had awakened him. He hadn't been asleep. As if he was going to get any sleep on the lumpy seat of the truck — not with all the noise that critters out there in the woods were making. In his previous life — he'd come to view it that way — he'd have found the eech-eech of the crickets and the harrumph-harrumph of the tree frogs soothing. Now, it grated on his nerves.

He opened the pickup door and climbed in, stretched out on his back on the seat with his head butting up against the passenger side door and his feet dangling off the seat on the driver's side, where he'd left the door open. Wasn't any way to fit his whole self into the truck with the doors closed.

Dawson McCade was six feet two inches tall. So, not "tall." Tall, he self-defined as anything six feet three inches and above. He was big, though — the definition being any man who wore a size XL shirt, and he needed a 2X because his shoulders were so broad and muscular.

Cade wasn't what he considered "real" muscular. Real muscular was the nomenclature attached to a man who had "earned" his muscles. A lumberjack, a longshoreman. Or any of the dozens of construction workers he'd known over the years. They were built like bulldozers because they worked all day at manual labor. He, on the other hand, had broad shoulders and strong arms courtesy of a personal trainer who knew what he was doing and the dedication of a former athlete — he'd gone through school at a small community college on a football scholarship — to stay "fit."

There was no judgement in any of those definitions, just what he considered a right reading of the nature of the universe. He had been a man comfortable in his own skin. Until he wasn't.

He tried to turn on his side, but then his legs stuck out into nothing, whereas on his back, they bent at the knee. So he flopped onto his back.

An owl hooted in the woods. Must have been calling out in the darkness because there was a response from the woods on the other side of the house. For the critters in the woods, this was just like every other night. I hoot at you. You hoot back. Maybe we get together later for a drink and spend the night hooting together.

This was not like any other night in the life of Dawson McCade. He hadn't had any *normal* nights since an ax had hacked into his life, sliced it top to bottom, cut one half so completely off from the other that the chasm in between was too wide to leap across, and he could see down into it from the edge, could tell it stretched all the way into eternity. Cade was on one side of the chasm. His life was on the other. And with every tick of the clock, he had less hope that he'd ever reclaim what he had lost.

KIDNAPPINGS SOAR IN LATIN AMERICA, Threatening Region's Stability. That was the headline on the story by James Brooke in The New York Times, *April 7, 1985.*

The image of the newspaper swims in front of his face as he tries not to inhale the exhaust fumes leaking into the car trunk. He'd found the newspaper in the seatback pocket when he settled into his first-class seat, had glanced at it, scanned it, picked up a couple of interesting factoids before the stewardess came around to take his drink order.

A kidnapping is reported in Colombia every six hours.

A kidnapping is reported in Rio de Janeiro every four days

Victims' groups estimate that over the last three years, $200 million has been paid in ransoms in Colombia alone.

"Fear of kidnapping has cost the country many economic growth points, thousands of jobs, millions of dollars. Who is going to invest and work to the maximum with such a high risk? It is absurd that one of the consequences of business success is to increase the probability of losing life, freedom, health and family peace. Kidnappings are a sword of Damocles hanging over the heads of all Colombians."

He'd liked that analogy. A sword of Damocles. Clever.

He remembered thinking at the time that it might be the good news that he was the low dog on the totem pole in this venture. Just bringing the offer from Spencer Refineries, a company that did off-shore drilling in the Gulf and operated refineries all over Texas and Louisiana. It was just the first date. Not even a goodnight kiss. Just see if La Luna Corporation had any interest at all in a partnership to build a mega-refinery in Bogota.

Cade should try to kick out the tail lights. Read that somewhere. If you were locked in a car trunk, kick out the lights, make a hole in the back of the car that you can draw attention to. Maybe a police cruiser will pull the car over for no tail lights.

Cade is on his belly, his hands tied with rawhide bands behind his back, his face jammed into the rubber of the spare tire. They are on some bumpy rural road in the guts of Colombia. Probably not a police cruiser within five hundred miles in every direction who would give a fig newton about a car with a busted tail light.

When the car suddenly stops abruptly, he hears staccato voices speaking Spanish so fast his three years of college Spanish classes offer him only a word or two here and there.

The trunk lid flies up, rough hands grab him by his bound arms and haul him out onto the ground and a filthy man with rotted teeth sticks a gun in his belly and tells him in heavily accented English that, "Nobody pay for you, you die."

He knows then that he will die here in this stinking jungle, with *human animals grunting and snarling around him. Nobody's going to pay for the messenger boy. They'd grabbed the wrong guy.*

CADE UNCONSCIOUSLY RUBBED HIS WRISTS, massaging away the remembered pain of rawhide bands cutting into his skin until his hands were slick with blood. He could sleep on this truck seat. He'd seen worse. If the experience in Colombia had granted him anything, it was a bottom-of-the-barrel life experience, against which any other calamity in his life would fall short by comparison.

Why, I can stand fill-in-the-blank. I lived four days in a squat hut in a Colombian jungle, crapping in my pants because they wouldn't let me go to the bathroom. I can survive anything.

Cade tried it now.

I can stand running for my life into the Twilight Zone where the world is turned upside down because I was a hostage … it totally didn't work. How could anything in life prepare you for the unexplainable?

He has come to a place where the entire population has vanished. And if he leaves, he'll forget he was ever here. And, oh by the way, he'll keep trying to come back until he has an aneurism.

Nope.

Nothing in life could prepare for that.

He tried rolling on his side again. Didn't work. It was going to be a long night. And tomorrow, he had to figure out how to build a chicken house.

Chapter Thirteen

THERE WAS nothing in her life for which Brianna was more profoundly grateful that morning than she was for the water in her grandmother's house. It was still on. All the furniture had vanished, along with her grandmother and every other possession. But the fixtures remained. The kitchen cabinets ... the toilet and the shower. Still there and functioning.

Without them, having Dawson McCade hanging around for the next twelve days would have been fraught with way more problems than it already was. She would go this afternoon to the storage building in Beaufort County from which she'd retrieved her grandmother's never-used — it didn't have a hundred miles on the odometer! — motorhome and gather up other equally unused camping equipment. Cade could pitch the tent in her grandmother's living room or wherever he wanted. A cot, a camp stove. Yeah, life would be ever so much less icky when she had those amenities.

He was already sitting on the back porch of Granny's house when she came out of the motorhome, looking a bit the worse for wear. No razor can add a scruffiness to a man's appearance that wasn't altogether unpleasing. But sleeping in your clothes, too ... he just looked rode hard and put up wet, likely hadn't gotten any more sleep than she had.

She started talking as she walked across the yard toward where he sat, carrying a thermos of coffee and a couple of granola bars.

"I've had violent nightmares all my life," she lied as she approached him, grabbing the bull by the horns and bringing up the subject of last night before he had a chance to ask. "Sorry if I got loud and woke you."

He merely grunted an unintelligible response and downed the coffee, and she watched it bring his torpid body back into focus, could see energy return to his face. She drank coffee because she liked the taste but the caffeine had zero rejuvenation effect.

"Why a chicken house," he said as he crunched on the granola bar. "Am I allowed to ask?"

"No, you're not. But I'll tell you anyway. When I was a teenager, I burned hers to the ground."

THE CHICKEN HOUSE smell fills every breath. Chicken crap, feed, dirty feathers and more chicken crap. Light from the cracks between the wall slats falls like the pinstripes on a suit across the nests. The nervous birds fluff their feathers. Brianna closes the spring-held wooden door softly behind her and walks carefully down the center aisle between the nests. As she passes, the birds flutter away from her like The Wave rolling across a stadium.

There's nowhere to sit down, unless she doesn't mind smearing chicken crap all over the back of her jeans, so she settles for leaning against the wooden bin where the chicken feed is stored.

Should have just gone out into the woods, found a place under a tree and sat down in the shade. Yeah, that would probably have been a better idea than hiding here in the chicken house. But the sense of secrecy associated with all things dope, marijuana, *makes plopping down out in the open and smoking a joint under a tree somehow an untenable idea.*

You don't smoke your first joint ever under the spreading bows of an oak tree.

She pulls the fat joint out of her shirt pocket. It's the size of her thumb. The marijuana wasn't exactly prime sensemilia, had a lot of stems in it, and it was hard to make it fit in the cigarette paper. She'd get better at rolling joints with a little practice.

She pulls a pack of matches out of her pocket advertising Saunders Wine and Spirits, strikes one, lights the end of the big-as-your-thumb joint and draws the smoke slowly into her lungs. It is only with the greatest effort, grabbing hold of her diaphragm and keeping it rigid, that she keeps from collapsing in a coughing fit.

Nothing. She feels nothing.

Somehow, she'd thought it would hit her immediately. Joey Pruitt, who sold her the weed, told her she might not feel anything at all, that sometimes people had to smoke two or three joints before they got high. She didn't have enough money to buy that much dope so this one had better do the job.

She draws in another lungful of smoke, holds her breath, listens to the indignant birds scratching around, angered by her intrusion into their domain. She lets out the smoke through her nose and tries to take another drag ... no, toke, another toke on the joint. But it has gone out. Cheap weed. She pulls out the matchbook and lights it again, tossing the match to the floor and stepping on it, wondering how long it will take before she feels any of the glorious sensations she has heard all her friends talk about.

"ON PURPOSE?"

"No, but I did hate chickens. Still do."

He looked at her questioningly.

"I don't like birds, period. Don't like that herky-jerky walk. Did you ever notice that birds only look at you with one eye at a time?" She demonstrated, putting her hand up to her nose to approximate a beak, then turning her head to look at him with one eye and then with the other.

"Never noticed, but you're right."

She turned up her coffee cup and drained it, then gestured to the bare spot that was only barely distinguishable from the weedy yard. "It used to be right there."

"How big?"

"About twenty feet by thirty feet."

"You planning on building one that big?"

"That was the chicken house and the fenced-in chicken yard, the whole thing. The chicken house itself will be on the back side."

"And do you have a plan?"

"More or less. I've been reading up on it." Quoting from *The Chicken Coop: Complete Guide for Beginners*, she said, "The whole point of a chicken house is to give chickens somewhere to sleep at night, a place to get out of the elements, and for the brooding hens to lay eggs."

"Just walls and a roof?"

"Nope, gotta have a floor, too. Without a floor, weasels, coons and foxes will burrow under the fence and enjoy their Sunday dinner on the hoof."

"Does your ..." he stopped and amended, "*did* your grandmother have chickens before the Jabber—" She could tell he didn't like using the word. Neither did she. "Were there chickens here that vanished with her?"

"If there were, they were homeless. I was going to buy her some chickens as soon as there was somewhere to house them." She walked into the yard and began to pace off a space.

"The book I read, the beginners' guide, says that as a general rule, a chicken house should have at least two to three square feet of space per chicken."

Something like a smile skirted the corners of his mouth.

"When I was a kid, I had a book that measured everything in chickens. You know, a giraffe is a hundred chickens tall, or an elephant is a thousand chickens heavy. So what happens if you make it smaller?"

"Apparently, the birds get persnickety. They fight, get stressed out and lose their feathers and most important, they stop laying eggs. There are certain features every chicken house has to have: nest boxes — you can use kitty litter boxes for those and I think I know where I can lay hands on some — roosts, walls, a floor and ceiling."

"And a chicken roost is ..."

"Anything. The book said it needed to be at least six inches off the ground, a flat surface where they can settle in for the night. A piece of plywood will do."

She stepped back and put her hands on her hips, recalling for him what she had seen in the books she'd read.

"We are *not* going for fancy. This book had pictures of coops that looked like a ski lodge in the Swiss Alps. One was a miniature house, painted yellow with the door frames and trim hot pink. One had this cutie sign: 'Chick Inn,' and another had a sign by the door: 'last one in's a rotten egg.'"

He did smile then and so did she.

"Show me the materials you have and your tools."

As soon as they started to work, it became clear that Brianna would be totally useless for anything more taxing than holding a board while he nailed it. Her cut fingers made it impossible for her to hold a hammer.

"You could buy a nail gun," he suggested. "Hold it with your left hand, brace it with your right."

When she left to go to Beaufort County mid-afternoon, the nail gun was on her list of necessary supplies. She'd get that at Home Depot, and stop by Walmart for the basics of human existence for her guest — clothing, from the skin out. *Work* shoes that didn't cost more than the gross national product of some Third World countries, toiletries, and a haul of groceries she hadn't thought she'd need.

She'd rented a Home Depot truck for the afternoon to haul the building supplies she'd already purchased — lumber, nails, tools, chicken wire — that lay beside the designated chicken house spot.

"It'd have been easier to haul the camping gear in the pickup truck," she said as she went around to the back of her Grand Am and began to loosen the duct tape holding her damaged trunk lid closed. Then she saw his stricken look. "I'm not serious. Your 'stolen truck's' no problem in Nowhere County — nobody here to see it, and nobody to report it to if they did." She began to peel up the tape. "Wouldn't take it across the county line, though. It's just that there's not a whole lot of room in a car trunk."

A haunted look washed across his face and he spoke softly.

"Nope, there's not much room at all in a car trunk."

Chapter Fourteen

AFTER BRIANNA WENT to a storage facility in a neighboring county and returned with camping gear, Cade was able to set up camp inside Bri's grandmother's house, opening a cot, unrolling a sleeping bag and blowing up the air mattress. Bri was more or less "camped" in the motorhome, too, since without hookups she'd had to rig up water from a hose and electricity through a big orange extension cord to the house. He had no idea how she planned to dump out sewage when the time came.

Cade's shoulders ached from working all day but it was a good ache. They'd decided to start with the chicken pen, the fenced-in area where the chickens could wander around and peck at whatever it was chickens pecked at. They constructed the fence in sections, laid out on the ground, made of two-by-fours formed into a square with an X of boards for support in the center. The first one was the hardest, and none of them was easy given that Brianna wasn't a whole lot of help except to hold boards while he nailed them together.

They completed two of the five panels. When all five

were complete, they would stand them upright and affix them to each other with metal brackets. Once they had three sides up, the structure would stand on its own and they'd string chicken wire around the outside. After that came the hard part — building the chicken house and the chicken runs up into it that formed the fourth side of the enclosure.

Cade built a bonfire in the front yard beside his pickup truck, with sticks, tree branches and leftover lumber, and when it got dark, Bri came out of the motorhome out back. They sat together then, Cade on the top step leaning against the railing post, Bri in the porch swing, engaging in that most ancient of communal human entertainment — looking into the flames of a fire.

Trying to make conversation with Brianna Haggarty was akin to walking through a mine field blindfolded. She clearly didn't want to have anything to do with him. Some of that was whatever baggage she was carrying, and the more time Cade spent with her, the more convinced he became that she couldn't have fit her personal baggage in the cargo hold of an ocean liner. But there was also the delicate subject of his crook-ness. He was a con man, a liar, a cheat, not somebody anyone would be interested in getting chummy with. And he had to keep up that persona, be careful what he said that might blow his cover. So they sat in silence, looking into the dancing flames.

Without appearing to, Cade studied her face in the flickering firelight. He hadn't thought so when he first met her, but now he realized she was pretty. Well, sort of pretty. If she'd made any effort to do the magical things women do to their faces, she certainly would have been. She had the right raw materials. Like location, location, location in real estate, beauty started with the basics. Her hair was a tumble of unruly curls that fell into her eyes when she was trying to work. He thought at first her hair was brown, then in the bright sunlight, he realized her curls were ... russet? The color of a chestnut foal, highlights of red and copper. In the firelight now, the highlights of red and copper caught the light and reflected it. Her eyes were hazel, that diaphanous shade of dark green that was a mixture of greens and browns and ... maybe gold. He hadn't done a great deal of looking into her eyes, though. She didn't like to make direct eye contact and always looked immediately away. Her eyes were almond-shaped, with delicate eyebrows that kind of turned upward at the corners. Even without a speck of makeup, you could see her long eyelashes as shadows on her cheeks. He suspected that hers might be one of those faces that is totally transformed by a smile. He wouldn't know that, because he'd never seen her really smile.

He didn't know how old she was, but would bet she was younger than she looked. There was a hard set to her features, a grim downward turn to her mouth, and those weren't facial attributes you were granted at birth. You earned those. Sometimes, she had a kind of puppy-opening-its-eyes-for-the-first-time look, like she had spent a long time in a dark place, and something as simple as a sunny day was a wonder to her.

But her most distinctive feature had nothing to do with her looks. Hers was a memorable voice, reminded him of the movie star, what was her name, the one who played Captain Janeway on *Star Trek: Voyager*? Mulgrew. Kate Mulgrew. The voice was a bit growly, with deep round tones that made him want to suggest she was missing a career opportunity reading audiobooks. But clearly Brianna Haggarty wasn't searching for career opportunities. He'd launched a conversation salvo across her bow earlier in the afternoon when he noticed the flat tire on the back of the motorhome, and came away from the brief encounter with the impression that the woman was not in immediate need of financial assistance — not with a brand new silver Grand Am and a thirty-foot motorhome that appeared to belong to her, too.

Nodding to a jagged piece of what might have been a broken beer bottle jutting out the side of the flat tire on the back of the vehicle, he'd said, "You could lose a finger trying to get that glass out."

"Yeah, it pretty much turned a 'mobile home' into a permanent dwelling at least until ..." They'd quickly established that parameter in their conversations. They didn't talk about the it, the thing, the Jabberwock that had sunk its teeth into Nowhere County.

"Surely, there's a spare." He looked over the vehicle. "Where's the trunk on a motorhome?"

She pointed to a panel on the side behind the door. "Cargo bay. There's a catch on the dashboard that won't operate without the ignition turned on."

"I'm impressed you managed to get this behemoth up here at all."

"I barely did. The mechanic I got to get the thing running after it had sat idle for ... I don't know, a couple of years, I guess, said I needed to drive it out on the road, put at least three hundred-fifty miles on it to 'blow the soot' out of the engine. I drove it the thirty miles between here and the storage building and parked it. So I doubt the engine will start now. Flat tire, dead engine. It's as stuck here as we are."

As he stole glances at her profile now, swinging slowly back and forth, making the porch swing sing out its rhythmic eech-eech melody, he tried to decide if he liked her and decided it wasn't even an askable question. It was like asking himself if he liked a Barbie doll. He sensed there might actually be a lot of *there* there, but she went to great pains to hide it under a bushel basket.

"You miss her?" he asked, to fill the silence that Bri wrapped around herself like a comforter, and that was probably the right word — *comforter*.

"My grandmother? Yeah, well, kinda. She wasn't some fairytale granny who did cross-stitch 'There's No Place Like Home' samplers and baked chocolate chip cookies — though her lemon meringue pie was epic! Granny Haggarty was a coal miner."

"You're kidding."

"*Had been* a coal miner. Not in my memory. When I was a kid, she drew a disability check and I never knew how she got disabled."

He shook his head, trying to make it fit.

"A coal miner ..."

"She was rough as a cob, chased my drunk grandfather around the house threatening to bash in his skull with a frying pan. She allowed that she had totally botched the raising of my father and that's why he'd run off to join the army at seventeen, so when the Department of Child Welfare deposited me at her door at age three after my mother bailed, she shoved me back at the social worker and told her to go find somebody who wanted to raise a kid."

"That's hardcore."

She smiled a little at that with a kind of pride.

"They told her they would, but the child needed some-where to stay until they could find a permanent placement."

With a little shrug, she continued, "I only heard the story from Granny and who knows what she added to or subtracted from it, but she said they just never found a place for me. I think … I like to think… that after a while she didn't want them to anymore."

"I'm still working on the granny-was-a-coal-miner part." He barked out a laugh. "Call my grandmother 'granny' and it'd be the last word you ever spoke. Not mee-maw or mam-maw, or anything else cutsie, either. She was 'Grandmother Sylvia.' She ran her own art gallery."

Bri held out her hands in front of her, palms up, as if she were weighing something. She lifted up one hand. "Art dealer." She lifted the other. "Coal miner." Then she joggled them back and forth again. "They wouldn't likely have had a whole lot to say to each other."

"Oh, I don't know. They might have respected each other, connected on the strength-of-character level."

After a beat of silence, both of them shook their heads at the same time and said in unison "Naaaa," and Brianna almost smiled.

"So how did you find your way from Nowhere County, Kentucky—?"

Brianna froze as solid as a glacier.

"I don't remember agreeing to a game of twenty questions."

The privacy doors that had eased open a crack slammed shut with a clang that was almost audible.

"Oops. Stepped in it."

She turned on him then.

"Look, stop trying to be charming. I'm sure you get a lot of mileage out the smiling good ole boy persona to pry open people's wallets. You don't need to manipulate me. I've already given you what you want — a place to hide. So drop the Mr. Nice Guy routine. Just … don't."

"I'm not trying to con you!" He hadn't meant to sound indignant, or like his feelings were hurt, but he heard both those emotions in his words and wasn't sorry. "I figure we're stuck here, adrift on the same lifeboat, and I don't see anything to be gained by icy silence."

He got up off the porch step and went to the fire, picked up a branch and stirred the burning pieces apart so they'd go out. When he turned around, she was gone.

Chapter Fifteen

THE SPLINTER CADE got in his finger Sunday morning ran deep into the meat of the middle finger on his right hand and up under the fingernail. Brianna noticed him picking at it, and as soon as she got a good look she knew he'd never get it out on his own.

"You should have left it alone," she said, when she held out her hand and demanded to see.

"What, just leave it in there?"

"I didn't say you should leave it in there. But digging around at it is just shoving it deeper. It's going to be even harder to get out now."

"I'll figure it out." He tried to snatch his hand out of hers.

"Don't be ridiculous. A first-aid kit came with the motorhome. There are tweezers in it with little bitty prongs I can use to get hold of the end of the splinter."

"And what if I don't want you to go digging around under my fingernail with a pair of pointy tweezers?"

"Don't make me have to hold you at gunpoint."

She hadn't intended the teasing, bantering tone to creep into her words. She was holding herself as aloof as she possibly could, made only minimal conversation and spent no more time in the man's presence than was absolutely necessary.

But the remark just slipped out, courtesy of their encounter yesterday when she'd hauled out the nail gun she'd purchased. She was proud of herself for selecting a good one, courtesy of the old man in Home Depot in Carlisle who could have built a functioning ocean liner out of popsicle sticks. It was a pneumatic nailer, the Power-Master, brand new off the assembly line this year.

The man had said they'd just gotten their first shipment a little over a week ago and they'd about sold out, that contractors were flocking to get one.

It was lightweight, didn't look nearly as clunky as the others on the shelf, and he'd said it was even more powerful.

"You got to be careful with this, little lady," he'd warned. "These things can fire projectiles fourteen hundred feet per second."

"Is this like a pistol?"

"You can't shoot it like a gun — pull the trigger and a nail flies out the end like a bullet, but it's as dangerous as one."

She'd been unloading it when Cade approached to help carry the supplies.

"I got one," she'd said, pointing it at him.

He had reached out a finger and gently pushed the barrel aside so it wasn't lined up directly with his heart.

"The salesman said you can't shoot a nail gun like a pistol," she'd said in her defense.

"Well, no ... I don't suppose you need a concealed carry permit if you put it in your purse, if that's what you mean. But the term 'nail gun' does imply that it actually shoots nails."

He took it from her, turned it over in his hands like this might not be the first nail gun he'd ever used, then said, "It doesn't have a sequential trigger, does it?"

He had her there. She hadn't asked the sales person enough questions so she had to suffer through Cade's description of the gun's functioning in explain-it-to-a-five-year-old language. She had figured out five minutes after they'd started to work that Cade did know a fair amount about construction — even if his only contact with the trade was "creative financing" to fund it.

"Nail guns come with different types of triggers — full sequential, contact, single sequential and single actuation trigger."

"Okay, I am sufficiently cowed for my lack of knowledge and impressed with yours. Just tell me how to use it."

"This one has a contact-trip trigger. It requires two actions to fire. You have to press the contact tip onto a piece of wood." He walked to a two-by-four lying on the ground and demonstrated by shoving the end of the nailer up tight to the board. "Then you have to pull the trigger."

With the contact tip engaged, he pulled the trigger and a nail fired with a resounding and impressive thump sound into the board. "Carpenters use contact tips to speed up the job. They just pull the trigger in and hold it, then bump the contact tip along the board and everywhere it hits, it puts a nail." He demonstrated again. Bam. Bam. Bam. Three nails in the time it would take her to get a nail in the proper upright position so she could hit with a hammer.

"That's why you have to be careful with this. If you have that trigger pulled, you can *accidentally* bump the tip into something — and it'll put a nail in it … like in your leg."

She came back out of the motorhome with the whole first-aid kit in her hands. It had been affixed with brackets to the wall in the closet that housed the hot water heater and the air conditioning unit.

She gestured for Cade to come and sit beside her on the bottom step of Granny's back porch. Setting the box on the next step up, she fished around in it until she found some cotton balls and alcohol to disinfect the area before she went digging around there.

He flinched backward when she held out her hand for his.

"You sure you know what you're doing?" he asked.

The question rebounded in her head like an echo in an oil drum.

"You sure you know what you're doing?" Jeff whispers, apprehension stamped on his handsome, tanned face. He looks down at the squirming child he's trying to hold still. "Is this going to hurt?"

She loves the concern she hears in his voice, tells herself to pack that away in a special room in her heart to haul out later when she needs it. Not that she expects to need it. They'd worked it out, things are fine now. They're a family. There won't be any more if-he-cared-he'd-be-here emotional rants.

But itchy reality points out that it's only blind chance he's even here today. She struggles to remember the last time they had dinner together, but can't go there, can't allow herself to put together in her head what she has never allowed herself to know — she is pregnant, carrying a child conceived the last time they made love ... *and she is due any day now.*

She also won't let herself know that Jeff won't be there when she goes into labor. Likely won't make the birth, either. He hadn't laid eyes on Winona until she was three days old. But maybe ... there was some degree of permanence to spring training, after all, though it is so grueling Jeff only swings by their beautiful Florida condo every couple of days to pick up clean underwear. There had been a fire last night in the training complex, however. The fire department had contained the blaze before it reached the locker room, but the stink of smoke was choking and there was water everywhere and the coach had actually sent the players home for the day while crews got it aired out and cleaned up.

So Jeff was seated on the deck drinking a glass of peach tea when Pooh took a header off her little push trike in the sunroom and landed in a potted plant. There was a decorative yucca in the pot as well as several small cacti.

Brianna'd almost had a heart attack when his panicked voice called out, "Briiiii, come quick, Pooh Bear's hurt."

"Hurt" consists of several cactus quills in her leg that Brianna needs to remove.

Winona had instantly picked up on her father's dismay, and little performer that she was, she had taken it as permission to throw a full bore fit. Not even two years old, she is already a master at manipulation.

"Hurts Daaaadeeee," she wails as if she is in imminent need of open-leg surgery.

The anguished look on Jeff's face is priceless.

"Jeff, you need to hold her still and ..." she spells it, "S-M-I-L-E." She smiles broadly as if he might not know what the word means. "You're S-C-A-R-I-N-G her."

He drapes a smile between his ears like hanging a sheet on a clothesline and it's all Brianna can do not to burst out laughing.

"It's okay, Pooh Bear." Surely even a two-year-old would pick up on the fake sweetness in his voice. "Daddy won't let anything bad happen to his precious little girl — ever."

"Put her in your lap over here in the sunlight so I can see what I'm doing."

Brianna is so ungainly that bending at the waist will not be an option for another couple of weeks.

Jeff holds the screaming toddler. Her ax-murder screeching is unnerving.

"Winnie, get a grip," she admonishes the child, with some measure of sternness in the tone.

The little girl lifts a tear-slathered face to her, lip trembling. "Can't fine dit," she chokes out through sniffles.

"Can't find what?"

Winnie shakes her head sadly. "I loss my gwip." And that *brings the house down!*

THE IMAGES WARMED HER. Moments in time with no sharp edges on them anywhere. She smiled, treasuring them. There were so very, very few of those.

"Looking forward to causing me excruciating pain, are you?" Cade asked.

The images in her mind still warmed her, hadn't faded away yet.

"I'm thinking amputation above the wrist. They do amazing things with prosthetic limbs these days."

"So you can't just … kiss it and make it well?"

It was probably because she'd relaxed enough for the Pooh Bear memory to surface, and it'd left the door open behind it. The image formed, as it had formed a thousand times. Just the single image, not tied to any memories before or after. It floated there, alone and brilliant, in clear perfection.

THE BABY'S SLEEPING FACE. The soft glow from the nightlight turning his cheeks rosy.

. . .

"His eyelashes were so long they made shadows, little fans on both cheeks, and he had a little bruise right there." She pointed to the space in the middle of her forehead above the bridge of her nose. "Just a little one, looked like it could have been a mark from Ash Wednesday. When I laid him down, I kissed it. Gently. He was sound asleep and I didn't want to wake him up."

The image vanished. She thought she could almost see a little sparkle in the air at its passing, like a soap bubble bursting.

The space that'd been occupied by the baby's face was filled with Dawson McCade's and she realized that she'd spoken her thoughts *out loud,* so she just blurted out ...

"Has your mind ever taken a snapshot, a still frame, one perfect image? You can pull it up and look at it, but it's just that one frame, nothing before or after?"

He merely nodded, no unasked questions, no response of any kind.

She was profoundly grateful for that and relief flooded through her. She focused her attention on his finger and the splinter. She would be careful not to hurt him.

Chapter Sixteen

CADE SET down the hammer and adjusted the Band-Aid that Brianna had put on his finger yesterday when she removed the massive splinter from under his fingernail. That was the first time he'd ever seen her smile, really *smile*, and he'd wanted to set off fireworks, maybe release a thousand colorful balloons, or hire the Mormon Tabernacle Choir to sing the Hallelujah Chorus.

He had exercised what he considered to be extreme good judgement in not asking her anything about the baby she'd thought of and smiled, but he had been *right* — when she smiled, it did transform her face.

But he would forget all about it.

The realization that slammed down on his chest — he wouldn't remember her or anything else about being here — knocked him back into that dark place where he'd been three days ago, so staggered by the reality of the unreal that his mind shied away from even thinking about it.

When he left here, he would not remember that he had ever met Brianna Haggarty. *How could that be?* How could a thing like that happen? Seriously. In the real world, not some stupid soap opera. To ordinary people.

Which reminded him uncomfortably that he'd had that same reaction when he'd learned on a bright sunshiny morning five days ago that he could either drop his life and run ... or die.

That had felt like movie script material, not real life. Not for the Dawson McCades of this world, an ordinary person, a man with a glove box full of parking tickets he kept intending to do something about, who had just signed one of the biggest deals of his life — a totally legitimate, honest business transaction, thank you very much, Brianna Haggarty! A man who was going to have to pay a late fee on the movie everybody was talking about — *Pulp Fiction* — and he hadn't even had a chance to watch the thing.

How did that happen? He didn't know how, but he did know how long it took.

It only took the blink of an eye.

AUDREY SHOWS the two men in suits with high-and-tight haircuts into his office. Law enforcement. Duh. His gut clenches in a sickeningly familiar way. What now? That part is over. Cade does not want to be reminded of that time now, wants to forget the whole thing ever happened, though God knows he has been so, so, sooo lucky.

They kept telling him that as he lay in a Florida hospital bed with a green jungle fungus growing on his foot, his wrists and ankles bandaged from where the ropes had cut into his flesh, and some kind of parasite in his gut that made social interaction a bit awkward because he couldn't get more than ten feet from the nearest bathroom.

He'd been lucky the kidnappers figured out they got the wrong guy three days after they abducted him. He had tried to tell them nobody was going to pay a hundred-thousand-dollar ransom for the dude who carried the briefcase, made sure the pencils were sharpened and all the contract-signing pens were full of ink. Didn't matter what he said, of course. They wouldn't have believed him even if they'd understood English well enough to know what he was saying.

He was lucky one of them did understand, though, lucky the guy was greedy, willing to cut a side deal of his own to sneak Cade into the hands of St. Vincent's Purse, a protestant evangelical group working to free kidnap victims.

He was lucky the whole horrible experience had cost him only four days of his life.

Soooo lucky. God, he's tired of that word!

It isn't true. The price tag on the incident was way higher than a mere four days of living.

It had cost Cade enough to put the kids of his psychotherapist through Harvard just so he could go to sleep at night without nightmares about cringing in a squalid hut in Central America with duct tape across his mouth and an automatic weapon pointed at his temple.

Nightmares of the man with dead eyes wielding a bloody chainsaw.

It had cost him his personal sense of safety — he never got into a car without looking to see who was nearby and might be watching him. He had a security system installed in his house so sophisticated that letting the cat out set it off.

It had cost him Melissa. Though, in truth, he and Melissa were heading for the reef before he'd taken the four-day detour in Colombia. His dysfunction afterward only accelerated the process.

It had cost him his job because for five years he flat-out refused to get on an airplane.

It had cost him the friends that went with the job.

It had cost him the lifestyle that went with the friends that went with the job.

It had very nearly cost him his life when he bottomed out ... before he began to climb slowly back out of the hole and into the light.

Now, he has to grudgingly admit that all the losses actually did, in the final analysis, amount to a net gain. His marriage needed to be over. He needed to become the man that three years of psychotherapy and two years of self-defense courses made him. He needed to lose that job, because it forced him to go into business for himself, and five years later he had a real estate investment firm that provided an income in the high six figures.

But even given how things had turned out, he has no desire to spend any time in the company of federal agents representing a government that had done absolutely zero to get him out of his predicament or to facilitate his return.

"What do you guys want?" That's not what he'd have said a decade ago. He'd have said something polite like, "What can I do for you gentlemen?" But four days in a hut fighting rats for food had pretty much burned the people-pleaser right out of Dawson McCade.

"I'm Special Agent William Holmes, from the Pittsburgh field office of the FBI, and this is Agent Jack Armstrong. May we sit down?"

"No. Forgive me if merely being in your presence makes my skin crawl."

The two men exchange a glance, then the first one opens a manila envelope Cade hadn't noticed he was carrying and withdraws a piece of paper. He places it on Cade's desk and scoots it toward him. It's a photograph.

"Recognize this man?"

"Never saw him before in my life," Cade lies. They can tell he's lying, but he doesn't care.

"His name's Juan Renaldo Santiago and he knows you. He was almost as much a nobody in 1985 as you were. But" — the agent looks around at Cade's impressive office — "his fortunes have improved, too, in the past decade. He made his way to the top of … his organization, and now he's turned his sights on politics. Has his eye on running for president."

"President?" *Cade may have said the word out loud. Or maybe not. He doesn't know.*

"Oh, there's a big field of candidates, but 'El Carnicero' is

particularly adept at eliminating competition," says the second agent, a man with the palest blue eyes Cade has ever seen. "He has to get his own house in order first, though, do some deep cleaning."

Cade says nothing because he has nothing to say and no voice to say it with.

"In the past eighteen months, he has been systematically exterminating anybody and everybody from his former life who might be able to connect him to the drug cartels, wants to distance himself from certain 'unfortunate incidents,'" says the first agent. "It's a big list."

"And your name's on it," says the second.

Cade swallows rapidly, fearing he might actually vomit all over his desk. In seconds, the world of safety and normalcy he has so carefully constructed in the past decade crumbles around him.

The first man is speaking, and a randomly firing synapse makes the connection — if these two guys were interrogating a suspect, the first guy would be Bad Cop, the second, Good Cop. Cade has to focus to silence the sudden ringing in his ears so he can hear what the man is saying.

"Where your name appears on the hit list depends on what you know, what you saw. You can lie to us, give us the monkey's hear-no-evil, see-no-evil, speak-no-evil crap. But we have reason to believe Santiago was in a compound run by National Liberation Army guerrillas in a village called Callista outside Bogota on March 15, 1985. You were there between March 13 and March 17. We know that for a fact."

The man must have caught the look on Cade's face because he held up a placating hand.

"I get it. We knew you'd been kidnapped and we didn't do anything to help. There's a reason for that, not a very good one, I'm afraid, but it wasn't just a random screw-up."

"Save your explanations for somebody who cares."

Dawson McCade had been a card-carrying American citizen and had naively expected all the rights and privileges that status conferred in foreign countries, had expected — laughable now — that the government would go to bat for him. Not! If it hadn't been for St. Vincent's Purse, he'd never have seen the outside of a squalid Colombian jungle hut.

"The U.S. government never even acknowledged the incident happened." Cade ground the words out through clenched teeth. "That's all I mattered — not a live human being, not even an incident."

"As it turns out, that's the only reason you're still breathing."

"You flew under the radar, nothing about you ever made it into 'official channels,'" says Good Cop. "So whatever sources Santiago pays for information didn't have your name to give him."

"He got other names, though. In the past eleven months, an Australian, a Canadian and three American businessmen who were kidnapped in Colombia in March of 1985 have been ... assassinated."

"The last American was Charles Spencer, who at the time was the CEO of Spencer, Inc. Refineries. That's the man Santiago's men thought you were, snatched you by mistake — isn't that right?"

Cade is too numb to speak.

"... and somehow you—"

"St. Vincent's Purse! They were there. They cared. They paid a whopping five hundred American dollars to some underling to sneak me out to them. Spencer, Inc. paid $350,000 for Charles Spencer. I wasn't worth but a buck two ninety-eight."

"We know you were there in that compound, but maybe you had a black hood over your head the whole time, saw nothing. We only know that Santiago is looking for you now, you specifically. So either he's just doing a really thorough housecleaning and wants to squash all the cockroaches — even the little ones hiding under the refrigerator — or he thinks you saw him, can testify that he was there, and ... well, he'd rather you didn't."

Bad Cop says, "I'll ask you again, Mr. McCade. Do you know this man? It's not like you could forget a face like that, though he's had plastic surgery, doesn't scare little kids anymore. If you don't recognize him ... then *we'll tell you to have a nice day and we'll leave. But if you do ...*"

And Cade does. Oh my yes, Cade absolutely does know the man, saw the man, and it occurs to him now that what he saw might really matter.

He finds that his voice is quiet, even though he's trying to speak up. He hates the interest he sees on Good Cop's face when he begins speaking, loathes the look of wonder that begins to form on Bad Cop's face as he tells the story. It doesn't take even a minute to say it, but in the space of those sixty seconds Dawson McCade becomes these federal agents' single most valuable asset.

They'd had no idea the jewel they had in him when they came calling ... not even a week ago! *It wasn't just that Cade could place a Colombian presidential candidate at the scene of the infamous Decimoquinto de Marzo Massacre. He could do much, much more than that. What he saw could actually bring Juan Renaldo Santiago down. Which catapults Dawson McCade from total obscurity to the top rung on their potential witness ladder, and to the top slot on the hit list of a man who had earned his nickname. El Carnicero. The Butcher.*

IN THE SPACE of that sixty seconds, life as Cade had known it ended and a new life of horror began.

Just the blink of an eye.

The impossible *did* happen to real people in the blink of an eye. Something impossible had happened to all the residents of Nowhere County. And would happen to Cade *again* when he crossed the county line on June 21. He'd forget he'd ever been here. He would never know he'd built a chicken house, would forever wonder where he got that scar on his finger where Brianna had pulled out the mother of all splinters, would have no memory of the first smile he had ever seen on the woman's face.

Then he realized there was something very "freeing" about that. Okay, so she didn't like him, was disgusted by his "criminal persona," wanted to have as little to do with him as humanly possible. What difference did all that make if he wasn't going to remember any of it anyway? What if he *did* offend her? What if he royally ticked her off by refusing to play by her ice queen rules and stopped walking on eggshells?

She had left to go looking for kitty litter trays, and when she got back, Cade intended to behave *normally*. He'd relax. He'd treat her like any other acquaintance, someone he made small talk with at a cocktail party or backyard barbecue. He'd be friendly. He'd *smile*.

They still had eight days to stay here together before he left to go to Louisville to testify and he was *done* being the Mute Boy.

When she returned from the Middle of Nowhere, he *did* smile, asked how her search had gone, and didn't care if she bit his head off.

Cade was prepared for whatever she might say. Except what she did say.

"I ran into a couple of real, live Away From Heres in the Dollar General Store parking lot. They were looking for the Butterfields' house, too. How's that for a coincidence?"

But he didn't think she thought it was a coincidence at all.

Chapter Seventeen

FOOL'S ERRAND LIKELY, but if it was, Brianna figured she was the woman for the job. And the Middle of Nowhere was considerably closer than going all the way into Carlisle.

It was a beautiful June day and Brianna rolled down the windows on Cade's "stolen" white pickup truck and smelled the fragrance of mountain air — so clean. She wasn't exactly a world traveler, but with his game schedule of 160 games a season, not counting exhibition, all-star games and playoffs, over the decade she and Jeff were married, she'd put in an appearance in just about every city in the country. Not just the ones with major league franchises, either, since Jeff had been the poster boy for all manner of products from aftershave to insoles; he spent much of his "free time" on Saturday afternoons in shopping mall parking lots across America, signing Jeff Nicholson on baseballs or the sides of kids' sneakers.

And in all those travels, Brianna had never found a place with air that smelled as fresh and pure as her home.

Not even the Rocky Mountains, where John Denver crooned about getting a Rocky Mountain high. The air there was crisp, but cold. Chilled, and the scents were overwhelmingly pine and spruce trees. The Appalachian Mountains in the spring and early summer were a feast for the olfactory nerves. Wildflowers lined the roadsides and grew in tangled abandon in every meadow and valley. Golden Aster, Sky Blue Aster, Bloodroot and Bluebells and frilly Queen Anne's Lace.

Honeysuckle abounded. So did kudzu, but it had no flowers or smell ... just covered up every other plant in sight. There were cedar and pine smells, too, but the hardwood trees had their own "woody smell" that was somehow hardy and invigorating and strong, as befitted the huge oaks, elms, sycamores and hickory trees. Factor in the blooming trees in the springtime — white dogwoods, pink dogwoods, redbud trees and tulip poplars, and in a few places oleander bushes grew wild — bright red, beautiful but deadly — as did pink and purple azaleas, their limbs so heavy with blossoms they bent all the way to the ground.

If Brianna got lucky, this trip would spare her the aggravation of building individual nests for each chicken in the chicken house, at least two, maybe three dozen of them. That would be time-consuming, even with the aid of the nail gun, which Cade had pretty much taken over using. The point of buying it had been to give Brianna something she could operate with her left hand, brace with her right. And she'd tried. She could use it, but was unutterably slow. Cade just put the thing on that automatic mode and bam, bam, bam, slammed nails into the floorboards, nailing them to the beams of the framework as fast as she could set them into place.

She breezed through the Middle of Nowhere intersection — nobody stopped at either of the four stop signs — but still glanced in both directions for oncoming traffic out of habit. The Middle of Nowhere was in a valley and the roads leading there from the four corners of the county were reasonably straight at that point, and you could see down them for a hundred yards.

Pulling into the parking lot conjured images of a hundred other times she had come to the plaza. It held the Healthy Pets Veterinary Clinic and a revolving door of other small businesses like flower shops, dress shops, a bakery and a video rental that each lasted a couple of years. Then the schools closed, the hospitals left, and so did everybody else. Only the Dollar General Store, which occupied a separate building, had weathered all the storms of economic tribulation and remained open.

At the bottom of the parking lot was a bus shelter that was miraculously still standing, its plexiglass walls so adorned with graffiti it was hard to see the bench inside. She supposed tourists would consider the "Middle of Nowhere" sign entertaining — if there'd been any tourists, and the last bus bringing any away-from-here people into the county, or taking any locals out, had pulled away from the bus shelter for the last time decades ago.

She drove around the empty Dollar General Store to the back, still creeped out by the vacant parking lot and empty building. She'd mostly stayed away from the Ridge, Persimmon Ridge, the largest of the unincorporated area not-towns, as she called them. She didn't like driving down Main Street, past the empty parking spaces and vacant buildings. The town had been, by anybody's standards, on life support for a long time, barely hanging on. But the courthouse was there, open and still functioning. So was the sheriff's department, and a handful of businesses were still operational — Willingham's Drug Store, the Hair Affair Beauty Parlor and Nail Salon, Stovall's Used Furniture. The post office was open, just no lobby service, and a lone employee drove the truck out back to the central post office somewhere to get mail.

Still, there had always been a few cars in the parking spaces. A handful of people on the street. The absolute emptiness now was as spooky as that ghost town, Gideon, out in Fearsome Hollow, that had been a real ghost town for a hundred years. Brianna had ventured inside a couple of the Main Street businesses and discovered that there were still tools hanging on the walls in Peetree's Hardware Store, and the soft serve ice cream spigots on the wall in the drugstore still functioned. But unless you were willing to eat ice cream as it dripped out — like drinking from a water fountain — you had to bring your own cup and spoon. All the cups and cones, hot fudge sundae and banana split bowls had vanished along with everything, and every*one*, else in the building.

The last time she had visited Granny Haggarty, she'd gone in search of cardboard boxes to box up some of her belongings that Granny had stored in her attic. A few things — a high school album, a couple of dead flower-pressed mums from football games, her ancient plastic tea set and several dolls with ratty hair and eyeballs permanently rolled back into their heads.

The manager had sent her around to the back of the building, said there might be boxes beside the dumpster. That's when she had noticed the rack attached to the back side of the animal clinic next door, stacked high with kitty litter boxes, gray plastic containers, dozens of them. She supposed an animal hospital/clinic would go through a lot of kitty litter, and apparently the bulk bags came with attached litter boxes.

Whatever it was that'd swooped into Nowhere County and snatched up all the people and furniture more than a week ago had left whatever was affixed to walls — pictures, mirrors or wreaths. So *maybe* that rack of discarded litter boxes was still on the outside wall of the animal clinic. Those plastic containers were the perfect size and shape to use as nesting boxes. She'd driven the pickup truck here, hoping to load up the whole back of it with trays.

She rounded the corner of the Dollar Store Building into the alley behind it and the animal clinic. There were several green dumpsters — for the Dollar Store, the clinic and the businesses that had at one time occupied the strip mall beside the vet clinic.

But no trays. Nothing but dumpsters.

She swung the white pickup around quickly — did *not* like looking at dumpsters! — and headed out across the Dollar Store parking lot ... when she spotted a car driving slowly down County Road 278. The car stopped at the stop sign, wouldn't have if the driver'd been local. That meant he was some away-from-here destined to yoyo in and out of the county once he got the lay of the land here.

The car was dark blue, a Pontiac maybe. No, a Chevrolet. The car that pulled to stop behind it was a Pontiac, though, black. There was only one person in each car. The car in front pulled away from the stop sign but didn't continue through the intersection. It pulled into the Dollar Store parking lot instead, heading toward her, and the other car followed.

She stopped and waited for the Chevy to draw up beside her truck. The driver rolled down his window and smiled at her.

"Hi," he said pleasantly. "My name's Joe Barnes," and he thrust out his hand to shake hers.

Bri was a little taken aback, but reached out her window, took his hand and shook it.

"Brianna Haggarty," she said.

"We're not from around here," he said, indicating the man in the other car. "You know where we might find a family — the Butterfields? Maude and ... Hal, or maybe it's ... Hurl?"

Chapter Eighteen

CADE MUST HAVE TURNED WHITE. Or green. Some color. He must have looked like he was going to puke or pass out or something because her face mirrored his response — surprise. Except dialed down below the speed of sound. She was surprised that he was stunned.

He could almost see the disdain welling up inside her.

"Chill out. This didn't have anything to do with you. *Did* it? This guy wasn't the type."

"Type?"

"Are we going to start the echo chamber again?"

He'd tried to speak more than that one syllable but the words seemed stuck in his throat.

"This man was nobody's corporate attorney. He wasn't a 'process' server in a tweed coat and a bow tie. There was nothing even remotely white-collar about him."

Then she started making connections.

"Besides, how would the lawyers looking for you know anything about the Butterfields? They're just the aunt and uncle of the guy you stole the pickup from? Right? How would lawyers looking for you know about the alcoholic who sleeps in your basement — what was his name, Jim Bob? And even if they knew about him, knew you stole his pickup — which, how could they? — but even if they did, how does that connect to his aunt and uncle in the mountains? That doesn't make any sense."

He had found his breath, at least enough to say, "I want to go back to the not-white-collar thing. What do you mean?"

"Just what I said." She was getting annoyed, and overlaid on a base level of disapproval, she came out snapping. "He wasn't a lawyer. He was just a guy, you know. Wasn't wearing a suit — just an ordinary button-down shirt, a work jacket and jeans. Just a guy. Said his name was Joe Barnes. Looked like ... oh, I don't know, a mailman, maybe. I didn't see the other guy."

Cade thought he was going to be sick. "Other guy?"

"There were two of them, one in each car, but they were traveling together because both of them were looking for the Butterfields."

"Was the guy ... did he look Hispanic?"

"Hispanic? With a name like Joe Barnes?"

Cade snapped. "Just answer the question. Was he Hispanic or not?"

She drew back like he'd slapped her. Her words after that could have fallen out of an ice tray. "If you're asking if he had black hair and brown eyes — yes, he did. But he spoke perfect English, no accent. He could have been ... Italian, maybe. Now, you answer *my* question — why would you think he's Hispanic?"

He ignored the question, his mind remarkably clear for how terrified he was.

"How do you know he — they — were looking for the Butterfields?"

"Because he asked me if I knew them and how to get to their house?"

"You *talked* to him — where?"

She was coming down the razor's edge of anger, only barely blunted by confusion and curiosity.

"He stopped at the stop sign at the Middle of Nowhere crossroads. Nobody does that."

He let it go.

"And ..."

"And he saw me in the Dollar General Store parking lot so he pulled up beside me and asked me if I knew the Butterfields."

This was the part Cade was dreading.

"What did you tell him?"

"The truth, of course. Why wouldn't I? Yes, I know the Butterfields. They live on Big Knob Road."

"That's it? That's all?"

Now, her interest and curiosity were morphing into suspicion.

"No, then he asked for directions to the place."

"And you—"

"I told him how to get there from the Middle of Nowhere, not the shortest route. That would have been totally useless because there are no road signs."

"Did you tell him that?"

"Tell him what?"

"That there were no road signs."

"No, because the directions I gave he wouldn't need road signs."

"*I* did."

"I'm sure the Butterfields told you how to get to their house the most direct route." Then she rattled off roads and turns and names so fast he could hardly keep up. "From the Middle of Nowhere south on Route 17 toward

Poorfolk, right on Gallagher Station Road. It forks and Pine Bluff Road veers off to the right, but you go left, don't turn on Cicada Springs Road or Hickory Stump Road or Sims Lane. The Gallagher Station dead-ends into Route 15, turn right and Little Knob road is the first road on the right. Big Knob Road is the first left off that. Is that what the Butterfields told you?"

He nodded. In truth, what he'd overheard the marshals say was a lot simpler than that.

"So why wouldn't this guy—?"

"Because I sent him down *state* roads. Danville Pike, well, County Road 278 West to Twig. Turn left in Twig on Route 15 and Little Knob Road is the first left."

Cade's head was spinning, but he managed to glean a couple of minnows out of the school of thoughts that swam by all bunched together. The guy would be going to the Butterfields' by a direct route, which meant he was already there. And would find nobody home.

That was comforting.

Then his heart seized up in his chest.

"You didn't mention ... me ... or where *you* live, did you?" He couldn't keep the raw fear out of his voice.

He couldn't imagine there existed some direct route to Brianna's grandmother's house. They'd turned and twisted so many times, he couldn't have found his way back to the Middle of Nowhere if he'd left a trail of bread crumbs. But if she'd *told* him ...

"Of course not. You think I want more Away From Heres on my hands who're going to freak out and go flying out of Nowhere County like their pants are on fire, and then come back and ..." She glared at him. "One babysitting job is enough."

He hadn't realized he'd been holding his breath until he let it all out in a whoosh. He felt weak-kneed, started to turn and go to the porch to sit down, but she grabbed his arm.

"Now you owe me an explanation!" Clearly, she was done with his runaround. "I get it that losing a financial empire, maybe even getting hauled into court is a frightening thought. But you aren't frightened. You're scared spit-less. What are you so scared of?"

He didn't have time to answer because they both heard it at the same time — the crunch of tires on gravel. A car was coming up the driveway.

Chapter Nineteen

THE CAR PULLING up the driveway was behind the bushes that blocked the view of the house from the road. Cade's eyes were huge and at that moment, he really did look like a deer caught in the headlights.

"Chill *out!*" What in the Sam Hill was Cade so afraid of? "It's some local — one of Granny's neighbors, has to be. Somebody who came home to nothing and is searching the immediate world looking for … anybody."

Brianna didn't care if the neighbor was totally freaked out, maybe wanted her to go with them to the authorities. She could deal with that. Just not another Away From Here, please! Not some random somebody who was lost, maybe saw her, where she was going. Maybe somebody three or four sandwiches shy of a full picnic courtesy of multiple trips into and out of the county.

How was Brianna supposed to deal with somebody like that?

The car pulled around the bushes and came out from behind the house. It was the black Pontiac from the Middle of Nowhere, driven by somebody who ought to be on his way to the Butterfields' right now with the buddy she'd given directions to.

What …?

Why …?

How?

How was the only question she could answer because there was no other possible explanation. He had *followed her.* But she had circled back through Persimmon Ridge, out the other side and along the winding mountain roads to Shagbark Mountain — that was impossible. She'd have seen him—

No, she wouldn't have.

When she drove away from the intersection she'd fallen into that space, the dark space, the place where all was ugliness and shadows. It only took a single image, a word or a smell or a melody. Her mind was a tinderbox, a forest after ten years of drought, where even a spark of static electricity will set off a blaze.

The spark was the billboard on County Road 278, only half of it was still readable but it was enough. *Kentucky Fried Chicken. Have Dinner with the Colonel Tonight.*

"You're from Kentucky and you don't want Kentucky Fried Chicken?" says the woman who'd been there when she first woke up, not the nurse but the one with frizzy red hair and quick little movements like a bird. Brianna hated birds.

"I'm from Kentucky and that's why *I don't want Kentucky Fried Chicken," Brianna counters.*

"Something wrong with it only the locals know? Like the eleven secret herbs and spices are actually ground-up chicken poop?"

That might have gotten a smile if Brianna hadn't been coming off a week of DTs and surgery to put a metal rod in her leg to hold the broken bones together.

"I don't want KFC or a Moon Pie or an RC Cola. My Southern accent notwithstanding, I'm not a hillbilly and I hate fried chicken."

All the air goes out of her and she slumps back on the pillow.

"Just go away. Leave me alone. It's not fair that you can come in here and park in my room and I can't" — she gestures at her leg in the sling cast dangling above her bed — "run away."

"Fine," the woman says and rises, doesn't appear the least insulted. "I'll swing back by tomorrow and see if—"

"I won't. I won't have changed my mind about you or fried chicken. All I want right now is to be left alone."

That night she found out about Jeff, though. And after that, she wanted to talk to the woman, begged the nurse to call the woman, to get her butt back here. Brianna didn't want anything in the world more than she wanted to talk to that woman, who held the key to the kingdom. The only key there was.

That woman was Brianna's only bridge from the hellhole of her existence to the other side where normal people went about normal lives — ate, slept, built houses, made love and raised their children.

Her name was Margo Adams, but her charges, as she called them, the drunks she sponsored, called her Sarge, paying homage to her drill instructor attitude — certainly not to her diminutive, baby-bird build — an attitude that brooked no, no, absolutely no opposition.

"You want to get sober, you do whatever I say, whenever I say it. We clear on that?"

"We're clear."

"I tell you ninety is ninety, you don't even blink, you down with that?"

Ninety meetings in ninety days. Yeah, Bri is down with that.

Then Sarge speaks in a quiet voice so intense it feels like she's shouting. "Understand this — if you never understand anything else in your whole life — booze will take everything you have and then it will kill you." She pauses, leans closer. "You work the steps or you die. It's that simple. Work the steps or you're gonna leave this life alone in some alley, lying in your own puke. And that's if you're lucky. That's if you don't take somebody else with you."

By the time she said that, she and Brianna had been getting together twice a day for a month, conducting what Sarge called PAA, or Private Alcoholics Anonymous meetings. Meaning there was nobody there but the two of them because Brianna was stuck in a hospital bed with her leg dangling in the air. In that time, Brianna had learned some of the lingo. There were trip phrases from AA recognized anywhere.

Sarge had hauled out one of them the night they lowered Brianna's leg to the bed for the first time — cause for great celebration because that meant it was no longer swelling. It was a step, a small step toward freedom.

"You're only as sick as your secrets," Sarge said.

"That's easy for you to say. You don't know my secrets."

Sarge had tilted her head back and let out a rumble of laughter so loud and abrupt that it reminded Brianna of a bowling ball slamming into the pins.

"Every drunk I ever met thinks she's got the biggest, baddest, meanest story in the junkyard." She must have seen Brianna's stricken look because she softened. "I'm not making light of your pain, sugar. I'm just telling you — whatever you've got to say, I've heard worse."

But she didn't say that anymore after Brianna told her, unloaded on her, said it for the first time out loud, tacked words onto the horror. In one, long semi-hysterical stream, Brianna described in graphic detail how she had killed her baby son. Sarge listened, let her spew it all out, but didn't feel sorry for Brianna, because sympathy was a waste of time for everybody concerned. She did understand after that, though, what drove Brianna, motivated her, she got it that Brianna would literally do absolutely anything to get sober and stay that way.

"Sounds like you got number four down pretty good, and tonight you got a leg up on number five." The fourth step in AA's 12-step program required that you make "a searching and fearless moral inventory" of yourself. Number five demanded that you admit to God,

117

to *yourself, and to another human being "the exact nature of your wrongs."*

In the months since that night, Brianna had progressed through the steps to numbers eight and nine. That's what she's doing in Nowhere County. Step nine had become a chicken house.

SHE'D BEEN THINKING of all those things, thrown back into that reality by the KFC sign as she drove home, and the dude in the black Pontiac could have been twenty feet from her back bumper and she wouldn't have noticed.

He *had* followed her.

Why?

And it was only then that Brianna thought to be afraid.

What possible reason could this man, with whom she had never had a single conversation, have for following her home?

Nothing good. Nope, could not possibly be anything good.

Chapter Twenty

"WELL, HELLO THERE," Brianna said, having decided in the five or six seconds she had to make the decision, that the only thing she could do was "act normal."

The man in the black Pontiac had followed her from the Middle of Nowhere and the only way that made any sense at all was if it had *something* to do with the man standing beside her, the guy running from process servers. *Or so he'd said.* The guy in the Dollar General Store parking lot had been looking for the Butterfields' and that's where Cade had been going. Duh.

But why hadn't this guy gone to the Butterfields' from the Middle of Nowhere with the other dude? If he was, if *they* were, indeed, looking for Cade, and thought Cade was there, why had he followed *her* instead?

And she'd gotten home five minutes ago, had been standing here talking to Cade. If the guy followed her, why didn't he come up the driveway right after she did?

Unless maybe he had ... what? Stopped at the bottom of the drive? Maybe got out and came upon it a little way to check things out? What was he afraid he might find here?

Now *that* was creepy.

The man pulled to a stop in front of them and got out of the car. *Unfolded* himself out of the car. He was ... enormous. Six feet seven or eight if he was an inch, maybe three hundred pounds, huge arms, massive hands, looked like a professional football player. Or hockey, yeah, he had the beat-up face of a hockey player. He said nothing at all as he approached, didn't even look at Brianna. Just stared at Cade with a cat-that-caught-the-canary look.

"You're kinda lost, ain't ya," she heard herself say, unable to keep herself from babbling, falling instantly back into her Eastern Kentucky dialect. "The Butterfields live down in Pine Bluff Hollow and—"

"Where'd you get the pickup?" he asked her, gesturing to the stolen vehicle she had driven to the Middle of Nowhere in search of kitty litter trays. He was looking at Cade, though, just ... toying with her.

"I ..." Her mouth froze shut. The man was standing only about three feet from her now, close enough she could smell his sickly-sweet aftershave.

"It's got Jefferson County plates," he said.

Well, yes, that would make sense, given that Cade had stolen the truck from a Louisville parking garage. *That* was it. The truck had been the hook the man had hung his suspicion on.

"It don't b'long to me," she bluffed, amazed she was able to form words. "B'longs to my brother and he works at the Ford plant on Fern Valley Road. You know the place?"

"You sure it doesn't belong to a fellow who reported one a lot like this stolen from a garage on Market Street in Louisville the other day?"

"What are you getting at? You think I stole this truck? Is that why you followed me here?"

"I don't think you stole it, but I think you know the man who did." He had never taken his eyes off Cade. And now she could see amusement there. He was enjoying this.

"You the law?"

He ignored her question. "So you're saying that if I look in the glove box of this truck, I'm going to see a registration in the name of ...?"

"My brother's name's Earl Haggarty. Who are you, anyway, and what—?"

"Let's just have a look," he said, and smiled.

The man started around the back of the truck to the passenger side.

Cade hissed, "Run!"

Brianna turned and bolted. Sailing past the end of the motorhome, she leapt over the side panels of the chicken run they had built but had not yet assembled, and tore out for the woods on the other side of the meadow.

Bam!

The sound of the bullet was not the crack of a rifle. That was a familiar, hunting sound. This was more a pop than a crack, and a tuft of grass right beside her right foot popped up into the air as if a gopher were shoving dirt out a hole with his back feet.

"You take one more step and I will put a bullet right between your shoulder blades," the man called out.

Brianna staggered to a stop and just stood, panting, terrified, no idea what to do next.

"Come on back down here," the voice called out. She didn't move.

"Now!"

She turned and stumbled back down the hillside,

almost tripped over the unassembled chicken-run walls and stopped by the front of the motorhome.

The man was standing with a pistol of some kind pointed at Cade and he gestured with it.

"Closer, come here."

She walked to within a few feet of him.

"I'm looking for a man named Dawson McCade." He was grinning a vicious smile. "You wouldn't happen to know a fellow by that name, would you?"

"There isn't anybody around here named—"

He took one quick step forward and slammed the barrel of the gun into Brianna's face, snapping her head to the side. She folded up in a heap at his feet.

The world grayed out. There was a sudden *whum, whum, whum* sound in her ears and she recognized it. She heard it when she opened her eyes after ... she had come to think of it as the "blow to the head" sound. She'd had more than one of those and knew her skull wasn't fractured. The side of her face had somehow caught fire, though, and it was screaming pain into her brain.

She saw shoes in front of her face where she lay with her cheek in the dirt.

"Don't lie to me!"

The words seemed to come from a long way off, and in some ways didn't really apply to her at all.

Then the man drew his foot back, preparing to kick her in the face. She wasn't completely tracking, because some ridiculously calm part of her wondered in an academic sort of way if he would break her nose with the toe of his shoe or just knock out her front teeth.

"Stop it!" Cade said. "You want me, here I am."

The feet turned and she watched the scene from the skewed angle of her face against the ground.

Cade's sneakers came into view. She recognized them,

of course. She'd had to search through half a dozen different brands to find the right size in Walmart, eleven and a half. There'd been size elevens and size twelves, but eleven and a—

"Dawson McCade?"

"Yeah, what can I do for you?"

"Die."

The man lifted the pistol and pointed it at Cade's head.

What happened after that was a blur of motion and sounds that Brianna couldn't connect to the images she could see. Cade lunged forward, and in a move too fast to follow, hit the guy's hand and the gun went off before it flew out of his fingers. She saw the pistol plop down into the dirt about ten feet away on the other side of the fighting men. They were almost on top of her and she tried to move out of the way but the world still spun when she lifted her head and reality was whizzing past way too fast for her to makes sense of it.

She figured it out later, when she had time and space to piece it together. She'd learned a long time ago that that was destined to be her lot in life, piecing together the sequence and substance of events from the random snatches of information her brain served up for her after the fact.

Cade had launched himself at the man, knocking the gun aside so the shot missed, and then they tumbled around on the ground fighting.

Though the man had six inches and probably a hundred pounds on Cade, and was clearly more experienced at the fighting thing, Cade was no slouch. He pistoned several quick punches, then landed a solid blow that must have broken the man's nose. Blood squirted out of it and he howled. More scrambling, with the man hammering blow after blow with his huge fists into Cade's midsection. He was either furiously angry or just enjoyed punching people, because even after he had the advantage, he kept hitting Cade again and again, over and over with fists the size of boxing gloves.

Her vision cleared then. She looked around for something she could fight with. And her eye landed on the only weapon in sight.

The man knocked Cade down on his back, then dropped to his knees on top of him, pinning him to the ground, smashed his huge right fist into Cade's face and then his left. He leaned back, with blood gushing out of his nose, down his lip and off his chin, looked around, stretched out his hand and picked up a two-foot-long scrap of two-by-four lying on the ground. Without moving off Cade's chest, he raised the board high above his head to bring it down with both hands on Cade's head.

"Drop the board or I'll shoot," she said.

The man turned her way and seemed to realize she was there for the first time. He looked at her, terrified for an instant — must have assumed she'd picked up his pistol. But it lay on the other side of the fighting pair, five or six feet away. When he realized that, saw what she was actually holding, he snorted in derision.

"A *nail* gun?" He was incredulous. "Those things don't shoot nails!" Then the humor left him and he changed the angle of the blow he was about to administer to Cade's face with the two-by-four, turned it sideways and swept the board at Brianna to knock the gun out of her hand.

What happened next was one of the pieces she had to fit together later because at the time it didn't make sense.

She had the manual trigger on the nail gun squeezed tight, ignoring the pain in her bandaged fingers — a ridiculous Hail-Mary attempt to do *something.* Maybe she could reach out, hit him with it in the leg, because she knew it wouldn't fire—

But it *did* fire.

A three-and-a-quarter-inch framing nail flew out the end of the pneumatic nail gun at 1,400 feet per second. It entered the man's chest just below his left collar bone and exited out his back, traveled another fifteen feet and ricocheted off the grille of the pickup truck before it landed in the dirt.

The man looked surprised. The look froze his features — his eyebrows raised, his mouth slightly ajar. His suddenly limp fingers dropped the board he had swung at her. The piece of wood had barely clipped the tip of the nail gun, but the impact had been sufficient to act as a trip. With the gun set on "contact tip trigger," that little bump was all it required to release the nail.

The man's eyes tracked down to his chest, where a growing circle of red was staining the center of his plaid shirt. He might have been trying to turn his head back to look at her, but before he could move, all the energy went out of his body and he slumped forward onto Cade's face.

After that, none of the pieces of reality fit together properly for a very long time.

Chapter Twenty-One

A BLACK PONTIAC pulled up beside the dark blue Chevrolet in the parking lot of the Dollar General Store as the white pickup truck drove off down the road.

"You thinking what I'm thinking?" Salazar asked, his eye following the pickup truck.

José Ortega, aka Joe Barnes, aka El Escorpión, didn't care what the driver of the black Pontiac was thinking. No, actually, it would be nice to know, to have a little advance warning when Salazar intended to stab Ortega in the back — either literally or figuratively. It was coming, though, he knew it was. Only a matter of time.

Sending Ortega backup when he'd neither asked for it nor needed it sent a clear message. And as Ortega was finishing last night's progress report, Salazar'd wanted to talk privately to el jefe. It was a thirty-second conversation Salazar'd said concerned an entirely different mission. He was lying. El Buitre, Juan Renaldo Santiago's "enforcer," had become indispensable by ruthlessly weeding out incompetence in the ranks, eliminating anyone who didn't measure up. Salazar was an ambitious man and right now Ortega was vulnerable.

He had no idea how McCade had made them, how their covers had somehow been blown — it hadn't been Ortega's fault! But it'd happened on his watch. The quail had been flushed out of hiding and into the wind. If Ortega didn't set it right, well, Salazar was at the head of a long line of wannabes itching for a chance to move up in the organization.

"Yeah," Ortega said, "the pickup missing from the parking garage was white." He nodded in the direction of the truck about to disappear from view. "And that one has Jefferson County plates. Follow her. See if there's anything to see. I got directions to the Butterfields'. Meet me back here in an hour."

Pépe Salazar's face darkened. He got it, knew he was being sent on a wild goose chase while Ortega went for the most likely target, the only lead they had. A stronger man might have stood his ground. After all, technically neither one of them was "in charge." But Pépe Salazar wasn't quite ready yet to make his move, to "pull the trigger," so he backed down.

Without a word, he tore out of the parking lot, peeling rubber and squalling tires voicing his protest, and flew down the road behind the pickup.

Ortega looked up at the road signs at the crossroads to get his bearings. He had grown up in Bogota. High up on the mountainside, which was where the city growth pushed the slums, up, up and up. El Paraiso, the name of the slum where he lived, was almost ten thousand feet above sea level. The air was thin. The nights cold. El Paraiso translated — Paradise.

But these mountains were not the mighty rugged Andes. They were steep, though, the valleys and hollows secluded, and the woman — Brianna Haggarty — had said the roads were winding, hard to follow, with few road signs. He headed out as she had directed him, didn't have time to get lost.

Ortega knew he'd found the right place when he saw the mailbox with the name Butterfield on it, confirmed by a sign on a fence post advertising Maude Butterfield's pies.

There were no cars in the driveway. He pulled his airport rental to a stop and checked his weapon — a .357 Magnum in a shoulder holster. He'd had all his jackets specially tailored to conceal the weapon. Their informant had identified this as one of the U.S. Marshals Service's safe houses. It was where they'd intended to bring McCade when he bailed out on them. There was no evidence to suggest that he had come here on his own. He lived in Louisville, had friends and connections there. Ortega was certain that Dawson McCade was *somewhere* in Louisville. But they'd spent three days beating the bushes there and came up empty. It was now time to check out the long-shots.

Ortega would make a clean sweep of the house, killing whoever he came in contact with. The silencer would muffle the sound, down to a kind of barking cough noise. Anybody who'd ever heard a silenced weapon would recognize the sound immediately, but if his information was correct, the McCade guy wouldn't recognize a gunshot if the pistol was right next to his ear.

He was what they called "a tourist," totally out of his element, and had been harmless even before that.

Drawing the weapon, Ortega rushed to the side of the house in a crouch, with his back to the outside wall, and inched to a window and took a quick peek.

The room was empty. Not even any furniture.

Fifteen minutes later, he had discovered that the rest of

the house was empty, too, as was an apartment above the garage which might be where the Butterfields housed their "guests."

It made no sense, and things that didn't make sense gave Ortega a crawly feeling at the base of his spine.

The feeling grew stronger and stronger as he looked for the Butterfields. Became an undeniable itch when he gave up that pursuit altogether and was just looking for *anybody*.

Anybody at all.

He checked fourteen different houses. They were all the same. Nobody home. Nothing in the buildings — no furniture, clothing, belongings, utensils in the cabinets, toothbrushes in the holder. Absolutely nothing.

The creepy/crawly feeling at the base of his spine had spread all over his body, because this wasn't just wrong — fifteen empty houses! — but *profoundly wrong*, wrong in a weird, sinister way that brought into his belly a sensation he hadn't felt in a very long time.

José Ortega was afraid.

Over the course of the next two hours, while he waited for Pépe Salazar in the parking lot of the Dollar General Store, he grew more and more scared.

The Dollar Store was empty, too. He noticed it from the parking lot — the plate glass windows revealing an empty interior. There were shelves lining the walls, but the shelves were bare and there was not so much as a gum wrapper on the floor of the cavernous structure. The veterinary hospital was empty, too, as were the three other businesses in the little strip mall, though from the looks of the outside of them, they'd been empty for a long time.

The Dollar Store had no pay phone, but who would he call, what would he say?

He didn't know yet, would know more after he talked to Pépe. Except Pépe never showed up. He found himself pacing back and forth across the parking lot, straining to see down the two roads that converged in the intersection, looking for traffic, for cars. For even a single car.

Nothing.

Where was everybody?

He clung to some sense of denial for a while, but after what felt like ten miles of pacing, he accepted the reality that clearly something had gone very wrong.

Something had happened to all the people in this county. Something had happened to Pépe, too, but Ortega knew what — at least *who* — had happened to him. Brianna Haggarty. Pépe'd found her and maybe McCade, too, might not have been such a long shot after all. How the two of them could have stood up to Pépe Salazar …

Finally, Ortega got into his car and headed back down the highway away from the Middle of Nowhere intersection, driving faster and faster, suddenly very *very* anxious to get away from this place. He'd seen a little convenience store, a Jiffy Stop a few miles before he saw the vandalized Nower County welcome sign. He'd go there and use the phone. Call in. Tell el jefe that Pépe had failed … and then what?

He was trying to figure out how he was going to explain what he'd seen to el jefe as he blew by the Welcome to Beaufort County sign.

José Ortega pulled into a little Jiffy Stop grocery store and gas station … but wasn't sure why.

He shook his head. His thoughts were foggy and that never happened. He was always alert, had to be. But he couldn't remember …

He was on his way to Nower County, Kentucky to find the home of Maude and Hurl Butterfield — that the informant had said operated a safe house — trying to find the mark El Buitre, the Vulture, wanted taken out.

But it was later than … He had left Lexington at …

He thumped his watch. It couldn't be right, couldn't be that late. He turned around, looking for the black Pontiac that held Pépe Salazar, who'd been right behind him, but now …

No Pépe.

Ortega waited, tried to clear his head. Then shrugged. Pépe was the one whose feet would be held to the fire for not showing up. Ortega hadn't been the one who'd invited him to this little picnic.

He turned his car around and headed out of the lot toward Nower County. He passed the welcome sign, where somebody'd added letters to make it Nowhere County.

As soon as the sign flew by, two things happened at once. First, Ortega suddenly remembered that *he'd already been here*, that he'd looked for the Butterfields but their house was empty. As were all the other houses he'd searched.

Second, he barely got his car pulled off the road onto the shoulder before he got violently sick, a fierce vomiting that was like his stomach was exploding out of this mouth.

He had no idea what was happening.

Chapter Twenty-Two

"... THE *OTHER* MAN ...?"

Brianna heard the words but couldn't assign meaning to them.

She was lying on her side in the dirt and Cade was kneeling beside her, shouting urgently.

"Brianna, tell me about the other man!"

Even with her wits blurred, she could hear the fear in his voice, saw him looking around, searching for ...

"I gave him directions to the Butterfields', so I guess ..."

"He went there, of course he did, and this guy followed you." It was a statement, not a question, and a good thing because she couldn't have answered a question. She just looked at him and said nothing.

She was lying on her side and then she felt Cade's hands under her arms, dragging her.

She grayed out then, went somewhere that had no form or substance.

"... keep the pressure on ..."

There was something on her face, pressing into her cheek and the pain of it shocked her, and she yanked back.

"You need to keep the pressure on," a voice said.

She opened her eyes and saw a man kneeling before her. He looked like he had been in a serious fistfight ... and lost.

The man had a cloth in his hand, holding it tight against her cheek and it hurt.

"Stop it." She tried to move away.

"Brianna!" The man's voice was stern. "I'm just trying to stop the bleeding."

Bleeding.

Her cheek.

The man with the pistol.

The nail gun!

Thoughts pulled out of the chaos of swirling images and painted reality in her mind.

A man had come. He'd had a gun and he'd hit her with it. He'd beaten up Cade.

And then she had shot him.

This time she pulled away enough to get her bearings. She was leaning against the front tire of the motorhome, her legs splayed out in front of her. She cast her eyes around, searching—

A gasp tore out of her throat.

There was the man lying on his side in the dirt a few feet away. He wasn't moving. He was ... dead.

She yanked her focus back to Cade.

"I shot him. I *killed* him!"

She wanted to scream, or cry or something. The thought was chasing its tail around and around in her head. *I killed him. I killed him. I killed him.*

Another thought stopped that one so abruptly it was like the engine of a train running into a brick wall, and all the cars behind it crashed into it and then fell off the tracks on their sides.

It's not the first time I've killed somebody.

She turned from Cade to the man and back to Cade.

"What's happening?" And then she did cry. Not heaving, gulping sobs. Just quietly, tears streaming out of her eyes and down her cheeks. Cheek. Just one. The other one was covered in the cloth Cade was holding against it. "What's going on?"

Cade had been on his knees, above where she sat, and now he leaned back on his heels, though he didn't take his hand off the cloth he had pressed to her cheek.

"Can we hold that question until later?" It sounded like he had a cold, and then she realized it was because his nose was swollen, fitting smoothly into the two black eyes above it, and the split lip below.

"But what—?"

"Hold this up to your face, can you do that — *tight*." He took her hand and placed it on the cloth he was pressing into her cheek. "I'm going to get some ice."

Her hand went limp and she dropped the cloth. He picked it up.

"Hold it!" he commanded, and she held it.

She watched him get to his feet. Slowly, one hand to his belly.

The huge man punches him and punches him, again and again, pummeling his midsection, should have broken every one of his ribs. It hadn't, though. Was it because Cade had what women called "washboard abs"? He'd taken his shirt off yesterday in the heat and she couldn't help noticing. Those kinds of muscles ... wouldn't that make a difference?

Still, he could have broken ribs — at the very least, cracked and bruised ones. And what else? Blows like that, so many ... what kind of internal damage could they do?

He turned carefully and put his hand out to the open doorway of the motorhome, then eased himself carefully up the steps.

Maybe a ruptured spleen. She'd heard about that, knew Cade would bleed to death inside if his spleen was ruptured, nothing to be done about a thing like that. Her thoughts, fueled now by fear, chased each other around and around in her head. A punctured lung? Maybe he had broken ribs and they'd punctured his lung. Couldn't do anything about that, either.

The real world settled around her — she could feel the dirt beneath her butt — she was sitting on a big rock, but when she moved to get off it, the pain in her face slammed into her again and she was still. Careful not to move, she looked around herself, trying to fit together the fragmented pieces of reality, of what had happened here in the past ... what? Hour? No, not that long. Half an hour. No ... it had all gone down in something like five minutes.

She had gone from standing in front of the motorhome arguing with Cade, to lying in the dirt with her face slashed open in minutes.

She looked at the body of the man, and pulled her eyes away.

She'd shot him. How had the nail gun—?

Cade was coming carefully back down the steps of the motorhome. He knelt beside her, moved her hand off the cloth she was holding to her face and immediately covered the blood-soaked cloth with — it was cold, an ice pack.

"Can you hold this?" he asked.

She looked at him, made eye contact.

"What's going on?" It was a plaintive whisper, not a whine, and he eased himself down beside her and leaned back against the tire. He swiped at the blood trickling down his upper lip, and it occurred to her that he was the one who needed the ice pack — to control the swelling on his eye and nose.

"You take this—" She got that much out and started to hand it to him, but he pushed her hand away.

"Hold it tight against your cheek or it won't do any good."

"Tight. Yeah, okay, fine. Tight. Now tell me what's going on!'

There was life in her voice now, energy. She must have been in shock, but that was passing, and the fuzzy wrapped-in-cotton inattention to reality was draining away. It was replaced by such a stew of emotions, she honestly didn't know which one to feel first.

Fear. Anger. Confusion.

She went with anger.

"Tell me!" she demanded, her voice stern.

"I am so ... sorry," he said, his words a little clearer. Maybe his nose had just been clogged with blood. "I didn't ... I never dreamed it would ... that this would happen. I never meant to drag you into it."

"Into *what*!" This time, she really did yell. "And don't hand me some line about process servers. What is" — she gestured at the man, and the air went out of her lungs so she couldn't do more than whisper the rest — "*this*?"

"Reader's Digest Condensed version: Ten years ago I went on a business trip to Colombia. I was just there for logistics, a glorified gopher, an assistant to the assistant to the CEO of the company — a nobody." He let out a breath. "But for reasons I still don't know, they thought I was Charles Spencer."

"They?"

"The kidnappers. I was driving down the street and a car suddenly pulled in front of me, cutting me off. I slammed on the brakes or I'd have hit him, somebody yanked my door open, dragged me out onto the street and threw me into the trunk of a car."

He took in a shuddering breath.

"And for the next four days I was a prisoner of ... somebody. I'm not even sure who that was either."

"Kidnapped?" The word did not compute anywhere in Brianna's mind.

"That year, 1985, there were more than six thousand kidnappings in Latin America — four thousand of them in Colombia. That's their definition of a 'thriving tourist business' — in three years, they cleared $400 million in ransoms."

Chapter Twenty-Three

CADE KEPT TALKING, but wasn't really aware of explaining it to somebody else. He was more than remembering it. He was almost reliving it, listening to the big Greek, Atticus Papachristodoulopoulos — just "Pop" — who directed St. Vincent's Purse, the Florida-based Protestant evangelical group working to free kidnap victims.

As he spoke, Cade sat shivering in a "safe house" in Cali, Colombia. It wasn't cold — he was shivering from shock, and fear, and whatever else it did to you to be terrorized for four days and then miraculously rescued.

Pop likely knew Cade wasn't really listening. He was just talking to fill the silence, to put words out there into the air so the world would seem real. Cade was surprised he remembered any of it.

"We recorded a conversation last February with Amelia Vargas, the wife of a 31-year-old farm manager kidnapped from his home at gunpoint on Christmas Eve. A voice said, 'the guy's already dead but we are going to charge you ten million pesos to deliver his corpse. If you don't want it, we'll feed him to the street dogs.' There are something like 200,000 wild dogs on the streets of Bogota. Mrs. Vargas paid the money, about $14,000 American, but she never got her husband's body."

Pop told Cade that the going price for an oil executive was $300,000.

"The police estimate that something like 14,000 Colombians have taken part in kidnappings in the past year. La Policia managed to arrest or kill three hundred and fifty. They rescued maybe three hundred of the three thousand hostages."

He said most of the kidnappers claimed to be "revolutionaries."

"Riiiiiight. The 'Revolutionary Armed Forces' kidnapped the editor of a scientific journal for the International Center for Tropical Agriculture and demanded a $6 million ransom. The ICTA didn't pay. Nobody ever saw the man again."

And Dawson McCade had been sprung for a measly $500. The kidnappers had figured out their mistake, were just going to kill him. But one of the 'soldiers' made a private deal with St. Vincent's Purse, whisked Cade out under the cover of night and pocketed the money.

"Why is somebody … trying to kill you *now*?" Brianna asked, and her voice brought Cade back to the real world, a hillside in the Kentucky mountains, sitting beside a woman who'd just used a nail gun to off a professional killer.

"While I was there, I saw something." He stopped, grabbed a breath before he continued. "It was … awful." Another breath. "Just one of a string of horrifying experiences that lasted … I call it the 'hundred hours in hell.'" He grabbed her gaze, noticed with a randomly firing synapse the streaks of bright gold in her hazel eyes. "Only it lasted longer than that. It lasted ... for years afterward. Years getting my head and my life back together."

Another pause. "And then, just a few days ago" — he almost laughed at that, *just a few days ago!* — "I had a visit from two special agents for the FBI. They'd been doing some digging, trying to warn people they were in danger, and they connected with St. Vincent's Purse. They wanted to know if I recognized a man named Juan Renaldo Santiago, said he had risen up through the ranks, climbed the company ladder, so to speak, and now was a serious player in Colombia. They said he planned to run for office and he needed to erase his past."

"And you're part of his past."

"Me, an Australian, two Canadians and three other Americans. At least those are the ones who have been successfully eliminated so far."

"These people have killed ... already *killed* ...?"

"They didn't get around to me because I didn't show up on any official records." There was a flash of sudden anger in his belly that he hadn't felt in a long time. "I was a very small minnow at the bottom of the pond, and my own government neither knew nor cared whether I lived or died."

He took a deep, shuddering breath.

"I'm a big fish now, though. The others who were killed, I don't know what they knew about Santiago, what they saw that he didn't want them to talk about. But when I told the agents what I had seen ... I rose to the head of the class, clap the man on the back and give him a Kewpie doll. Not only could my testimony muck up Santiago's resume, I could put him away for good."

"How did he find you?"

"He has tentacles that stretch waaaaay beyond Colombia. He didn't know I existed until the feds came to warn me he was offing people. Then I suddenly landed on the top of his kill-this-man-*quick* list. Obviously, there's an informant, a fly in the U.S. Marshals Service's buttermilk. I bailed before Santiago could get to me in Louisville."

He looked her square in the eye, his own eyes pleading with her to believe him.

"And I promise ... I *swear,* I thought the Butterfields were *safe.* I'm sure the whole Federal Bureau of Investigation, the Marshals Service ... shoot, maybe even the CIA are looking for me by now, but they aren't looking at the Butterfields because the marshals know they never even told me their names, let alone where they lived." He grimaced from the pain the effort of talking was causing. "If I'd had any idea ... I never would have—"

"What did you see that man do in Colombia?"

"You don't want to know."

"I'm sure I don't, but tell me anyway."

"I watched him kill a man ... more than one man." His chest was suddenly constricted and it was hard to breathe.

"Go on," she prompted.

He didn't want to, absolutely one hundred percent did *not* want to talk about it. But this woman had earned the right to hear the story.

"It was called the Decimoquinto de Marzo Massacre. March 15 in Callista, a village outside Bogota. It happened in the compound of one of the drug lords, where the kidnappers had thrown me into a dark hut and forgot about me. There was an attack, a gunfight, Santiago's guys won, so they marched the losers out into the center of the compound, told them to get on their knees."

He took a breath. Tried to speak and couldn't. Took another breath.

"Then they killed them all. I watched through an open

doorway. One by one, Santiago butchered them, cut them to pieces … *with a chainsaw.*"

Chapter Twenty-Four

As Brianna listened to Cade's story, she grew more horrified with every word.

His nose was still bleeding, running down his upper lip, and she handed him the cloth he'd used on her face before the ice pack. He used it to unconsciously dab at the blood. She watched his expression as he talked, knew instantly when "Dawson McCade left the building," went to the dark place. Oh my, yes, did she know that place! Had the address and the nine-digit zip code, could provide directions down to the longitude and latitude lines.

It was the place in the heart and soul of every person where they store the most awful things that have ever happened to them. Some people are able to lock the door to that place and never go back in. Or she supposed some people could. She had never been able to. She couldn't lock the door ... shoot, most of the time she couldn't even get it to shut.

He was apparently handier with a deadbolt lock than she had ever been, though he had had more practice, a decade to figure out the best locking combination and the most secure place to dispose of the key. She didn't think he had hauled these images out of that room in a long time, probably not in years, and some part of her felt a tinge of envy that he could put such space between himself and his nightmares while hers were always right there, two or three eye-blinks from the surface.

Picking out a casket. Babies' caskets are so small; how could he possibly fit in there?

As she listened to his story, her emotions swung like Tarzan on a vine. She felt sorry for him. She was furious at him. She felt sorry again. Back and forth. Clearly, nothing that had happened to him was his fault, but still, she had to make the mental adjustment from her assessment of him as a crook who cheated little old ladies out of their life savings.

Why didn't he tell her in the beginning?

Why had he made up that cock-and-bull story about process servers, for crying out loud?

He described his near-miss in Louisville—

"It was just a guess, not a guess, a gut reaction. I was standing by the window and saw these guys crossing the parking lot and ... there's no reason I should have known, could even have ... but the way they walked, their whole demeanor ... it was so hauntingly familiar. A kind of cultural thing, maybe, South American. Or maybe they just exuded danger. It wasn't like either one of them had 'I am a killer' on a flashing neon sign above his head. But I just ... I knew. Or thought I did. So I booked."

He shot a glance at the man lying on his side in the dirt.

The man she had killed. *Killed!*

"And you didn't tell me all this in the beginning because ...?" She didn't try to keep the anger out of her voice.

"Would you have let me stay if I had? Hi, my name's Dawson McCade, and there are hired killers looking for me who want to put a bullet in the back of my head and will likely take out everybody else for a hundred yards in every direction."

"So you tricked—?"

"I didn't *know!*" There was genuine anguish in his voice. "I would never have put you or anybody else in danger if I had thought ... but how could anybody have found me *here*? Up in this remote little hollow in the mountains? I thought they'd just sent hitmen to pick me off at the federal building before I ever got into a car. But ..."

"But somehow they found out about the Butterfields, too—"

"Which means ..." His face blanched. "There's nowhere I can go that's safe."

He looked at Brianna and seemed suddenly to see her for the first time. His eye went to the ice pack she held to her cheek.

"I have to get away from here — from *you*. I never meant to put you in danger—"

"Away ... and go where?"

He said nothing. Then mumbled, "... somewhere."

Her cheek was screaming in pain. Aspirin. There was a bottle in the medicine cabinet. And Cade needed an ice pack a whole lot more than she did. She started to get up. When he tried to stop her, she snapped "move!"

She stood, the world dipped and dived and cartwheeled around her for a moment, then steadied. "You're not going anywhere right now. The other guy ..." They both looked at the body lying in the dirt and she lost her breath for a moment along with her train of thought. "If he was coming here, where is he? What's he waiting for?"

Cade said nothing.

"I gave him directions to the Butterfields' and he went *there*. Of course he did — they were looking for *you* and that's where they thought you were."

"They spotted the white pickup truck and split up. *He*" — she nodded to the man on the ground — "followed *me* ..."

Cade nodded, still didn't speak.

"So the other guy's at the Butterfields'. That's on the other side of Bishop Mountain in Pine Bluff Hollow, fifteen, maybe twenty miles from here down roads with no signs. He could only get here, *find* here, by following me and he didn't. There's no possible way the second guy could know where I am, where *you* are."

As the words left her mouth, she grasped the truth of them. It was blind luck the men had spotted the white pickup truck, pure chance. But only one of them had followed her home and he was dead. Nobody else could find them, not snuggled up here so close to the edge of the county you could almost throw a rock into Beaufort County, high up on the side of Shagbark Mountain. Nobody else would know where to look.

"It's safe *here*," she said. "And we need to do something about your face."

Chapter Twenty-Five

BRIANNA LOOKED at her face in the mirror over the sink. There was a two-inch-long slash across her right cheek that absolutely needed a stitch or two. That wasn't going to happen. So she did her best to clean off the dried blood down to the ragged skin where the sight on the top of the barrel had gouged deep. It was swollen now, puffed up into a chipmunk cheek and every touch caused a reflexive cringe.

But it would have been a lot more swollen if Cade hadn't put the ice pack on it.

Butterfly bandages. She'd learned how to make those from Sarge, who, when she wasn't ordering her girls around like a drill instructor tearing into Marine recruits, was an Emergency Medical Technician. That's how she had first come upon Brianna. She'd been part of the crew that tended to her after the Jaws of Life cracked open the compacter of the garbage truck and extracted her and her squashed leg.

"Cut half moons out of the tape on both sides, just leave a little bitty piece between them to hold the sides of the tape together," Sarge had said, demonstrating with the butterfly bandage she was using on the healing wound of Brianna's leg surgery. "Stick the tape down solidly on both sides of the wound and stretch that little bitty piece over the wound itself — so when you take the tape off it won't pull the wound open."

Stepping back, Brianna appraised her work with her left eye, which she could open all the way. It wasn't bad. It would hold. And yeah, she was likely to have some Frankenstein-monster scar on her cheek as a result but right now she didn't care.

Cade looked worse. One of his eyes was swollen shut and the black was edging across to grant shiner status to his other eye. His nose might not be broken ... might not. His bottom lip was split wide open and swelled up like a golf ball, and there were both top and bottom teeth so loose he'd have to be careful not to swallow one or more of them the first time he tried to get a drink of water.

And she had no way to know if perhaps he had fractured cheekbones, punctured sinuses, a broken jaw. She wasn't a doctor. She wasn't even an EMT. Cade needed to go to the emergency room, but that wasn't going to happen.

After she washed her hands and dried them, she made her way back to the living room of the motorhome where Cade sat on the couch.

He didn't mince words.

"There's a body out there. A dead man."

Body. The word hit her in the belly, and she sank down into the kitchen chair she had just stepped past.

"I ... killed him. I killed a man."

"If you hadn't, we'd both be dead right now." He was all business. "What we have to figure out is, now what?"

"Now what *what*?"

"What are we going to do about it? Are we going to call the police?"

"No!" Her response was an instant knee-jerk. Brianna wasn't completely certain about such things, but she was reasonably sure the state didn't grant custody of small children to mothers who were murderers.

At least not murderers they knew about.

It had been self-defense, but the mere fact of it — she'd *killed* somebody. Even a minor brush with the law — a speeding ticket — was chancy.

And who was to say it'd been self-defense? Cade — who didn't dare stick his head out of a rabbit hole or he'd be shot?

She barked out a grunt that might have been something like laughter.

"Wouldn't do any good if we did call the police. They could come here, do their whole police dance, complete with bright lights and buzzers — but they'd forget all about it as soon as they left."

Cade nodded and she suspected he'd already reached the same conclusion, maybe hadn't gotten there by the same route she had, but the destination was the same.

"Okay, then, we have to get rid of that body."

"What? Like dig a grave, is that what you're talking about?"

"I was thinking more like ... get him into the back of the pickup and take the body somewhere and dump—"

"That white pickup truck is not moving one inch out of that driveway!" She almost yelled the words.

"You're right. Of course. So what else ...?"

"The well. Granny had a well. The last time I saw it, she had a wooden topper over it. We could drag ... throw the body down the well."

For some reason, that sounded funny — "throw the

body down the well." She recognized it as tiptoeing very close to the edge of hysteria, so she stifled the response and concentrated on the logistics. A wheelbarrow. She'd bought one for the construction project that—

Build a chicken house. One simple chicken house.

That was the mantra that was supposed to keep her sane and sober. Brianna couldn't imagine that everything would go on as planned *after they'd tossed a dead body down her grandmother's well!* Not likely. The chicken house project … who knew?

Right now she knew only one thing for lead pipe certain — she would never again in her life be able to pick up a nail gun.

"I've got some cracked ribs, I think," Cade said, his breath tight. "I've never had cracked ribs before but this hurts like … it hurts, but I believe it'd be worse if they were broken."

"Never had broken ribs, but I did" — she looked down at the leg with a metal rod inside — "break my leg, and I'm here to testify that if you'd broken something, you'd know it."

"The thing is, with these cracked/broken ribs, I don't know if I can drag a body up a hill …"

"The car!" she said. "We have to get rid of his car, too." The blue Pontiac sat outside in her grandmother's driveway. "Let's kill two birds with one stone." *Kill* two birds. "Put the body in the trunk of the car, and I could hide the car in the woods. Drive it up an old logging road and just leave it there."

Cade nodded. "Okay, that works." He got to his feet slowly and carefully. "I'll—"

"*We'll*," she corrected. "It'll take both of us together to lift him. There's an old logging road less than a mile that way." She paused. "What about the gun?"

"We keep it! We might … need it." His words were so chilling, she felt like she was the one trying to breathe with broken ribs. He must have seen she was freaked out, and added, "Stick it under the front seat of the pickup. Just in case." She tried to read his eyes, but couldn't. Trying to read any expression on a face as ruined as his was futile.

"When we get back here, we need to talk about—" he started.

"No! We're not talking about anything until the morning! Put the gun under the seat, dump the body in the trunk, dump the car in the woods … and talk in the morning. I can't deal with anything else today … I'm done."

∼

LIGHT SUDDENLY STABBED into José Ortega's eyes and he squinted as he opened them.

It was morning. Where was he? What …?

He reached up and swiped at his upper lip and his hand came away bloody.

Trying to sit up, he felt an ice pick of pain in the center of his forehead. It radiated out in all directions, pounding and pounding.

It made his teeth hurt.

His sense of direction was off, he couldn't seem to find "up" but he finally made it to a sitting position.

The front of his shirt was soaked in blood. And he had … wet his pants. When did …? He shook his head and the pain was so staggering he went momentarily blind.

"… all right in there?"

He heard a voice, and turned toward it. But he couldn't make it out. He slowly turned the left side of his head in that direction and caught the words. Apparently, his right ear was deaf.

A face swam into and out of focus. Someone was speaking. Ortega's thoughts were muddled, sluggish. It seemed to take a whole minute to think of a response.

Was he all right? No, he was not.

Forcing his mind to focus seemed to rob him of his senses. He could either think or he could hear, but he couldn't seem to manage both at the same time.

A man was standing beside the door of Ortega's car.

"... help you?" the man asked.

Fumbling for the handle, he finally managed to open the door and tumbled out onto the ground, spilling out onto the grass a lapful of vomit.

"... really tied one on!" the man said.

The fresh air revived Ortega. He didn't remember how to ... Ortega's mind formed thoughts, but each one stood all by itself, and he couldn't manage to connect any of them together to form understanding.

One swam into sharp focus, though, and he grabbed it, held on with all his will.

"Yes, you can help me. I'll pay you $100 if you can tell me how to find ..."

What?

Who?

Other thoughts swam through his mind then and images floated by as disconnected as photographs on the surface of a creek.

A woman's face. Brown hair. Green eyes. He's holding her hand in his, squeezing, as she says, "Brianna Haggarty."

He concentrated to make his mouth form words.

"... how to find Brianna Haggarty."

Another image floated lazily along behind that one.

El Carnicero is splattered in blood, smiling so there's blood on his teeth. He is holding up a human nose that's no longer attached to a face.

Then Ortega knew what he had to do. The thought became clear, as the single image caught in the reeds on the edge of the creek, floating there for him to study.

Yes, *that*. That would seal his place in the order of things forever. He grabbed hold of the shirt of the man leaning over him, the man who thought he'd "tied one on." He pulled the face up close.

"And two hundred more if you make a phone call for me, give the man who answers a message."

"That's it? Give you directions and make a phone call — for $300?"

Ortega nodded. The man grinned, revealing a mouth without a single whole tooth in it anywhere.

"What's the message?"

"Tell him his package is at Brianna Haggarty's house," Ortega said. "And tell him I'm going to cut it into little pieces and bring him one."

Chapter Twenty-Six

CADE GOT UP RIGHT after sunrise. Or what passed for sunrise here. He had discovered in the short time he'd spent in the mountains that their shadows covered the hollows and valleys, shades of night clung to nooks and crannies, pooled beneath trees and gathered in the darkened interior of the woods long after the sun had cleared the horizon in the rest of the world. He eased himself up onto the edge of the cot, allowing himself to moan and groan because there was nobody to hear him. And it *hurt*!

Maybe he actually *had* broken a rib, but that didn't seem likely. Brianna had found an ACE bandage in a bathroom drawer of the motorhome and had wrapped it tight around and around his chest and belly, securing his diaphragm in place. He could barely breathe, but that was the point because breathing was what hurt. And bad as that was, he figured it'd be a whole lot worse if a jagged rib were poking into a lung.

He sat on the side of the cot for a long time, staring at nothing, his mind so exhausted his thoughts didn't even have the energy to spin around and around in his head. He could reach out and pluck any one of them from the pile and think it for as long as he wanted.

But he was too tired to pluck up thoughts, too tired to think them, in so much pain — physical and emotional — that the act of thinking seemed like way, way too much trouble.

The light grew outside. He had left a window open in the kitchen and he sat listening to the early morning sounds. Birds. Creatures of some kind. Though he had lived much of his life in a city, with the sounds of honking horns and sirens and the smell of exhaust and somebody cooking something somewhere always in the air, he had grown up in the suburbs, in a neighborhood with trees and birds. He had never spent any time in deep woods, though, and was surprised by how noisy it was here.

He took a long time to get all the way to his feet and walked carefully barefoot across the cold wooden floor to the bathroom.

When he saw his face in the mirror above the sink, he genuinely did not recognize the man staring back at him. Two black eyes, a nose so swollen it was painful to look at and a lower lip he was sure would split back open again if he tried to talk. His right eye had swollen shut yesterday, but after an evening with an ice pack, he could open it halfway now. The other eye was functional. He felt his teeth gingerly with his tongue. Loose. Particularly the ones on the bottom. But he hadn't lost any. The dentist so concerned about his jaw grinding would be glad about that.

He bowed his head over the sink to splash water in his face and the world tilted and swayed a little. Of course, he hadn't slept. Who sleeps with broken ribs? Okay, certainly bruised and maybe cracked ribs? And all those awake night hours had been filled with the scenes he had kept locked away, snug behind a barred door.

What he needed was a shower. A long, hot shower.

He turned toward the bathtub with the bar above it for a shower curtain. There was no curtain. How crazy was that? There wasn't a stick of furniture in the house, but the water was turned on and apparently, so was the electricity or gas that fueled the hot water heater.

He was about to make a royal mess on the floor.

He had no wash cloth or bath towels. Brianna had gotten supplies for his "camp trip" in her grandmother's house, but she hadn't thought of everything. So he could take a shower, with water splashing on the floor, and drip dry. He'd take that.

He turned the nob and watched the bathroom fill up with steam as he carefully removed the ACE bandage from around his chest and poked it down into the pocket of his jeans so he could get Brianna to put it back on later. His chest and abdomen were a mass of bluish-purple bruises, and even the water hitting them when he stepped into the tub was painful. But in the way of hot showers, good painful.

It was a small bathroom and a loud shower. The running water masked the soft sound of tires on gravel as a car pulled slowly up the driveway. It even masked the sound of Brianna's screams.

Chapter Twenty-Seven

THE WARRING SENSATIONS were evenly matched, two boxers battling for the championship, both with the same strength and level of skill. Brianna Haggarty's desire for a drink had never in her life been stronger than it was as she lay in the growing dawn light in the motorhome in her grandmother's backyard in Nowhere County. And her gratitude that there was nothing to satisfy that craving, not a single thing, not so much as a bottle of cough syrup, was just as powerful.

She seesawed back and forth between a craving that literally made her mouth water and a growing sense of strength, a little more every day. But it was enough.

Or it had been, as long as her job had been nothing more complex than concentrating on the right-here, right-now. Start small, Sarge had said. One baby step. You have to take that step, succeed, before you can move on.

Sarge had called it the top-button-of-the-shirt principle.

When you buttoned a shirt, you had to make sure the top button was in the proper hole. If you did that, every button after it would line up. But if the top button wasn't fastened properly, all bets were off. Leave it that way and none of the rest of them would ever line up properly.

Build a chicken house. A simple chicken house. That was the mantra, the life vest that kept her afloat. Simple. Easy. Build a chicken house and stay sober and she could rescue her little girl from the monstrosity who walked around in the human being suit of the child's grandmother.

But that had been before the man had slammed the barrel of a gun into her face, before she'd shot him. Killed him.

Now what? dangled out beyond that.

She should call Sarge, no matter how crazy her sponsor would think she'd gone with a tale of vanishing people and wiped-out memories. She really should, but she didn't have a phone.

Of course, Brianna could get in the car, drive out of the county to the Jiffy Stop in Beaufort County. There'd been a pay phone on the wall there, she'd seen it. The phone was right next to the display of booze.

Yeah, she could leave the county and make a call and still keep all her current marbles. Cade couldn't, but she could. Only she didn't dare.

Alright, maybe she did dare. She felt a surging confidence that she could handle that kind of temptation if she had to. But she didn't and why tempt fate?

She took a breath, hated the itchy-all-over feeling of need. Wanted the only thing that seemed to soothe that away.

Music, to still the savage beast.

Sarge had not led a particularly privileged life, the daughter of a longshoreman who drank his family into poverty and beat his wife and children every Saturday night at ten o'clock as soon as the bar closed — you could set your watch by it. She'd had no appreciation of the music Brianna had fallen in love with the first time she'd ever sat in a concert hall. It was back when things had been good. She'd met a handsome man, who, oh by the way, was also rich and famous. Back when it'd been new and glittering and glamorous, a new city every couple of days.

Jeff had actually gone with her to the concert, the first one, anyway. He had fidgeted in his seat, but when the music started, she wasn't aware of him at all. That first time, the Pittsburgh Symphony concert opened with Rhapsody in Blue, and Brianna Haggarty didn't breathe from the first note to the last.

After that, music soothed her when she was lonely, or angry, or sad, or ... mostly lonely. She always kept her Walkman loaded and charged.

She got up and dressed as light grew outside, selected her Gershwin favorite on the Walkman, slipped it into the pocket of her jeans, put her headphones on, and began to make a big pot of coffee as she listened.

Though the music always managed to ease, temporarily, her ever-present itch, it was not a magic eraser that wiped her mind clean. Her thoughts again hopped on the merry-go-round, spinning as they'd done while she lay in the bed last night, unable to sleep.

Who sleeps after they've killed a man?

Who sleeps with a gash on her face that needs stitches — where a killer hit her with the barrel of a pistol?

Who has somewhere in their minds to put things like that?

A professional *killer*.

A body in a trunk.

A car ditched in the woods.

And Cade.

In her mind, he was a crook, an embezzler, cheated little old ladies out of their—

Except he wasn't.

He was a man who'd been dragged out of a car in Bogota, Colombia and had been trying to put his life back together ever since.

She could relate to the put-your-life-back-together part. Trying to figure out how you went on after some horrible thing, an event that killed your soul and should have killed you along with it. You didn't walk away from a thing like that.

What happened to Cade hadn't been his fault.

What happened to Brianna had absolutely been her fault. She was to blame for everything.

So how could she not have sympathy for someone whose life had been destroyed by a catastrophe not of his own making?

Lifting a mug off the coffee-cup tree on the cabinet, she poured the black liquid from the pot into it and—

A monstrous shape was standing in the living room of the motorhome.

She dropped the mug of coffee, watched the black liquid splash out of it when it hit the floor, felt it burning the top of her foot.

And then someone was screaming. Shrieking. Making a horrible wailing sound that didn't even sound human.

It mingled in her ears with Rhapsody in Blue.

Brianna staggered back, slammed into the refrigerator, knocking the potato chips and the half-empty loaf of bread off onto the floor.

The screams — her throat was raw, *she* was the one who was screaming. Music wailed in her ears, her own screams tore out her throat and the monster appeared to be laughing.

She reached up and yanked off the headphones and the music was replaced by shrieking wails and maniacal laughter. Then she watched in horrified amazement as the shape shambled out of the shadows into the light. It was only then that she saw the pistol aimed at her.

"Shut up that squalling," he said. The words rode a spray of blood out the creature's mouth. He had gone from insane laughter to blinding rage between one heartbeat and another.

"You're Brianna Haggarty — right? The guy with no teeth gave me directions. Where's Salazar?"

It was the man from yesterday in the black Chevrolet in the Dollar General Store parking lot. *Hi, I'm Joe Barnes.*

Except it wasn't.

Blood poured in a steady flow out his nose, over his upper lip, down his mouth and dripped off his chin. The whole front of his "ordinary button-down shirt" was soaked. So was the left shoulder of his jacket, where his ear had been bleeding, but now only dripped. Bloody tears streamed down his cheeks, and he had suffered some kind of stroke or brain bleed or something because the left side of his face wasn't lined up properly with the other side. His voice was the sound of chains dragged across a metal floor. Cold and ragged and fearful in every way.

"Asked you a question." He spit blood out as he spoke. And she could smell … had he … he had wet himself and fouled himself, too. "Pepe followed you yesterday." He sneered and gestured to the bandage on her cheek. "Is Pepe what happened to your face? What'd you do with him?"

The left side of his body didn't appear to be affected by the stroke or whatever'd happened in his brain. He held the pistol firmly, finger on the trigger.

Brianna couldn't speak, couldn't have forced a sound

out between her lips if her life had depended upon it, as well it might.

But the intensity suddenly left his eyes; something had shifted.

"McCade. Dawson McCade. Where is he?"

If she said the wrong thing, he would shoot her. He might very well shoot her no matter what she said, or didn't say. This man was insane. This was what happened to people who went back and forth across the county line, what the men in the coffee shop had been talking about.

"Who's Dawson Mc—?"

He lunged at her and she was stunned that a man in his condition could move that fast. Slamming her up against the wall, he held his forearm across her neck. "He in here?" He nodded toward the back of the motorhome.

"No ... nobody's here," she managed to reply, though the pressure on her throat was producing black spots before her eyes.

He shot a glance down the hallway into the bedroom, a straight line of sight. It was clear nobody was there. Stepping back, he took his arm off her neck and grabbed a handful of her shirt in his fist. Flinging her toward the door of the motorhome, he said, "Then let's go find him."

Surely, Cade had heard her screaming, had run to the truck for the gun under the seat. Was waiting now to open fire on ...

Or maybe he had just run out the door of her grandmother's house into the woods and kept going. Once he got into the trees, this joker would never find him. And what would he do to her if he couldn't find Cade?

Chapter Twenty-Eight

CADE WIPED at the steamed-up mirror to clear a spot so he could see to shave. Drip-dry was fine, as far as it went, but putting on socks and underwear, a tee shirt and jeans without drying off first reminded him of what his older sister used to say when the weather was hot and he complained about the lack of air conditioning.

"Until you've tried to squeeze a sweaty butt into a pair of pantyhose, you don't have a dog in this fight."

When he finished shaving, he'd get Brianna to wrap the ACE bandage back around—

"Dawson McCade — Yo, McCade. Come out, come out, wherever you are."

Cade froze; his razor slipped out of his numb fingers and clattered to the floor.

The voice was coming from the backyard and he rushed to a window, ignoring the protest of his bruised ribs at the sudden movement. A dark blue Chevrolet was parked in the driveway.

Nausea and dizziness swept over him that had nothing to do with yesterday's beating. He went to a different window, peeked out around the frame and could see a man standing in front of the motorhome, holding a gun on Brianna.

"Come on, McCade. Give it up and come on out where I can see you."

Who—?

This had to be the other guy from the Middle of Nowhere, the one named Joe Barnes, who'd asked her how to get to the Butterfields'.

How had he found them? The other guy'd followed Brianna, but this one hadn't. How — something was wrong with him. He was swaying, holding onto Brianna's arm as much to steady himself as he was to keep her from running off.

The other man had fit her description of just a regular guy, not a lawyer type. It had been an accurate description as far as it went, simply missing key interpretation. The man Brianna had shot with a nail gun had not, indeed, been the type to be hauling a leather briefcase into a court-room, but he had by no means been anybody's definition of a "regular guy," hadn't carried himself like a normal, garden-variety schmuck, had carried himself like a man who had no patience for the garden-variety schmucks of the world. He'd been arrogant and mean. If Cade had been casting a hitman for a movie, he wouldn't have picked that guy because he hadn't been beefy enough, not muscle-bound, but his demeanor had fit the part perfectly.

This man was tall, muscular, thick black hair — a casting director's "hitman" dream. Or would have been except ... it looked like maybe he'd been in an accident, like he had been hit by a car or something. He was bleeding out his nose, and around his mouth. His speech sounded like he'd been to the dentist and one part of his mouth was still numb.

Or like somebody who'd suffered a mild stroke.

Bam!

The sound of the gunshot went through Cade as if it had been carried along by the bullet. Brianna had screamed, but the guy had just been firing into the air. Maybe that was the same gun he'd used to take down the Australian, the Canadian and the other three Americans.

"I know you're around here somewhere and I'm not in the mood to play hide-and-seek," the man called out. "Come out here, show yourself right now or ..." He pointed the weapon he'd been waving around in the air at Brianna's temple. "I'll blow her brains out." He paused. "You've got to the count of three. One!"

Until that moment, Cade had detected no accent of any kind. But those words — the slight trill on the r — betrayed his origin.

What could Cade do? The man was standing ten feet from the cab of the pickup. There was no possible way for Cade to get the gun out from under the seat.

"Two!"

He heard himself call out before he even thought what to say.

"Let her go, then I'll come out."

The man whirled around toward the window where Cade stood, but the motion unbalanced him and he swayed.

"Why should I let her live? Where was I? Oh, yes — Two!"

"She doesn't know anything. She's not involved in any of it. Just let her—"

"Fine. Deal. You have five seconds."

"Okay, okay. I'm coming."

He saw the man turn around, searching, like he couldn't tell where the voice had come from.

Cade made his way through the house to the back door like a man in a trance. He was coming up on the last few minutes of his life and he didn't know how to think about that. Hadn't known a decade ago when he expected to die every second of every day.

Brianna was going to die, too, of course. They all three knew the bargain was a lie. Cade was only buying her a few more minutes. The man was a killer; he wouldn't let her go.

Cade had come bumbling, barreling into her life, lied to her about everything, and now he was going to get her killed.

Still, the guy was unsteady, maybe Cade could …

When Cade got a good look at the man's face, he understood, figured it out. This guy had gone back and forth across the county line and it had done something to him. A stroke or something. One eyelid and the side of his face drooped just a little, but the hand holding the gun appeared firm. Cade walked in sock feet across the weeds and grass of the backyard toward the driveway, where the nan had hold of Brianna just outside the door of the motorhome. He was surprised that he didn't just fold up; he felt like the tops of his legs were attached to the bottoms with bags of water.

"Bri—" he said, as he approached. She looked so scared. He probably looked the same way.

"Shut up!" The man spat blood when he said it. He smiled a lopsided smile as Cade got closer, didn't let go of Bri but was no longer pointing the gun at her head. He was pointing it at Cade's chest.

Acknowledging the ruin of Cade's face, he said, "I see Pepe worked you over pretty good. So where is he?"

Neither Cade nor Bri spoke.

The man looked from one to the other, then roared in Brianna's face, "I said, where is he?"

And she blurted out the truth, "In the trunk of his car."

"And where might his car be?"

"In the woods." He shook her, clearly wanted more than a three-word answer. "We drove it up that logging road by the big stump, you passed it, a couple of miles from here."

He turned back to Cade.

"How'd you kill him?"

"I didn't kill him."

The man's look demanded an explanation. Cade said the first thing that came to his mind. "I don't have a gun. I'm not a killer!"

"Well, Pepe *is* a killer! So why are you still alive?"

The man turned on Brianna, screamed in her face in a maniacal rage. "Answer me!"

"I shot him with a nail gun."

The man looked surprised, then barked out a bleat of laughter.

"You can't kill someone with a nail gun."

"She didn't." Cade blurted out the words, suddenly unwilling to let the guy know it was Brianna who'd killed his partner. It might go worse for her if he knew. Cade would find a way to take the blame.

"She didn't say she killed him. She just shot him."

"What's he talking about?"

Then he shook a reply out of Brianna. "He hit me with the gun." She touched the bandage on her cheek. "And he was ... he hit Cade and kept hitting him and hitting him." The horror in her words rang true. If the man had needed verification, he had only to look at Cade's face. "He had a board and was going to hit Cade with it, so I picked up the nail gun, and …"

Cade saw a tiny glimmer of hope and went for it.

"She shoved it up against his arm and shot him. A three-inch nail, all the way through." Cade was winging it. "And I took his gun away. It's under the seat in the pickup truck."

"You telling me you didn't kill him!"

Cade was sure that if this man had been firing on all cylinders, he wouldn't have bought the story. But his engine was barely running at all. He looked like he might collapse. His reflexes appeared to be in no better shape than his thinking. If Cade could have moved fast … but that wasn't going to happen, not with his bruised/cracked/maybe broken ribs.

He had always heard that the best lie has an element of truth.

"I told you, I'm not a killer. You might be able to put a gun to somebody's head and blow them away, but I … we … couldn't."

"You just shoved him in the trunk and left him there?" The man was incredulous — but not because he didn't believe it. He shook his head and mumbled. "Tourists." Then he looked at Cade. "What were you going to do with him?" It was a genuine question, though, not a challenge.

"I don't know!" Cade cried, allowing real emotion to color his words. "We didn't *have* a plan. We were going to … come up with something this morning. But then you …"

"Rained on your little parade."

Without a word, the man turned toward the pickup truck and walked slowly to it, never taking the gun off Cade. It was then that Cade realized the man had … messed in his pants. The man appeared oblivious. He opened the truck door, felt around under the seat for the gun and pulled it out. That seemed to confirm for him the truth of everything they'd told him. He looked at the gun and shook his head again, then drew back his arm and threw the weapon as far as he could into the weeds of the meadow.

He looked around, seemed to be considering something, figuring something out. Cade's mind raced. The guy thought the other guy was still alive, a prisoner somewhere in a car trunk. What did that mean? How could Cade …?

The man gestured to a pile of tools beside the boards they were using for the wall of the chicken run. He looked at Brianna.

"Get one of those ties, put it around your ankles and fasten it."

She looked at him like he'd just grown a third eye.

"Do it!"

She stepped over to the pile of tools and fished out a zip tie from among them. She took the tie, pulled it around her ankles, then stuck the end through the hole and pulled it tight.

"Tighter," he said. She pulled on it again.

He turned to Cade. "Put your hands behind your back."

Cade did as he was told, looking for some kind of chance to … But for all his impairment, the man never left an opening. Maybe he had just done things like this so often he didn't have to have all his marbles to get it right, to stay just out of Cade's reach, to keep the gun level and steady.

The man instructed Brianna to use one of the ties to fasten Cade's hands together.

"Tighter!" She pulled it another notch. "Tighter!" She pulled it again and Cade could feel the plastic digging into

169

his skin. Then the man shoved Cade hard and he lost his balance and went down. With his arms bound so he couldn't brace for the fall, he landed on his side in the dirt and moaned from the pain in his cracked ribs.

"Get two more ties," he told Brianna and she dropped to her knees, feet bound, and dug through the pile of miscellaneous tools and fasteners, finally came up with one and held it out to him.

"This is all there is," she told him.

He shrugged. "Make a loop, put your hands through it," She started to do as he'd instructed. "Behind you!" She performed the same procedure behind her. Then the man stepped forward quickly, grabbed the piece of plastic and yanked it through the loops. He pulled it so tight Brianna cried out, but he ignored the cry, just shoved her over sideways and she toppled onto the ground beside Cade.

He looked down at the two of them, lying side by side in the dirt, facing each other. Then he turned to Brianna's car, the shiny Grand Am.

"Nice car," he said, then pointed the pistol at the right front tire and fired. The explosive shot was deafening, seemed as loud as a cannon. He moved to the pickup and disabled it, too, then slipped his pistol back into his shoulder holster.

"I'm going to go get Pepe," he said. "Where are the car keys?"

"I ... I threw them into the woods."

The man spewed out a string of expletives. "I'd better be able to get that trunk open with a tire iron, and if that car's not on that road, I will come back here and—"

"It is. It's there, the road right next to that big stump. About half a mile up, you can follow the tire tracks into the trees after that. I swear it's there." That seemed to satisfy him. He seemed to know she wasn't lying. The car and

Road To Nowhere

Pepe would be right where she'd told this guy to look. Only when he opened the trunk, he'd discover that his friend had, indeed, been killed with a nail gun. And after that—

But the man didn't leave, apparently wasn't finished. Instead, he went to the motorhome, climbed the steps and went inside. Brianna looked at Cade, so terrified her eyes mostly showed only whites. "What's he …?"

They heard him rummaging around inside the cabin, then he came back down the steps. He was carrying a meat cleaver.

"This will do." He ran his finger along the sharp edge, and drew back when a thin line of red formed. "Excellent. This will do fine."

He smiled at Cade.

"I understand you've seen El Carnicero … pull the wings off a fly, yes?"

Cade couldn't breathe.

The man nodded to Brianna. "Has he told you the story of the butcher?" She didn't answer so he landed a vicious kick on her thigh and she cried out.

"Yes, he told me," she gasped.

"Then you know what to expect."

He looked at Cade and said, "I've used all the zip ties but I can't have you running off before Pepe and I get back and start the party."

Without preamble, he reached into his jacket and pulled his gun out of the shoulder holster.

Cade knew he had only seconds to live. He closed his eyes.

Bam!

Brianna screamed and all the lights went out.

Chapter Twenty-Nine

HE *SHOT HIM.*

The man pointed the gun at Cade and just shot him. Point blank in the leg.

Then the man got into his car with the meat cleaver and backed down the driveway to the road.

"Cade!" Brianna cried, her eyes fixed on the growing circle of blood beneath his leg. "Cade!"

He moaned, had passed out but was coming around. As soon as consciousness hit him, so did the pain and he cried out, continued to yell, his eyes squeezed shut, whipping his head from side to side.

"Agggghhhh!"

She watched the pain wrack his face, could do nothing, was terrified of how badly he was bleeding. He could bleed out ... before the man got back to kill them both. Maybe that wasn't such a bad idea.

Cade fought for control, squeezed his eyes closed and gritted his teeth. When he spoke, his voice was breathy, just in spurts of sentences that he could force out through the agony.

"The tire," he gasped and tears ran down his face.

"Tire?"

He opened his one functioning eye and looked at her then, focused.

"Listen to me," he gasped. "You don't have much time."

He was on his side, but rolled onto his back, cried out, and panted, swallowing more screams. Then he spoke, breathy.

"The tire. The piece of glass in the tire." And he gestured with his chin toward the motorhome.

At first she didn't have any idea what he was talking about, then he cut his eye toward the front left tire and she got it.

"Crawl over there." He was gasping out the words. "Use it to cut the ties on your hands." Another gasp. "Hurry."

She heard him grinding his teeth to keep from screaming.

The tire was about fifteen feet away and at first she couldn't figure out how to move toward it with her hands tied behind her and her ankles bound. She was on her side facing Cade. She couldn't just roll — she wouldn't go the right direction. So she scooted, using her legs to shove her, craning her neck to see, adjusting her direction by scooting her shoulders.

Finally, she bumped into the tire. The piece of glass was sticking out of it, imbedded in the rubber near the rim, and she studied the position, trying to figure out how to get her bound hands up—

"Hurry!" Cade called. Using her knees, she raised up and shoved her shoulder onto the tire, then scooted upward along the side of the tire until she could balance on her knees, every motion digging the zip ties into her skin. Scooting forward, she turned her back and wiggled closer to the rim of the tire, trying to get her hands in a position where the piece of glass sticking out of the tire would cut through the plastic.

Leaning carefully toward the glass, she positioned it on the zip tie and began to saw back and forth across the plastic. She lost her balance momentarily; the glass cut into her arm and blood flowed out over her hands. Now the plastic was wet and slick, making it even harder to get the glass into position and use it to saw back and forth.

"Brianna … hurry."

She sawed frantically, nicked a finger, cut her palm, feared that when she finally cut through the plastic, she would slice into her wrist with the glass and hit the vein.

Then her hands were free, and she almost collapsed back onto the tire.

Her ankles. She dropped to her butt, lifted her legs and sawed through the zip tie holding them together. It came off quickly now that she could see what she was doing and saw effectively back and forth with her legs.

When her ankles came free, she fell backward into the dirt.

Cade.

Leaping to her feet, she ran to where he lay and knelt beside him.

"Run!" he gasped. "Run now. He'll be back any minute."

Ignoring him, she raced into the motorhome and returned moments later with wire snips. She turned him on his side and one pinch of the snips freed his hands. He reached down reflexively to his bloody pants leg, groaning.

"You have to stand up."

"I can't. Bri, you have to run. He'll be back——"

"And he's going to find both of us still here unless you

get up." She grabbed his arm, lifted him to a sitting position with his legs splayed in front of him.

"I can't!"

She got down in his face, inches from his nose and yelled at him.

"Yes, you can. You can do anything if you have to. You told me that. Now come on."

She stood up, grabbed his arm again and pulled. He cried out, shifted his weight to the right side and tried to push up off the ground with his left foot.

He wobbled, fell back to the ground, cried out again.

"You want me to drag you? Now come on!"

This time he made it all the way upright on his left foot, holding his right leg bent at the knee. The bottom of his jeans was soaked in blood. She draped his arm around her shoulder and took a step. He hopped to stay with her, groaned at the pain and almost collapsed.

"Come on! One more." She took another step, he hopped along beside her, swaying.

It was no use, at this rate they wouldn't even get to the meadow, let alone into the woods. And they had to make it into the trees to hide ...

Or did they?

She turned, hauled him another two steps to the front of the motorhome and leaned him against it.

Then she leapt up the steps, turned the key in the ignition and flipped the switch on the cargo bay door latch. She heard the latch click, yanked the key out of the ignition, stuffed it in her pocket and jumped back down to Cade. The panel fit invisibly into the side of the motorhome. Closed, you couldn't tell there was an opening of any kind.

The killer would think they'd run away. He'd look for them in the woods. He wouldn't know there was a compartment in the side of the vehicle, wouldn't know how to open it if he did, and couldn't open it even if he knew how because it required that the ignition be on and she had the key in her pocket.

She stood in front of the side panel of the vehicle, running her fingers along the underside, searching frantically for the release. Her fingers grabbed, probing. Where was it? She'd only opened it one time.

She found it, pulled, and the panel opened. She lifted it up, revealing a compartment maybe six feet by three feet. A brand new spare tire and jack lay at one end.

Cade had figured out her plan, didn't like it, begged her. "Run. Leave me and just run!"

Brianna had neither the time nor the energy for an argument.

"No!" She grabbed his arm, draped it around her shoulder, and the two of them walk/hopped to the opening. Brianna couldn't help snatching glances at the driveway, the spring inside her winding tighter and tighter. Cade leaned into the opening and she shoved him the rest of the way in, hurt him, was sorry about that, but hurt was better than dead.

When he fell, she noticed the tip of the ACE bandage dangling out of his pocket.

Thank God!

She thought she heard a sound from the road.

Leaping in beside him, she turned to pull down the bay door.

Two things demanded the full attention of her consciousness at the same time.

There was a bloody trail in the dirt leading to the side of the motorhome.

And there was a car pulling off the road into the driveway.

She dived out of the compartment on her belly into the dirt, doing a bad imitation of making a snow angel face down. She swung her arms and legs frantically, leapt to her feet and jumped back into the opening. Reaching up, she pulled down the lid as she heard the crunch of gravel in the driveway. A car careened around the house, throwing gravel and dirt, and then the slice of light was gone and it was dark.

But she didn't need light to see what was going on out there. She could hear it.

Chapter Thirty

José Ortega could only see now out of his right eye. His left had gone blind, had just ... gone blind. He didn't know when. But he didn't need both eyes to find the stump where the Haggarty woman had said there was a logging road. Didn't need but one to drive up the road into the trees, twist and turn and ... there it was!

Pépe Salazar's black Pontiac was parked about fifty feet off the side of the road in the trees, and he could see tracks where another car had turned around in the leaves and dirt.

He pulled to a stop. Smiled.

He had briefly considered leaving Salazar to die in the trunk of his car, would have done just that if he hadn't needed the man's help. Ortega's brain wasn't functioning right. Something was very, very wrong with him, but his mind wasn't sharp enough to figure out what it was. Everything was crazy, his thoughts jumbled, so tangled up he couldn't order them. But he would never be able to do what he needed to do alone.

He wondered briefly if Salazar's mind had gone loco

on him, too. Maybe it had, no way to know because Ortega couldn't have said what was wrong with his own mind. Everything was blurred, the world was smeared, the colors all running together, the sounds too loud, too soft or gone altogether in one ear when it started bleeding.

Ortega had left, driven away from Nower County. And then he came back, and realized the instant he crossed into the county that he had been here before, done this before. He was violently sick, almost wrecked his car trying to pull over so he could heave and heave and heave.

With the understanding that he had been to Nower County already that day came the equally horrifying understanding of what he'd found when he got here. A nightmare, except he didn't wake up. Nobody was here. All the houses were empty. Everyone had vanished.

Vanished!

And he had to get help, had to call el jefe.

So he turned around, raced down the highway to get to a phone to …

He had to find Dawson McCade, had lost Pépe Salazar somewhere along the way, but Ortega *had* to …

Time vanished, and he'd found himself back on the side of the road, almost in the same place, throwing up blood. Nose bleeding. Feeling like he was dying.

Everything jumbled up after that.

He left again to get help. Then it was suddenly night and he and Pépe had come looking for their prey in the morning. How could it be night? He had to find McCade, had to go to the Butterfield house …

And then he was vomiting. Vomiting and vomiting by the side of the road.

Morning.

A face in the window.

Are you all right?

He was finally able to order his thoughts after the hill-billy told him where to find the Haggarty woman who had done something to Pépe. Ortega'd gotten his act together then. He'd found them — the woman and McCade — would go back and finish the job as soon as he got Pépe to help.

With Pépe's assistance, he would do what he knew el jefe wanted done, could see it so clearly it was almost real enough to reach out and touch. He would cut the man into pieces and take the best pieces to El Carnicero. The Butcher.

Not McCade's head, of course, that was too big. But there were other choice bits. His nose, his ears or thumbs ... or his—

A voice spoke into his mind. He recognized it as the José Ortega who'd come driving into Nowhere County ... today, maybe yesterday ... a strong man, in charge, capable. That voice wanted to know how José intended to get body parts onto an airplane. He didn't know the answer to that question.

How would he keep Pépe from taking all the credit?

He didn't know the answer to that question, either.

How would he ever escape the nightmare of this place with vanished people and memories that yo-yoed into and out of his mind, sliding in with the ease of a wave washing across the sand onto the shore? And sliding out of his mind just as easily.

Did he realize that he'd crapped himself? Couldn't he smell it?

"Shut up," he screamed at the internal voice. "Shut up or I'll kill you." He literally reached for his gun to put it to his own temple ...

No. No, no, no, no.

He needed help. He needed Pépe.

He got out of his Chevy and walked through the blanket of forest leaves to the black Pontiac parked in the trees.

"Yo, Pépe," he called out as he approached the car. "You will owe me the rest of your life for this."

He banged the tire iron on the trunk.

"Taking a nap in there?"

That was funny and so he laughed, except it didn't feel funny, and when he laughed, he blew blood all over the trunk lid.

"Pépe!"

Nothing.

He fit the end of the tire iron under the latch of the trunk, pried upward. It only took a couple of tries and he was smiling when he opened the trunk lid.

Then the world went black again, not because his memories had suddenly been slammed back into his mind so recklessly that they crashed into everything else inside. The world was black with his rage.

He didn't remember getting into his car, turning it around on the steep, slick hillside, roaring back down the logging road and then the highway and then up the driveway.

He would cut them both into little pieces *slowly*. He would start with fingers and toes. He would keep them alive to experience the pain. He would ...

They were gone.

Standing beside the open door of his car as the dust his tires had stirred up slowly settled out of the air, he stared in stunned disbelief at the place where he'd left them. He closed his eyes, opened them again slowly, expected them to appear there, the way his memories had appeared in his head as he drove along the road, on his way to a place he'd already been.

He screamed, let out a single violent cry that was as much animal as human. He wouldn't cut them apart. He would *chew* them apart. He would bite off their noses and their ears, their fingers, he would ...

They were *gone.*

He ran around screaming for a time. He ran into the empty house that had a cot and a camp stove in the living room, but no furniture, as empty as all the other houses he'd searched. He tore through the motorhome, destroying the place, ripping down curtains, throwing pillows and clothing, pots and pans and dishes.

Then he was standing, panting in the doorway.

They weren't here, obviously. They'd run away into the woods. He staggered, trying to run, but his balance was all off, across the meadow and into the trees, screaming that he'd return with an army, describing what he would do to them. But he stopped, knew he'd never find them in the trees.

His mind went blank then. The next thing he knew he was standing beside his car in the driveway as understanding flooded through him.

Horrible, terrifying understanding.

A primal fear rose up in his belly as he got it, as he knew, and he would have vomited, did heave, but there was nothing in his stomach to throw up.

McCade and the woman had vanished.

Vanished!

Just like all the other people who weren't in their houses anymore had vanished.

When that realization hit him, he became suddenly aware that the sun had dropped behind the mountain, and the long shadow of the peak was reaching out to him.

The puzzle pieces fell into place.

The two people he had left tied up here so he and Pepe

could slice them into pieces had disappeared *just like he would vanish* if he didn't escape.

The mountain's shadow darkened, slinked through the trees toward him. If the shadow got him, touched him, he would be gobbled up and vanish off the face of the earth.

He had no memory of leaping into the car, of careening down the driveway, banging into the pickup truck. He flew down the winding roads in a race for his life, trying to outrun the shadows that were coming at him from every side. He drove faster and faster, gripped by a terror that knew no bounds. Fifty. Sixty. Seventy miles an hour.

He might have been doing near eighty when he missed the hairpin turn and sailed through the broken guardrail on the Antler Creek bridge. The car went airborne. Ortega stared through the windshield at the emptiness opening up below him. Screamed at the trees rushing toward him. Tried to claw his way out of …

Antler Creek lay ninety feet below the level of the road, swollen by spring rains to more than three feet deep. Ortega's car hit the hillside, then tumbled end-over-end down it, rolled over and over until it finally came to rest upside down in the water. The car filled quickly, the water running in the broken windows and windshield. It was dark water, like the shadow of the mountain was dark. It flowed into José Ortega through his nose and ears and mouth, filled him with the blackness. It mingled with the blackness of his own heart and he was no more.

Chapter Thirty-One

BRI AND CADE lay in the darkened interior of the cargo bay, listening to the maniac charge around in a rage. He ranted and raved. They heard him in the motorhome, breaking things. Heard his voice from the meadow and the woods beyond, screeching at them.

Then he was right outside again. They heard his running footsteps, the door of his car slam shut. Then they heard a crash. He must have slammed into one of the other vehicles, the pickup or her Grand Am on his way down the driveway. They heard the grind of gravel as he tore down the winding driveway to the road.

And then there was silence. Neither of them was willing to break it so they sat motionless for what seemed like an eternity but was probably only a minute or two.

They were holding their breath. Bri let hers out in a quiet sigh.

"You think he's really gone?" she whispered. "He could have—"

Boom!

Even in the enclosed space of the cargo bay, it was

clear what the sound was. An explosion of some kind, nearby.

Their eyes had adjusted to the darkness of the interior, the light shining around the hatch that allowed access to the bay from the cabin. Bri could see Cade's pain-wracked face.

"What was that?" he asked.

Bri had no idea what could possibly have made a sound like that. How could the guy have left, and then set off an explosion? Or he could be out there somewhere now, the whole leaving-the-scene an elaborate ruse to get them to come out of hiding.

She didn't think so. His had sounded like real panic. Something had spooked him and he'd gone tearing outta here like his hair was on fire. She had to chance it, had to do something about Cade's bleeding leg. Feeling for the internal catch that released the hatch lid, Brianna eased it upward, peering out around it in reflexive fear, though it was clear the man's car was no longer parked in the driveway.

She rolled out into the dirt, stood and looked around. Stood still. Listened. Nothing. Turning, she pulled the hatch the rest of the way up. Cade lay on his back, panting in pain. From his perspective, he was looking over her head and he pointed at something in the sky.

"Look," he gasped. She turned to see a plume of smoke rising over the trees on the other side of the road.

What on earth could that ...?

Then she put it together where the smoke was coming from. The other side of the ridge ... rising above Antler Creek. She turned back to Cade.

"I think I know what that is ... but we can figure out for sure later."

Snatching the ACE bandage she'd seen dangling out of

his jeans pocket, she made a tourniquet above his knee. There was a hole in his blood-soaked jeans right below his knee. The guy'd likely been aiming for the knee and missed, but what kind of damage the bullet had done to wherever it did land was something Bri could deal with once she stopped the hemorrhaging.

She looked at the dark red stain in the dirt where Cade had been lying, the puddle of blood in the cargo bay. She wasn't sure how much blood there was in the human body, but Dawson McCade had lost a ton of it.

"I'll be right back."

She plowed through the mess of broken dishes on the floor to the hall cabinet, grabbed a handful of dish towels, snatched the roll of surgical tape and the scissors out of the bathroom, and raced back to where Cade still lay on his back in the cargo bay. Using the scissors to cut through the fabric of his jeans, she removed the pant leg. There was a bloody hole in his calf, about an inch below his knee. A hole in *both sides* of his calf! That meant there was no bullet buried somewhere in there to dig out.

Using the dish towels as pressure bandages, she covered both of the wounds and taped the bandages securely in place. Tight. Then she untied the ACE bandage. Waited. Blood didn't soak through the towel bandages and she heaved a huge sigh of relief.

She knew next to nothing about first aid, only knew her way around a bandage from watching the nurse change the dressings on the incisions where metal rods had been placed in her leg to hold the broken bones together. But it seemed reasonable to assume if Cade was still breathing … and she had stopped the bleeding … then he wasn't going to bleed to death. Right?

Well, she'd go with that.

Cade had closed his eyes as she bandaged his leg and

she didn't know now if he was sleeping or unconscious. She used other clean towels to wrap around his leg, then affixed those in place with the bloody ACE bandage she'd used as a tourniquet.

When she was done, Cade still hadn't opened his eyes, but his breathing was steady. And his pulse felt ... well, strong. Shoot, she didn't know what a strong pulse felt like but his was rhythmic, not hammering away, and she would have to go with that, too.

Finally, she stood on shaky legs and looked around, surveyed the two vehicles in the driveway. The guy had shot out the front right tires on her car and the pickup, then had banged into the pickup as he tore out of the driveway. Neither was drivable in its current state. She'd done everything she knew to do for Cade; now she had to find out if her suspicions were true.

"I'll be back," she told Cade, but he didn't open his eyes. "Don't go anywhere while I'm gone." She thought she saw his eyelids flutter.

She ran down the driveway, crossed the road, leapt over the little creek that trickled down beside the rutted asphalt, and began climbing up the hillside on the other side of the road. It was getting late, the shadows long and deep by the time she reached the top of the ridge. The black smudge was still there in the sky, trailing a tail downward. A meadow opened up a break in the trees and you could see for miles.

Even though she'd been convinced that she knew what she'd find, she still sucked in a gasp at the sight. From her vantage point, she could see only the end of the hairpin turn on Baxter Trace, but all of the bridge was plainly visible. The guardrail had been knocked completely off, now dangled in a mangled necklace along the top part of the ridge. Smoke was rising in a thready plume of black from the heap of metal that now lay upside down in the water of Antler Creek. She couldn't tell much about it, but she didn't need to. A small, dark-blue spot on the trunk was visible. It was springtime, so the undergrowth was green and moist. If an explosion like that'd happened in the autumn, it could have started a forest fire. She imagined she could smell the smoke rising off the scorched metal from where she stood, but the wind was carrying the smoke the other way.

As she sat on the bottom step of the motorhome hours later, looking up at the Big Dipper and the white spray of the Milky Way overhead, she imagined she could still smell the stench of smoke. Cade made some kind of groaning, moaning sound, and she got up and went inside to the bedroom where he lay sprawled on her bed. He was so beat up, banged up and shot up, she wondered how he knew what hurt. When she'd gotten back, he'd been sitting up in the cargo bay of the motorhome and she'd literally had to force him to take two of the oxycontin tablets the doctor palmed off on her for her cut fingers. But they'd done the trick. She got him inside before he went out again — deep sleep, she thought, not unconscious — but how would she know? She wasn't a doctor. Cade had needed a doctor's care after the beating he'd taken yesterday. That was before he got shot today.

"He's gone?"

His voice was a whisper on a breath but it startled her. She'd thought he was out cold. His eyes ... eye ... sought hers, caught and locked. She sat down on the bed beside him, careful not to jostle his injuries.

"Yes. I told you before. He's gone."

"I thought ... maybe I dreamed it."

"You weren't dreaming. His car crashed through a

guardrail, went off a bridge, fell ninety feet into a creek and exploded. He's dead. It's over."

"No, it's not over," he whispered, his eyes still locked on hers. "There will be others."

"Not in the next half hour there won't be," she said, "so take a half-hour nap."

"We need to talk, to figure out—"

"No!" she hadn't meant to bark, but that's how it'd come out and that was okay. "Not now we don't. Later." He started to protest but she held up her hand. "My house. My rules. Shut your mouth and go to sleep. Now!"

He shut his mouth and went to sleep.

Chapter Thirty-Two

CADE BELIEVED there was a warp and woof to life, a cadence, a rhythm. Like waves on the shore, coming in a little farther with each wave as the tide came in, and stopping a little shorter when the tide went out.

His days had that kind of rhythm to them now, and he understood it was partly because he might have a mild concussion from the beating Dude Number One had given him, had lost something like a gallon of blood when Dude Number Two shot him, and because Brianna kept poking those narcotics down him like they were candy.

Okay, not that. But he was reasonably sure she wasn't being particularly careful to observe the every-four-to-six-hours rule printed on the bottle. She could tell when the pain was bad and she gave him a pill, and the pain receded. Like the tide going out.

In the beginning, the pills merely blunted the sharp edge of the agony in his leg where Dude Two had shot him.

Just shot him.

Brianna didn't know how to think about a thing like

that, but he did. There was a time when he wouldn't have, but … when you'd seen worse. That'd been her line. She'd been changing the bandage on his leg — obsessing over keeping it clean "because we only have a few cut-finger antibiotics, so if you get an infection you'll just … well, die." He hadn't been able to hold onto the groan and she'd told him that "Anybody who can survive being kidnapped by monsters … well, you've seen worse."

"Sounds like the voice of experience."

Cade had hit a nerve there, was always doing that because he didn't know where the bare wires were.

"If you mean have I seen all the boogeymen under the bed, yeah. So me, too. I've seen worse."

She wasn't a particularly chatty sort, that's for sure, though given his condition — high on drugs, a concussion, major blood loss and oh, by the way, he'd been *shot* — he wasn't the best judge. But some things were clear. He'd tried, drunkenly, to get her to go away, to leave him, that the monsters would never give up.

"It's not safe. There will be others."

"But they won't come here."

"That's what you said the last time. And they found me … *twice.*"

"I didn't know there was a toothless wild card in the deck."

His mind was too muddy to follow.

"Think about it. Two guys—" She stopped and Cade could see her make herself say it. "Two *killers* cross the county line into Nowhere County on their way to the Butterfields' to … looking for you. They stumble upon me in the Dollar General Store parking lot in the Middle of Nowhere." She shook her head. "Where, friendly-South-ern-girl-to-the-bone that I am, *I introduced myself.*"

She held up a single finger — the index finger that'd had stitches, healing nicely.

"Then the first, the guy I ... shot, followed me here because I was driving a white pickup truck like the one you stole. The second guy ... he probably waited for his partner who never showed up, or maybe he looked around and got freaked out or — who knows? For whatever reason, he left. He crossed the county line and forgot he was ever here, just remembered he was *on his way here looking for you at the Butterfields'*. So he turns around and comes back ... and remembers he was here before, leaves again — wash, rinse, repeat. At some point, along came the wild card. The guy was probably beside the road puking his guts up, some local missing key teeth felt sorry for him and he asked Mr. Helpful for directions to my house. He was half dead by the time he got here. Now, he's all dead. Those two men were the only people on the kill-Cade squad who ever heard the name Brianna Haggarty."

"But the second guy, when he left, he could have told ..."

"Told who what? The minute he left here, he forgot he'd ever been here. He forgot my name and everything else about what happened here."

Cade had begun to see it through the muck.

"The only two killers who know anything at all about me are dead. You're safe, snuggled up here in — well, not the middle of nowhere, but close. As safe as you were the day you asked me if you could stay."

She paused.

"They could send the whole Colombian Revolutionary Army to the Butterfields' since they all seem to know *that* location, but like I said before, Maude and Hurl live in Pine Bluff Hollow, which is fifteen miles from here—"

He finished for her, "Over roads with no signs."

After that, he'd more or less relaxed, well, relaxed as much as a man could who knew there were murderers turning over every leaf, rock and twig looking for him.

The tide had rolled in. It had rolled back out.

Again and again.

His mind had been clear enough this morning to do the math, and unless he'd lost a day — which was entirely possible — today was Saturday, June 17, four days *after* Dude Two had shot him and four days *before* he'd have to drive out of here to go to Louisville and testify before a grand jury about how he had watched Juan Renaldo Santiago become a butcher — literally.

Cade could hear Brianna outside working. She must have taken the stitches out of her cut fingers at some point, or maybe they just fell out. With surgical tape wrapped around them now, she could hold a hammer. He could hear her banging away with it.

A hammer, not the nail gun. He got that.

Building a chicken house.

When she came back in later that afternoon, she was genuinely surprised. He had gotten up, managed to take what passed for a shower in the tiny little motorhome shower, and was mildly presentable in clean clothes — sitting at the table, which he had set for dinner. That consisted of dealing out paper plates, plastic spoons and forks and paper-towel napkins, and setting the bread and sandwich makings on the table.

"Well, look at you!" she said, and smiled.

The transforming smile, the one Cade had seen peek out the day she'd taken the splinter out of his finger, the day she remembered kissing the baby he'd never asked her about. The little boy had been her son, obviously. You don't get that kind of look on your face kissing somebody else's baby. And if she wouldn't talk about the child …

"Not exactly dressed in my party best but" — Cade didn't mean to blurt out the rest, which was probably why it fell right out of his mouth — "you've seen me wearing less."

Her face instantly flamed scarlet and he wanted to rip out his tongue.

"I mean… well, I *didn't* mean …"

She turned her back, suddenly very interested in the dashboard of the motorhome.

"Brianna, I'm so … that was rude, and I didn't mean to embarrass …" He paused. 'I'm usually a bit better at putting words together than I am demonstrating now. I was just … you took care of me and I was trying to thank you. I owe you my life."

She didn't turn, spoke over her shoulder.

"Actually, it's the other way around. I owe you my life."

"How you figure *that?*"

She did turn around then and looked at him. The shadows by the front seat of the motorhome hid the finer points of her features.

"When Dude Number Two showed up, you could have left. He didn't know you were in the house. You could have hightailed it into the woods and never looked back. But when he threatened to kill me, you came out." He held up both hands. "Whoa there! I don't think I get points for saving your life when I was the one who put it in danger in the first place."

"Fine. Let's call it even." Clearly, she did *not* want to talk about it and he could see her scrambling to find something else to say, *anything* else to say, to change the subject.

"Uhhhh … did I mention there's still soft-serve ice cream in the drug store in Persimmon Ridge — comes out of the wall spigot. I could go get us some later, it's BYOBS, bring your own bowl and spoon."

He could think of no response to such a non sequitur.

She hurried on. "That can be dessert ... so tell me" — she gestured at the table settings — "what fine cuisine you've prepared for our dining enjoyment tonight."

He picked up the ball and ran with it.

"Well ... I'm thinking bread as a first course. Laid flat on a plate and then add just the right amount of mustard."

"Mayo."

"Just the right amount of *mayo*. Ham or cheese can come next, but I am of the opinion that ham first adds a certain ... exotic quality—"

"Exotic? It's a pig."

"Work with me here." He pointed to the jar of pickles. "Sweet or savory. The choice determines the whole bouquet of the meal."

"Ham and cheese, sweet gherkins and a side order of barbecue potato chips."

"Ahhhh, such a refined palate."

The smile again. Brief, but it definitely did light up her face.

Chapter Thirty-Three

THOUGH HE'D BEEN UP and about, hopping around the motorhome like some crazed bunny to get strength back in his leg, Cade hadn't actually gone all the way down the steps yet, and decided tonight was a good time to try his wings. He was anxious to get *out of Brianna's bed* — which she'd put him in when he'd been incapable of protest — and get Brianna off the couch. If he made it all the way to the dirt today, tomorrow he'd demand to return to his cot.

"I'll do the dishes," he said, when she stood and started gathering up the trash.

"Dishes?"

"Outside. I'll make a fire. Wish you'd picked up some hot dogs for later. It's hard to cook lunchmeat on a stick."

Brianna'd changed the flat tire on her Grand Am that the gunman had shot out so she could go into Carlisle, which was apparently the closest still-functioning town, for real bandages and other miscellaneous medical supplies — including a crutch. From the look on her face when she'd rushed into the bedroom as soon as she got back, he was sure she'd believed he'd dropped dead while she was gone.

After that, she only made quick trips to a convenience store — not the Jiffy Stop with the mechanic who'd fixed her trunk, a little place that carried only the bare necessities. And an air pump. Her spare had a slow leak.

He made a fire and they sat by it in silence, though it was companionable silence now. The fire crackled and popped. Brianna had gone up into the edge of the woods and brought some windfall limbs down to add to the left-over pieces of lumber, some of it cedar and the smell was divine. It was dark now, with a canopy of stars overhead so bright they looked like Christmas tree lights, so close it felt like you could reach out and pluck them like blackberries.

He looked over at the chicken house, which was actually kinda sorta beginning to take shape. While he was out there in the na-na land of a gunshot wound and almost bleeding to death, she had somehow managed to complete construction of the remaining sections of the chicken-run fencing, but it would take two people to lift them up and attach them to each other to form an enclosure.

She gave him an appraising look.

"Your face is ... looking better."

"I look best in flickering light, so there are equal periods of darkness between the sparkles of light during which you can't see me at all."

"Seriously, it is."

And it was. he could open both eyes now.

"I'll return the compliment." He indicated her cheek. "You did a great job with the Band-Aids."

"It'll leave a good-sized scar," she said, in a much more matter-of-fact way than most women would have said it.

"Not a big deal in your life?"

She snorted out a response. "I have waaaay bigger fish to fry than a mark on my face." She realized she might have opened a door so he watched her close it. Though she didn't slam it, she did ease it shut. "I have a chicken house to build!"

"Sorry I'm too weak to help lift those sections."

"You're entitled to be worn out. Growing millions of new red blood cells is hard work. I'll worry about putting the fence together when the time comes."

"Why?" He was risking a door slamming, but he wanted to know bad enough to take the chance.

"Because there's no sense in worrying about it until—"

"No, why the chicken house?"

"I told you. I burned down my grandmother's chicken house when—"

"And so one day you were suddenly seized by an uncontrollable desire to replace it … what? Twenty years later?"

She didn't say anything.

"I know it's none of my business, but I—"

"I'm doing it to make amends."

"I get that, but why—"

"Not just 'oh, I'll apologize to Granny after all these years.' It's not like that. It's not that kind of amends."

He was about to ask, and then he thought he knew. She was looking at him, saw understanding on his face, lowered her head and looked into the fire.

"Made a list of all persons we had harmed and became willing to make amends to them all." She said the words, a rote recitation, in a soft, emotionless voice. She looked up, caught his eye and held it for a moment, then looked back into the fire. "That's step eight, actually. The chicken house is step nine, the 'made direct amends' part."

"My father got his thirty-year chip two weeks before he died." Cade started to reach into his pocket, then remembered. "I used to carry it around with me for luck." He offered a little smile. "Didn't put it in my pocket and look what happened."

He thought he could see tension draining out of her posture. He didn't say anything else. She'd tell him about it if she wanted to. If she didn't want to, she'd shut him down.

"It's because it was simple, see. A simple thing you could hang onto. Nothing complicated. That's what Sarge said, that the first amends needed to be straightforward. Because they build on each other. One amends builds on the next." She glanced up at him then, but immediately averted her eyes. "So you have to get the first one right."

"And the chicken house was your first."

"Build a chicken house. One simple chicken house. I said it over and over. Hung onto the words."

"And how could you know you were coming home to a completely insane, impossible world in which to build your chicken house?"

Her eyes snapped up then. "Nope, had no idea ... just like you had—"

"But you stuck to your guns anyway. Even after the Jabberwock bit you on the butt." He could tell she was trying to read his face, trying to judge if he were serious. "That took some stones." She let out a kind of shuddery breath. "How long?"

She knew what he was asking.

"Eleven months, three weeks, two days and"— she looked at her watch — "six hours. Not that I'm counting or anything."

"Like I said, that took some stones."

"Not stones, desperation. If I build a chicken house ..." He watched her consider whether or not to take the plunge. "I get my little girl back." He said nothing, didn't allow himself to hold his breath, either. Didn't move. "Not just get her back, *save* her. I have to! *She can't stay where she is.*"

She looked up at him.

"You a baseball fan?"

"Pittsburgh Pirates. I bleed black and gold."

She smiled, but it was wan and didn't light her face.

"Then you've heard of Jeff Nicholson."

Chapter Thirty-Four

AT FIRST, Brianna watched Cade's face in the flickering light, trying to gauge his reaction to the story she was unraveling.

Hillbilly-girl-in-the-big-city fairy tale. She meets a famous baseball player, falls in love, and they get married.

They're happy. They have a little girl.

But he's never home, and so the marriage starts to go south.

Somewhere in the telling of the story Brianna stopped watching Cade's face to gauge what he thought about what she was saying. She fell into the reality of it, and his opinion didn't matter.

DR. LAWRENCE ABERNATHY looks across his desk at Jeff and Bri, sitting side by side in uncomfortable chairs in front of it.

"I'm afraid I can't help you," the marriage counselor says.

"Can't help us?" Brianna is both incredulous and outraged. This guy costs like a bazillion dollars an hour, was recommended by "all the right people" and has a reputation among professional athletes for

putting broken relationships back together on the north side of a divorce court ... and all the accompanying property division that entails. "I realize we've got some pretty nasty issues — that's why we're here, for crying out loud — but surely ours isn't the worst case you've ever dealt with."

The shrink doesn't look at her. He looks at Jeff.

"I can't help the two of you as a couple until you deal with your own issues, Jeff, the issues relating to the abuse you suffered as a child."

If a hole had opened up in the floor beneath her and Brianna had fallen into it and dropped all the way through it to China, or whatever country was on the opposite side of the globe, she couldn't have been more surprised than she is by the statement.

Jeff doesn't look surprised, though. He looks horrified. For about two seconds. Then he looks angry. She'd only seen Mr. Nice Guy's anger flash a handful of times — and you did not want to be on the receiving end of it.

"Child abuse?" He roars the words. "I have no idea what you're—"

"The child who only watches is abused, too, just in a different way," the counselor says evenly. He looks at both of them then. "Child abusers are usually selective. They don't abuse all the children in the family. They pick out one, or maybe two, depending on their proclivities. Some select a single child — the oldest, or the youngest or the weakest. Some select a single sex, and abuse all the little boys in the house. But in abusive households, more often than not the majority of the children suffer no actual damage. Except they do, of course. Witnessing the abuse of a sibling is in itself child abuse. Watching helplessly as an adult torments a child is just as corrosive to the development of the character and personality of the observer as it is to the actual victim."

He turns back to Jeff.

"I know you weren't actually physically harmed, but watching what your mother did to your sister amounts to the same thing. And *until you resolve those pent-up emotions, deal with the rage and impotence you felt, there isn't any sense in doing marriage counseling. You aren't emotionally healthy enough to sustain a relationship until you do."*

Jeff leaps to his feet, utters selective profanity like she had never heard — *her husband was one of only a handful of baseball players, of men in general, who don't curse* — and storms out of the room.

The silence that remains seems to gather around Brianna's head like a swarm of gnats.

The counselor shakes his head. "It appears Jeff lied," he says. "I'm sorry. He said he'd told you about his mother and his sister."

Brianna gapes, has difficulty forming words.

"All I know about his sister is that she's ... she has all kinds of mental problems. Bipolar disorder, depression, drugs, she's tried to kill herself a handful of times ... she's a mess."

"You would be, too, if you'd suffered what she did as a child."

When Brianna gets home, Jeff is there — drinking. He never drinks. That's one of the margins she has built around her own growing craving — that Jeff never has alcohol in the house. But he has come by a bottle of vodka somewhere and he pours a glass half full of it and fills the remainder with coke.

"Jeff ...?" It's all she can say, and he turns on her. Lashes out in an anger she has never seen, railing at her for demanding they seek marriage counseling, for selecting Dr. Abernathy, for forcing him to go with her. None of that is true and they both know it. Jeff had suggested marriage counseling after he talked to some teammates, who had told him bluntly that the widening gulf between him and Bri wasn't going to go away on its own. They were friends trying to help. They'd suggested Dr. Abernathy, said he was the best. But reality doesn't seem to matter now.

Over the course of the rest of that evening and into the night when Jeff eventually passes out, she is given a guided tour through hell. His mother, Ophelia — *whom Brianna had only met a handful of times and totally loathed, was an aloof ice queen who wrapped herself in* her collection of china dolls, her social gatherings and her charitable causes. She was also a monster in a human being suit.

Jeff was planned, the son Ophelia's Hall of Fame baseball player husband, Big Jeff Nicholson, had always wanted, and father and son delighted in man things, from playing catch in the front yard to professional coaching lessons to help Jeff get the most out of his swing.

But two years after Jeff was born, his little sister Amanda was born. She had not been planned. Her mother had wanted to get an abortion as soon as she found out she was pregnant but Big Jeff was Catholic, not particularly devout but definitely vehement and he had absolutely forbidden it. Ophelia developed preeclampsia. Her legs and feet and ankles swelled so badly she couldn't walk. She had headaches, blurred vision and gained more than fifty pounds. All of that, of course, was the baby's fault and Ophelia already hated the child before she ever laid eyes on her.

Her husband ignored Mandy in his determination to turn his son into a professional athlete. Jeff didn't ignore her, though. He had thought she was the most beautiful thing he'd ever seen when his mother brought her home from the hospital, assumed his mother would adore her, too, because the baby was a live doll — even though she wasn't perfect like the dolls in his mother's collection. Mandy had a disfiguring brown birthmark on her nose and lip. Her mother called her Booger Lip, Queen Ugly and Monster Face when no one was around to hear — except Jeff, of course.

Throughout his whole childhood, Jeff watched his mother torture his little sister. Not in ways anybody could see. His father was scouting at the time, never home, so Jeff was the sole witness to the nightmare. It escalated from banging on the sides of Mandy's baby bed in impotent rage when she was an infant to locking her in a dark closet when she wet the bed, making her sit there all day in her own excrement.

Did Bri know, he'd asked her, his words so slurred by this time that she could barely understand him, that shoving needles under a *child's fingernails didn't leave a mark. Neither did shoving something into an ear. His sister's hearing was so damaged by the time she got to grade school that she had to wear hearing aids.*

After those revelations, Jeff passed out.

The next morning, he emerges from the mother of all hangovers to some kind of reset on reality. It's like the whole thing never happened, like they'd never been to the counselor, and he'd never vomited out the reality of the hell of his childhood.

But their marriage is better for a time, a year, maybe eighteen months, so she's willing to live with the conceit of playing the it-didn't-happen game. Jeff is attentive. Actually flies home from a couple of away-games so he can spend the weekend with her. He sends her flowers. Writes her love letters. It might have been the best couple of years of the whole ten years they spent together.

It wears off, of course. It isn't real change, so it didn't, couldn't last. Bri never went to the therapist again, but she did call him, just to ask what kind of damage had been done to her husband. He'd been blunt. Jeff would never be able to form a real emotional attachment to a woman. He did love her, to the extremely limited extent he was capable of loving any woman. He was a good man and he would try to be a good husband. Theirs was the perfect lifestyle to practice his lack of attachment. A marriage he didn't have to show up for because he played a 160- game season — plus spring training, exhibitions and playoffs. Most of his teammates didn't show up for their marriages, either.

BRIANNA FINALLY LOOKED up at Cade's face. And she had, of course, been blessed/cursed with an ability to read people, to see their real reactions, regardless of the emotional exterior they tacked on for the rest of the world to see.

All she saw in Cade's face was compassion. But then, maybe that's all she wanted to see there.

"Baseball was Jeff's life. I didn't even come in a close second. Though he did adore Pooh Bear." She stopped to explain. "Eastern Kentucky name — Winona, which quickly became Winnie ... and that ..."

He nodded understanding.

"He couldn't love a woman, but he absolutely *could* love a little girl who — I'm guessing here — was some kind of stand-in for the little sister he couldn't save. I knew he'd take good care of her, he and our nanny, Elena, who adored her. So I didn't worry about Pooh ... well, of course, I worried, but I knew she was ... *safe* with him while I was ... away."

She stopped talking then, couldn't go on because a bottomless black chasm had opened up in the chronological order of her memories. All the meanies lived down in the depths of that hole in a tangled mass of writhing horror.

The *thing*, the horrible, horrible thing Brianna had done.

The days after.

Suicide.

Of course, she'd considered it in the beginning. It had been so tempting, the go-to act that would rescue her from the jagged guilt and grief that ripped her insides to shreds with every breath.

But Brianna Haggarty knew there was life after death, believed it to her core. If her grandmother had done anything for the little girl the social worker shoved into her life years ago, it was ensure the child "was raised by the good book." Church every Sunday morning, Sunday night and Wednesday night for prayer meeting. No exceptions, no excuses.

Unlike so many people who'd had spirituality jammed down their throats as children, Brianna hadn't rebelled.

She'd merely believed. She knew on a gut level that every word the minister had ever said about life, death, heaven and hell was true. And she understood the implications of that reality. She was destined to spend eternity in hell. That's what happened to mothers who *killed their babies.*

And she was afraid of that. Terrified. She would die someday, certainly sooner rather than later given her life-style, and when she did she would burn in hell. But she couldn't help running from that reality.

Without the relief of death, what other escape was there?

She couldn't take a chance that she would ... that somehow she'd harm Pooh, too. Pooh was definitely *not* safe with Brianna, because her mother was not safe inside her own skin.

And so Brianna ... backed away.

The slide was swift and ugly. As long as Elena and Jeff were there to make sure everything was loving and good and *safe* in Pooh's life, Brianna was unhinged. Unhooked.

She drifted.

She drank. She sobered up, remembered what she had done to her son that kept her away from her daughter, and drank some more. She wanted nothing but to crawl into a tequila bottle, curl up beside the worm and forget.

There was a quiet divorce. Jeff was, after all, a famous baseball player and what had happened to his Poor Baby Son and his Poor Beautiful Wife was sad, oh so very sad.

Living on the streets, sleeping under bridges ... until the night she had curled up in the bottom of a dumpster to get out of the rain. And the next morning she'd had a close encounter with a trash compactor that shattered her leg.

That memory was a bridge across the black chasm and Brianna leapt across it and continued the story from the other side.

"Then, about a year ago, I was in an accident." She gestured toward his chest. "It's how I know what a broken bone feels like. I broke my leg and while I was in the hospital, that's when Jeff's plane crashed."

"I remember. He and another teammate. There was a lot of press coverage."

She opened her mouth to say she knew exactly what the press always said, about "Poor Jeff" the famous baseball player and his "Poor Beautiful Wife." She'd experienced their cloying pretense of sympathy.

"So I was lying there in a hospital bed with my leg in a cast watching the news and I saw ..." She lost her breath and had to stop before she could continue. "There was a picture of Pooh Bear and *Jeff's mother* at the funeral! And it hit me then — *she'd get custody.* And I couldn't ... I had to ... Pooh wasn't safe with me, but she'd be safer with me than with that monster!"

"And so the chicken house."

"Yes, eventually, the chicken house. And it's the first step. I have to get it right, it's the foundation for the rest. I have to or ..." She stopped and started again. "I have to have a 'record of sobriety' before I can sue for custody. That's what my attorney says, and I hired the best money could buy." She shrugged. "Huge divorce settlement and not much to spend it on for a lot of years. I have a big nest egg. My next appointment with the lawyer is July 15 and if I show up there ... in good shape, he'll start the ball rolling."

She looked at the construction in progress out there in the darkness.

"Between now and then ... I have to build a chicken house. One simple chicken house."

∾

CADE WATCHED the woman in the flickering light bare her soul, he listened, but that was all. He asked no questions. She would tell him whatever she wanted him to know and the rest was none of Dawson McCade's business.

But he did know there was a whole lot more to the story than what she'd shared. He knew that the Pirates' legendary center fielder Jeff Nicholson had had *two* children, a little girl and a little boy. And he knew that the little boy had died.

Chapter Thirty-Five

BRIANNA WAS up near the top of the ridge, royally ticked off. She'd climbed all this way up here this morning because she was certain there was a blackberry bush beside the big rock in the meadow. Of course, she wasn't even sure she remembered how to make blackberry cobbler. And maybe she didn't even have all the ingredients, though as she recalled, it was mostly just blackberries, sugar and pie crust, and none of those required any elaborate preparation. She'd serve it with big blobs of ice cream, go get some of the soft-serve she'd mentioned to Cade last night.

But when she got to the rock, there was no bush in sight. No sign there'd ever been a blackberry bush there. Had she gotten the place wrong, or had something happened to the bush—?

She spotted movement out the corner of her eye and her eye snapped to the road. From here she could see a half-mile stretch of it. A car was coming down it.

It was driving slowly.

Well ... people drove slowly on these roads, these were mountain roads, after all, and ...

Locals didn't drive slow.

She watched the car, a dark-colored sedan of some kind, as it wound in and out of her sight, behind trees and reappearing around bends. Her heart began to hammer so hard she could feel her vision pulsing with each beat.

The closer the car got, the more sinister it looked.

That was ridiculous. The mere presence of a car on the road did not automatically mean it was …

She remembered Cade's description of his near-miss in Louisville.

It was just a guess, not even a guess, a gut reaction … there's no reason I could have known, should even have suspected. It wasn't like either one of the guys had "I am a killer" on a flashing neon sign above his head. But I just … I knew. I knew. So I booked.

Brianna *knew,* too.

And she was up here on the side of the mountain. At a dead run back to the motorhome, she still had time to warn Cade and—

Yeah, and *what?*

What could they do?

They had no weapons, unless you counted a nail gun. Dude Two had thrown Dude One's pistol out into the meadow and they'd just left it there.

But Cade was in no condition to run anyway. Oh, sure, if she barreled back down there now and warned him, the two of them could take off through the woods … Cade wouldn't make it two hundred yards.

The car came around the final bend and headed toward Granny's driveway.

Closer.

Closer.

Then it drove past and kept going.

Brianna almost choked on her relief, gasped and tears

squirted down her cheeks. Of course, it wasn't somebody looking for Cade!

Paranoia, thy name is Brianna Haggarty.

She tried to still her runaway heartbeat, took a couple of deep breaths and let them out slowly, shook her head to refocus.

Maybe the mystery blackberry bush was in the smaller meadow halfway up. She turned and trotted down the mountainside, careful not to lose her footing on the glaze of fallen leaves.

The recipe, the pie crust part, might require baking soda and she didn't have any. As she stepped out into the meadow overlooking Granny's house, she tried to figure out what you could substitute for baking soda if—

She almost missed it.

Far down the road, a man was moving stealthy through the woods about fifty feet back into the trees, coming this way. She could see only that he was dressed in dark clothing, and had a shock of white hair that blazed in the afternoon sunlight. He was not dodging from one tree to the next or anything like that, but moving warily, slowly and carefully. He'd obviously gone down the road and around the curve, then parked and was returning on foot to ...

To kill them.

To put a bullet in Cade's head. And in hers too, if she went back down there. Sudden terror grabbed her guts and squeezed. The man sneaking through the woods was a trained killer.

She couldn't *save* Cade. It would do no good to rush down the mountainside so she could die with him.

What would happen to Pooh Bear if something happened to Brianna?

Bri was safe up here, could step back into the trees,

vanish into the undergrowth and he'd never know anybody'd been there.

The man was coming up on a rocky ravine. Unless he went back out of the woods to the road and skirted it, he'd have to clamber down into it and back out and that would slow him down. It was almost completely covered with kudzu vines and you couldn't even see it from the road. He wouldn't know it was there until he got to it. He wasn't familiar with these woods but Brianna—

She knew the woods and he didn't. She knew where—

She took out at a dead run across the meadow toward the motorhome, was gasping for air when she burst through the door and found Cade practicing with his crutch.

He didn't even ask. He could tell from the look on her face.

"Where?"

"On foot" — gasp! — "coming down the roadside. A couple of minutes."

"You've got time. Get out of here, get in the car and—"

"Tire's flat." She'd noticed it when she'd started on her blackberry quest earlier. The slow leak in the spare had finally flattened it.

"The woods, then. Hide. Leave me and go—!"

"No!"

He was standing on his good leg and grabbed her by the shoulders, literally shook her and shouted into her face.

"Get out of here! Do you *want* to die?"

She heard her own words and marveled.

"A decoy—"

"What?" He was still yelling, incredulous and angry and scared. "That's insane."

"Mother birds ... pretend they're hurt, lead—"

Now he was screaming.

"Listen to yourself, Brianna. I'm not your baby bird! What good will it do to lead him—?"

She was catching her breath.

"I know these woods and he doesn't."

"What difference does—?"

She yanked out of his grasp, the motion almost knocking him down, and pointed up the mountainside.

"The Beaufort County line is *less than a mile* that way!"

He knew instantly what she was planning.

"He'll kill you. He'll shoot you down before you—"

"He wants to find you and I know where you are! He won't kill me."

She just said that. She didn't really believe it.

Cade was still babbling but she wasn't listening anymore. She opened the little coat closet, yanked a jacket off a hanger, stuffing her hands through the sleeves as she headed for the door.

"What …?"

"Red. He has to see me to follow me."

"Brianna …" The word was a strangled sob. "*Please, don't*—"

She missed the rest of it by leaping down off the last step and shoving the door shut behind her.

Chapter Thirty-Six

How COULD Brianna get his attention?

Turned out that wasn't hard at all. She raced across the backyard, through Granny's empty house and out onto the front porch that faced the road. She let the screen door bang shut behind her, took two steps out onto the porch and a voice from below her and to the right called out, "Freeze. Stop right where—"

She leapt off the porch and raced across what once had been a rose garden up next to the house, expecting any second to feel a bullet in her back. Then she ducked behind the hedge and tore out for all she was worth along it to the trees. He couldn't see her through the hedge, would have to climb the steep incline of the front yard to chase her, even to get her in his sights to shoot her.

Not daring to look back, she raced into the woods, through the trees and up the hillside.

"Stop!"

The voice was much closer than she'd thought it'd been and she almost stumbled. A chunk flew out of the bark of the tree beside her, though she heard no gunshot.

He was shooting at her!

She staggered sideways, trying to zig-zag, when a chunk flew out of another tree on the other side.

She was a big target in a red jacket and he'd missed twice. Maybe he was trying to hit her *without killing her*, which would be a tricky shot. She dived behind the big oak tree where she'd carved her initials when she was ten, instantly flattened up against the trunk and edged the rest of the way around it, a hand over her eyes to keep from being blinded by the monstrous firethorn bush's vicious thorns, like three-inch hypodermic needles along every stem, curved to puncture, rip and grab. The needles cut into the back of her hand, snagged the sleeve of her jacket and her pants, clawed at her forehead.Leaping out from behind the bush, she ran as fast as she could up the hillside to the cover of an outcrop of rock, where she used to sit when she was a little kid, pretending it was a pirate ship and she was the captain, sailing it off through the green sea of woods.

Grunts, then a muffled cry came from the space by the oak tree.

It'd worked; the man had come barreling around the tree after her and ran smack into the firethorn. It would come close to skinning him alive if he hit it full blast. It would at the very least cut him up good as he fought through it, and hang on his clothing, slowing him down, giving her another couple seconds of lead.

She scrambled over loose rocks and fallen leaves, stumbled, fell and tore out the elbow of the red jacket she definitely didn't need to be wearing for him to keep track of her. She saw no more flying chunks of wood knocked out of trees, so he must have stopped shooting.

The limbs of a huge weeping pine tree about twenty

feet up the hill hung down so low, you had to duck your head—

She heard a scrambling sound and realized he was right behind her! She sneaked a look and he'd lost his footing in the same spot she had, maybe thirty feet away. The image froze in a frame in her mind when he looked up and she saw him.

The face had been a nightmare of scarred flesh long before he ran into the firethorn bush that had sliced bloody claw marks across it. He had no right eye, wore a black eyepatch, it looked like there were scarred holes in his skin where flesh was missing, and a chunk of his nose was … gone.

The white hair was on the head of a man in his mid-40s, big, muscular and strong — long legs and broad shoulders. He was wearing a dark tee shirt, a black vest and camouflage pants, with a holster strapped to his leg. Taking all that in between one heartbeat and the next, Brianna turned, dived as she was turning, slid like on snow across the bed of needles and leaf fall under the big tree's limbs. Her momentum carried her almost all the way out front under the low limbs and she scrambled to her feet on the other side of the tree. Hunching over, she raced for the creek bed just up ahead. Big laurel bushes lined both banks, but right up at the top, there were what she called tiptoe rocks, ones she'd placed there years ago so she could hop from one to the next and go up the creek instead of plowing through the bushes on the bank.

She made the creek. Hopped rock to rock to rock, aware of how slick they were with the springtime moss and lichen slathering their surfaces. Wet, too, of course. One misstep. Leaping out of the creek bed at the end of the stand of bushes, she ran at right angles to it, seeking an outcrop of tumbled boulders beyond.

Splash!

Yes!

The sound was like rocket fuel, propelling her forward. She reached the rocks and dived in among them. They ranged in size from as big as a washing machine to bigger than a house, jumbled up there in the woods. She'd asked Granny once how that had come to be, and the old woman had favored her with a withering look.

"How would I know how them rocks got up on that hillside? Seems more peculiar to me that there's a layer of coal runs all the way through this mountain like the icing in the middle of two layers of cake. How'd *that* get there?"

She paused for a single gasping breath, considering ...

It wasn't like she knew exactly where the border was in the woods, like there was the dotted line on the forest floor and across the limbs of the trees. She knew that the Pendergrasts, who lived in the hollow on the other side of this bluff, had gone to school in Beaufort County. She'd had a crush on the oldest, only saw him at football games. So somewhere—

A chunk of rock flew out of the boulder right beside her nose and she leapt forward, ducking down, ran bent over, trying to take advantage of the small stand of bushes that ran from the rocks up to the embankment at the top of the bluff. It provided scant protection. If he really wanted to shoot her, now was the—

A flame of pain exploded in the back of her head and the world went black.

Whum!

Whum!

Whum!

The thrumming sound in her ears was so loud and pronounced it muffled every other sound.

Rocks were stabbing into her back and her head was

lower than her feet. Must have tumbled down ... took a header off the embankment.

"... did not kill you ... que bien."

She opened her eyes and the man in the tee shirt, vest and camouflage pants — *wet* camo pants — stood about twenty or thirty feet above her on the hillside, pointing a pistol at her. The others hadn't had Spanish accents, but this one did.

Reaching her hand up to the top of her head, she drew it back with her fingertips bloody.

"... will live. Come here."

The world was spinning. She was breathing in strangled gasps, terror so constricting her chest she couldn't seem to get in enough air. The man above her was scratched up — bleeding from a dozen cuts — and wet, but he didn't even appear to be breathing hard.

"Now!"

She tried to obey, but couldn't seem to figure out how to get up. Her head was below her feet. She had to get to her knees somehow, but no movement seemed to work.

"What did you do with Ortega and Salazar?"

Without answering — what could she say? — she concentrated on figuring out that she'd have to roll over onto her belly, scoot her legs around until they were downhill and then get to her knees. She tried, creating a cascade of leaves and forest floor debris down the hillside. Rising up on her knees, her back and hair coated in leaves, she tried to rise, but her feet slid out from under her and she went down.

"Do not make me come down after you." He didn't frame it as a threat, a simple statement. "If you do, I will put out one of your eyes."

She looked up at him in terror and saw no emotion of any kind on his ravaged face, knew with absolute certainty that if she didn't do as he said, he would indeed blind her. She leaned forward and clawed at the incline, digging with her hands as well as her feet. But it was steep and slick and harder to climb than it looked and she mostly scrambled and slid in place.

"I tell el jefe, send no one else. By Wednesday, I bring back a souvenir. I do this job per-son-al-ly." He pronounced each syllable separately.

He held something in front of him. She couldn't see what it was but he made some kind of motion and then she recognized it as a small knife, there and gone, a switchblade.

"Sharp — to cut through cartilage ... an ear, a nose."

He dropped it into the side pocket of his vest.

Redoubling her efforts, Brianna scrambled frantically upward, slid down, clawed her way back, crawled, groped, dragged herself.

"Ortega's hillbilly, he tell me 'Hag-gar-ty,' where to find. Is *you*, yes?" She was more than halfway up, struggling to keep going. "Answer me!"

She slid backward a few feet.

"I'm Brianna Haggarty," she panted.

He made a come-on gesture with the hand not holding the gun. "Twenty seconds or you lose an eye." Propelling herself upward with a mighty shove, Brianna clawed the leaves, digging her hands and feet deep, crawled upward frantically and finally collapsed in a winded heap on the edge of the embankment in front of him.

"Get up."

He kicked her hard, the blow merely aimed at her body, nowhere in particular, and it connected with her hip. She yelped in pain, tried to rise.

It wasn't planned, if "planned" meant more than a second or two of premeditation. He reached down and grabbed her by the hair to drag her to her feet and she got halfway up before she began to lose her balance, felt herself falling backward, began to pinwheel her arms to stay upright.

He still had hold of her hair and she sensed his own balance faltering. In response, she pushed off and launched herself backward with all her strength. He let go of her hair but it was too late. She dragged him off his feet with her and together they tumbled head-over-heels down the hillside. He started grabbing for her before they even came to a stop. She shoved at him with her feet, pushing him farther down, rolled to her left and began crawling frantically sideways to get away.

He'd grab her any second. An iron fist around her ankle. A bullet in her back.

She made it to a tree trunk and looked back.

The man in the wet camouflage pants was lying at the bottom of the hill on his back. Just lying there.

Bri leapt up and bolted away, angling along the hillside rather than climbing up it. Ran maybe fifty yards to a big sycamore tree and dodged behind it.

There was no sound behind her. Gasping, she tried to hold her breath so she could hear better. Two seconds. Three. Five.

The breath burst out of her lungs.

Still nothing.

Peeking around the side of the tree, she could see the embankment they'd tumbled down, but bushes blocked her view of the bottom of the hillside.

She stood frozen, undecided on what to do. Then the man appeared, getting slowly to his feet below the bushes and she was afraid to move. He didn't look to either side, merely stood, his clothes and hair matted with leaves and dirt. He took a single step down the hillside and his feet immediately went out from under him. He went down, slid ten or fifteen feet. Then he got back up and kept going.

He made no effort to turn sideways and dig his feet into the hillside for traction, just walked, *staggered* downward, stumbled, fell, got up, fell again, and kept going — moving forward in the direction he was pointed, which was down the hillside.

Brianna stayed out of sight, but moved around the tree as he descended so she could watch his progress. He never turned from one side to the other. Never made any effort to change direction. He merely walked with his arms limp at his sides, his hands empty.

She waited until he was completely out of sight. Even then, she crept low to the ground to the spot where they'd landed, looked around. Yes! Lying in the leaves, there was his pistol. She reached out trembling fingers to pick it up and when she lifted it off the leaves she saw the knife he'd been holding, too, a small switchblade dangling beside a single key from an unadorned keyring. She picked it up as well, then turned and let go of her terror, raced across the side of the hill below the embankment, over some rocks to a creek bed that she could clamber up to the top of the hill. From there, she made it all the way to the motorhome at a dead run.

Chapter Thirty-Seven

CADE HAD SAT FROZEN after Brianna came rushing in, grabbed the red jacket and ran off into the woods to be a mother bird.

He called out to her once, then made himself be quiet. He didn't know where the killer might be.

She'd run off ... just run ...

What could he do?

He turned and grabbed the crutch he'd dropped on the floor, started for the door, took a hopping step, put the toes of his bandaged leg on the floor and shifted as little weight as possible to that leg in an effort to limp rather than just hop. But the pain was a flamethrower in his leg, and the jostling was sending shockwaves through his bruised/broken ribs.

What was he going to do — hop down the steps and go chasing after her like he was on a pogo stick?

Nooooo!

He screamed the word in his head, turned and swept everything off the countertop onto the floor in frustration.

Think. *Think.* What could he do?

The killer would come back here. Cade hadn't heard gunfire, though the killer probably had a silencer on the gun, probably sounded like a cough when it fired.

Say he caught Brianna — *didn't shoot her,* Cade couldn't allow his mind to countenance that — he would drag her back here. Cade had to be ready for them when that happened. He crutched into the kitchen, opened the silverware drawer and selected the biggest, meanest butcher knife he could find.

There was nowhere in the motorhome where he could hide and then leap out at the killer, surprise him. Okay, then, he would ... hide in the shadows behind the motorhome,

He made it around to the side of the motorhome that didn't face the woods, flattened up against it. You'd have to come all the way around it to see him.

He waited, listened.

This was crazy, absolutely futile. He was on a crutch with broken ribs and a butcher knife.

What was that saying — never bring a knife to a gunfight.

Was there something else he could do? Anything?

Maybe he could crutch out into the meadow, search the grass, find Guy Number One's pistol that Guy Number Two got out from under the seat of the pickup and threw away.

Cade hadn't been looking when he threw it, didn't notice where it went. He'd intended to go up there and find it as soon as he was moving around a little better. You didn't just leave a loaded .357 Magnum lying around in the grass. A maybe-gun was better than a useless butcher knife. He dropped the knife, moved as fast as he could around the motorhome, crutch/hopped across the construction site and out into the meadow and was about to drop to his knees in the grass.

A sound. A voice.

"Cade! Cade!"

He looked up into the trees searching, saw her pinballing from one tree to the next in the forest, running dead out. She came out of the woods into the meadow.

She was alone!

Spotting him, Brianna cried out his name, and then raced toward him and only aborted throwing herself into his arms and bowling him off his feet at the last second. She skidded to a stop in front of him, dropped what she was carrying, and he grabbed her, held her.

She began to sob, cried out random words he couldn't connect, the sound of her voice rich and velvet. She made no sense but that didn't matter. Sense didn't matter. She was *alive!*

A few minutes, five hours, a lifetime passed and she finally cried herself out, the first burst of hysteria over. She stepped back, still panting.

"He went over. Must have. Had to, I guess. He fell down a hill after he shot me—"

"*Shot* you?"

"Nothing. It's …" She reached up into her hair where he could see it was matted with blood, and kept babbling. "Then he wandered away down the hillside, staggered, like he was a zombie."

Her mind was obviously ping-ponging. She leaned over and picked up what she'd dropped. A pistol and a keychain with something long and slim, maybe a knife, attached to it.

"He's lost his gun." Then she tapped the only other thing besides the knife on the keyring — an ignition key. "And his wheels."

"But he'll be back."

"Not for a while he won't."

"How long?"

"I don't know. We need to figure that out. When you forgot, what was the first thing you remembered?"

Cade forced himself to calm down and concentrate.

"It was like waking up from a dream, fuzzy, like my head was full of static. I don't know any other way to describe it. And I was driving down the road toward Nower County to get to the Butterfields', but something was wrong. The time wasn't right. I looked at my watch and freaked. I had lost three hours."

"So your first memory was ..."

"That I was on my way to Nower County. But I was already driving toward it by then, and I don't remember turning around, so there had to be some period of time when I figured it out, changed directions, then gradually ... *came to*."

"But somehow you *reset* to going down that road."

"I guess."

"Okay, so in a couple of hours, at least that long, probably a lot longer, this guy's going to come around and remember he was looking for you. He'll be somewhere on Shagbark Mountain." She glanced up the hillside. "There are thousands of acres of woods on that mountain. You could get lost for *days*. He won't remember how he got there, but he *will* know that he was on his way to Brianna Haggarty's house in Nowhere County."

"And he'll find a way to get back to that. He'll steal a car, buy a car, pay somebody to give him a ride, *something*."

"The guy in the Waffle House said ..." Brianna's brow creased and she repeated the man's words, complete with mountain dialect. "Them folks get into some kinda loop. They leave, forget they was ever here, so they minds reset, go back to whatever they last remember and they start all over."

"So they have to somehow make their way to a road leading into Nowhere——"

"Not just any road. A specific road. They remember they were going into Nowhere County *on a specific road*."

"So what road would this guy——?"

"Baxter Trace. He was coming from the north. If he'd crossed the county line on Blue Spruce Pike or Henryville Lane, he'd have been coming from the south. He'll reset to 'going down Baxter Trace to Brianna's Haggarty's house,' he'll cross the county line and——"

"He'll get sick, pull over to the side of the road, puke his guts up ..." Cade paused, "... and keep coming."

"Right. So what's your point, Cade? In an hour or three hours or two or thirty minutes, he'll come back — and we *have to get out of here* before he does! I'll have to change the tire on the pickup, bend the side of it back out where the guy banged into it, then we can go——"

"Where?"

"*Anywhere!* Go to somebody's house." She barked out a laugh. "*Anybody's* house. There's a whole county full of empty houses here, in case you hadn't noticed. Take your pick. We have time to grab a few things before we go, supplies, stock up, because when he hits the county line and gets his marbles back, he'll remember chasing me through the woods, *remember my face* — so we'll *both* have to stay out of sight from now on."

"Not if we stop him."

That stopped Brianna.

"*Stop* him?"

Cade nodded.

"How? He's a professional killer and so far" — she made a sweeping gesture that took in her face and head wounds, his face, chest and leg wound — "those guys are better at this than we are. How could we possibly—?"

"Because we know the future and he doesn't."

"Say again?"

"We know what's going to happen."

"How does that help—?"

"We know he's going to cross the county line, pull over and get desperately sick."

"And ..."

"And we'll be waiting for him when he does."

"*Waiting* for him?"

"Yeah, the mouse that roared and all that. The worm that turns."

Rage erupted like lava through a crack that went all the way to the center of the earth.

"I *won't* be the victim anymore! I didn't ask to get kidnapped. I didn't ask to be tied up, gagged, terrorized and dragged through filth for four days, didn't ask to crap my pants because they wouldn't let me go."

He didn't mean to say that last part out loud.

"I watched a man butcher another man. Literally. *With a chainsaw.* And for the past two weeks, I've been running in blind terror. I'm *done* running."

He turned, his gaze boring into her hazel eyes.

"When he comes back, when he crosses into the county, I'm going to be waiting for him. And while he's too sick to defend himself ... I'm going to put a bullet in his brain."

Chapter Thirty-Eight

"Just ... *shoot* him?" Brianna was having trouble catching the train of Cade's thought. It'd pulled out of the station before she was ready. "Are you suggesting, we just ...?"

"Shoot him down in cold blood? Yeah, that's *exactly* what I'm suggesting." He took the pistol out of her hand. "He's unarmed, remember."

"He could get another gun somewhere."

"Why would he stop for a gun if he doesn't remember he lost his?"

"I don't know! I don't understand how this whole mind-wipe thing works. How will he figure out he needs a car if he doesn't remember he left his here? When you left Nowhere County, how did you know you were going the wrong direction so you had to turn around to go back? You did, though. You turned around, even if you don't remember doing it."

"I can't answer all the questions. I don't even know what I don't know. All I do know is I need your help."

She must have looked horrified because he rushed on.

"Not to kill him. I don't mean that. I'm not asking you to kill him. But I can't ..." He gestured down at the leg with a bullet hole in it. "I can't get there under my own steam."

She said nothing.

"Please."

All the air went out of her and she settled back against the hood of the motorhome, might have collapsed if it hadn't been there.

"You're crazy. We can't ... he'll ... what if he *does* get another gun? He'll shoot you."

"Even if he hadn't lost his own gun, he won't be in any shape to shoot anybody, to do anything but heave his guts up. Been there, done that! I *guarantee* he'll be totally incapacitated."

"For how long?"

He concentrated.

"A couple of minutes."

"Are you sure? How long is 'a couple"? Two minutes? Three?"

"It ... passes gradually, doesn't turn off like a spigot. You come back around slowly."

"*How long?*" she demanded. "How long were you so totally out of it you couldn't have stopped somebody from shooting you?"

He didn't say anything, then looked her in the eye.

"At least a minute. *At least* that long. I think it was *a lot* longer than that — like five, maybe even ten minutes. But when you're that sick ... time flies when you're having fun."

She gave him a dirty look for the lame humor.

"Even if it's only half that long, I'm willing to take the chance. But I am *not* asking you to risk your life." He might have been trying to grin but couldn't pull it off. "I just need a lift. Give me a ride to the place where he'll cross the line, let me out and drive away. I'll take it from there."

She studied him, realized to her horror that he was absolutely determined, that she wasn't going to be able to talk him out of it.

"And leave you just sitting on the roadside for hours, maybe all night, just waiting ..." She stopped. "You're really going to do this, aren't you?"

"Yes, I'm really going to do this."

She made a humph sound in her throat.

"Hopping on one foot? Riiiiiight."

And they left it at that.

Cade went back into the motorhome to put shoes on both feet, the hopping one and the other. She went out to the meadow and looked around. It didn't take long to find the gun in the grass.

When she came back inside with it, he said, "You think we need a second gun?"

"I'd take a bazooka if I had one."

She put the pistol beside the other one lying on the table. She knew nothing about guns, but it was easy to see they were different kinds. One had a sight on the barrel that had gouged a hole in her cheek and a revolving chamber for ammo. The other was flatter, more stream-lined, the kind she'd watched countless television cops slam a magazine into the bottom of the grip.

"Can you shoot either one of these?"

"You pull the trigger — bang! bang! — how hard can it be?"

"You don't really mean you've *never*—"

"Sorry. Lame attempt at black humor. My bad. Yeah, I know how to fire them. After ... when I got back, I bought several firearms, pistols, a couple of shotguns, learned how to use them all. Got a concealed-carry permit and for years

I never went anywhere unarmed." There was a hardness in his voice and she noticed that teeth-grinding thing she'd seen the first day she met him. TGA. Teeth Grinders Anonymous.

Then he shrugged. "A couple of years ago, I figured out that carrying the gun was fear reaching out from the past to bite me in the butt. I wanted it all to be over, so I weaned myself off ... first, I didn't carry it, but kept it in the car. Then just in the nightstand by the bed. About a year ago, I locked it in the wall safe."

He reached down and picked up the gun that didn't have a sight, hefted it from one hand to the other.

"This one is a suppressed Glock 17, 9mm with a 17+1 capacity, and high-set night sights."

Okay. She was impressed.

He picked up the one that'd torn a hole in her cheek.

"This is a Ruger Security-Six, .357 Magnum with serious knockdown power."

Indicating the sightless pistol — "You want this one in a gunfight. You'd have to reload the revolver three times to get the number of rounds in only one Glock magazine." He paused. "Magazine, not clip. Clip is Hollywood-speak."

Then he put the Glock back down on the table. "I'll take the Ruger. I think it might possibly stop a charging rhino. My firearms instructor said he'd dropped a bear with one." He smiled a little. "I won't shoot my foot off."

She thought he might be about to add some crack about not having a foot to spare, but either he wasn't or saw the look on her face and thought better of it.

Looking around for something to carry food and water — they would have to wait for hours, might even be tomorrow before he showed — her eye went to the top of the refrigerator, to the cutesy little contraption containing plastic plates and utensils, a big thermos painted in rainbow hues and a red-checked tablecloth to spread on the ground.

A picnic basket.

The irony was fitting.

But before she could start work changing the pickup tire, Cade suggested they use the killer's car, instead. They had the key. And with the back side of the pickup bed mashed in, it might prove very difficult to change the tire. It'd be quicker and easier to use the other car. She didn't like the idea but couldn't come up with a reasonable excuse not to.

She ran all the way down the road to the spot where she'd seen the killer skulking through the woods. About seventy-five yards farther up the road, a black Lincoln Town Car was pulled off into the trees. She unlocked the door, opened it ... and didn't want to get inside. This car wasn't some airport rental. This was *his* car, had New Jersey plates.

She shook her head, no time for nonsense, got in, fiddled around with the seat to readjust it forward so she could drive. She could smell him, a raw man scent. Not aftershave or scented bar soap. The killer's smell.

She drove it up Granny Haggarty's driveway and around to the back. Which had become a veritable parking lot, with the motorhome, her car and Cade's stolen pickup truck. There was also a black Pontiac on a logging road with a body in the trunk.

Images flashed through her mind like a comet and were gone. *Jew got some 'splainin' to do, Lucy.*

Brianna leapt out of the car as soon as she came to a full stop.

"It's *his* ... it ... smells." It was a ridiculous thing to say, but it was true. Cade crutched around to the passenger side, opened the door, rifled through the papers in the glove box. When he read the name on the car title, all expression fell off his face.

"Describe this guy."

"Had a black patch over his right eye, big and strong — too young for white hair. And his face was ... he had scars all over—"

"His mother ran away from his abusive father, took her four children and tried to cross the La Tatacoa Desert. He was the only one who survived, had to fight off the scavengers. The birds pecked out one eye and chunks of his face. He was three years old."

Brianna shuddered.

"He's Santiago's right-hand man, his second in command. El Buitre ... the Vulture. He ... was there that day in the hut, he helped Santiago ..."

Cade leaned over, pulled the key out of the ignition, hobbled around to the back of the car, punched the key fob and opened the trunk. Then stood staring at the contents. Brianna started around the car to look, but he slammed the trunk lid down.

"Let's go." He tossed her the keys and got in on the passenger side.

As they drove away from her grandmother's home, Brianna told Cade that where he had planned was "actually a pretty good place for ... an ambush."

She'd been considering the geography of the spot on Baxter Trace where the imaginary dotted line split Nower and Beaufort counties.

"No matter how big a hurry he's in, he won't be going fast at that point. That stretch of road — for about two miles it's coming down off Shagbark Mountain to the North Fork of the Rolling Fork River, turns and twists and switchbacks. It's really narrow, too."

She slowed as they made a sharp turn, then pulled off

the road in front of the sign that said "...ufort Co..ty." "Beaufort County" riddled with bullet holes.

"This is it." He got out of the car, leaned on his crutch and hobbled clumsily toward the sign.

"Be careful. If you trip and fall across that line, you won't remember why you came here."

The enormity of that statement hit both of them and they were silent.

If he took one step past that sign, Cade would hit the Jabberwock and wouldn't remember he had ever been in Nowhere County. He wouldn't remember how he got beat up, how his ribs got cracked, how he'd got shot.

And he'd forget all about Brianna Haggarty and her chicken house.

Chapter Thirty-Nine

THE REALIZATION ROLLED AROUND in Cade's mind like a bowling ball in a rain barrel.

Not *if* Cade crossed the county line ... *when* Cade crossed the line. *When* he did, he wouldn't remember.

If he survived the next few hours, Cade *would* be crossing it to go back to Louisville to show up as the surprise witness at a grand jury hearing, where he'd testify under oath about watching a monster butcher another human being. He and Brianna hadn't talked about it, didn't have to, they knew what day it was. By some mutual, unspoken agreement, neither one of them had brought it up, though, and he couldn't really tack a reason on why that was. They just ... hadn't, and they *would* have to talk about it — the logistics of it.

But that was then. This was now. He had to focus on now.

Looking around, Cade could see why Brianna thought the spot might be a good place for an ambush. Coming from Beaufort County, a car would come upon the county line right out of a curve, no warning. Beyond the road sign, the road was straight for less than a hundred yards before another sharp curve to the left. The road and shoulders were narrow, the hillsides on both sides steep, and the forest came all the way down to the road.

They'd decided not to wait in the car, didn't want the killer to notice *his own car* parked on the roadside up ahead with two people sitting in it, feared he might pull off the road in Beaufort County to get the lay of the land, maybe get out and try to circle through the woods to investigate or something — not likely, but he was a *trained* killer. Brianna let Cade out, and while she drove the car down the road and around a bend out of sight, he worked the math in his head, eyeing the distance. A car traveling twenty miles per hour took about fifty feet to stop. Say he was going twice that — forty miles per hour — it'd take at least seventy-five feet.

Somewhere between the stand of yellow wildflowers — fifty feet in — and the big crack in the asphalt at seventy-five feet, the killer would pull over to the side of the road, desperately sick. Cade needed to be somewhere in the middle, so he wouldn't have far to run — hobble, *hop!* — to where the car had pulled off.

Searching the woods beside the road, they found some cover that was about halfway. It wasn't a lot of conceal-ment but the killer wouldn't be eagle-eyeing the woods for danger at that point. Two rocks about the size of a matching set of Volkswagens protruded from the leaf-strewn hillside. One rock stuck out from the hillside farther than the other, blocking the line of sight for cars coming from Beaufort County. The other rock would provide a bench of sorts to sit on while they waited.

Cade gauged the distance he'd have to cross to get to the car, thinking like a football player, a running back. He'd have to make more than a single first down … maybe almost three first downs. On a crutch. Or hopping on one foot.

Brianna would wait for him there, sitting on the rock, while he …

They settled in, sat side by side on the cold stone, mostly hidden from view by the big rock, and waited. It grew quiet. Not a car passed. Now that they'd stopped making noise, the forest sounds picked up again — birds calling, a couple of cicadas in the bushes around the sign.

Cade checked his watch. It was only half an hour later than the last time he'd checked it. It could take a long time for the killer to find wheels and take up again the task of murdering Dawson McCade and Cade would just have to wait patiently here until he did.

The sun in a cloudless blue sky shined down into the hollows and valleys between the mountains, casting long shadows on the road. They didn't talk much, just sat, staring, each a prisoner of their own thoughts.

Mid-afternoon passed. It grew late.

The shadows lengthened, spread out east from the mountains as the sun crossed the sky.

"My granny used to tell me 'the shadder'll get ye,'" Brianna said, indicating the darkness moving across the valley toward them. "'When it's yore time, the shadder'll come and take ye away.'" She shook her head. "Granny Haggarty didn't believe a word of that, but I'm sure *her* granny did."

He leaned forward and took the pistol out of the back of his waistband, turned it over in his hand, saw that Brianna was staring at it in wonder.

"Yeah, I know," he said. "This can't be real. None of it."

Then her body started to shake, like she was sobbing,

but there were no tears on her cheeks. He reached out wordlessly and put his arm around her shoulders.

"And I'm not even talking about the Jabberwock! I'm talking about *us*, here, you and me. Dawson McCade and Brianna Haggarty. We're sitting here waiting to ..." He paused and drew a deep breath. "I've never *killed* anybody."

"*I* have."

"That doesn't count — you didn't plan to kill that guy. It doesn't count if it was unintentional."

The wind whispered through the trees, sighed among the branches. Her velvet voice had the timbre of green leaves rustling and she spoke so softly, he wasn't sure he'd heard her.

"Yes, it does. Even if you didn't mean it, it counts. They're still dead."

He didn't respond, didn't say a word.

Chapter Forty

SHE DIDN'T KNOW why the floodgates opened then, and all the putrid water came streaming out. Though at that particular moment in time, there was certainly justification for any human response on the spectrum.

... CLINGING to sobriety with her fingertips ...

... Granny Haggarty's gone, poof, along with every other man, woman, child, cat, dog, canary and goldfish in Nowhere County ...

... there's a thing, a Jabberwock, out there, eating memories, making people forget ...

... a man comes who's a crook, except he isn't, and she shoots a paid killer with a nail gun to save the man's life ...

... they're safe, except they aren't, a second killer gone mad drives off a bridge, and she's been shot — shot! — she can feel the raw groove where blood dried in her hair ...

... now, she sits in a quiet forest, waiting for a car to—

. . .

"I WAS ALREADY a killer when I got here," she said, surprised to hear the words come out of her mouth. Once she started, it was like pearls on a string, one attached to the next, each one pulling the following one along after it.

She'd been a good mother, she told him. She *had*! The children were her first priority. Her only priority. She took good care of them, was loving and kind, played princess and had tea parties with Pooh Bear, got up for middle-of-the-night feedings with Li'l J.

All. By. Herself.

Jeff wasn't there for any of it.

He had never been there for any of it.

He had missed his namesake's birth, showed up ten hours later with blue roses — lord knows where he got them or what he had to pay for them. He had to leave the next day, of course, but he'd be there in the morning to take them home from the hospital. He wasn't, of course — schedule change, earlier flight.

That was the day the baby became Li'l J. She'd just gotten settled in, after a cab brought her and her newborn son home into the loving arms of … Elena, the nanny. No Jeff. But Elena was there with an off-the-wall-excited Pooh Bear. Jeff's famous father had been Big J, Jeff was Jeffry Dean Nicholson, Jr., but somehow dodged "junior" and went through life as plain "Jeff." They'd decided if the baby was a boy, they'd name him Jeffry Dean Nicholson III and call him Trey. But Jeff's father had called from Orlando that afternoon, wanted to know how "Li'l J" was doing and that was all it took.

They figured they'd drop Li'l J when the boy got older.

But he never got older.

"I'm not really sure what happened." She paused. "Yes, I am. I know. I'm the only one who does know what happened."

There was a nightly routine, though it varied. Some nights, Elena would give Pooh a bath while Brianna got Li'l J ready for bed. Other nights, Bri bathed Pooh, and Elena took care of Li'l J. That night, Brianna read a story to Pooh and she begged for another. And then another.

"By the time I got her in bed, Elena was laying Li'l J in his crib. She turned and put her finger to her lips as I came in and I stopped. She whispered that Li'l J had bumped his head — just a little bump, but he'd been grumpy so she'd had to rock him to sleep. I blew him butterfly kisses from the doorway. Elena was right across the hall with the baby monitor."

She stopped then. She could hear the sound of the cicadas in the bushes, but they sounded a long way off.

She continued in a voice that didn't have any emotion in it at all, like she was reading aloud the recipe for bean dip or the assembly instructions on a backyard barbecue grill.

She told Cade that every night after the children were snug in bed, under the watchful eye of the nanny ... Brianna went down into the basement to Jeff's man cave and drank. It had evolved, started with her going down there because she was lonely, she missed him and that room was the essence of all things Jeff. But there was a fully stocked bar down there, too, and after a while ...

That night was no different from any other night, except it was different from every other night Brianna had ever lived. She had to piece events together later from the murky shapes and freakshow images, an intricate puzzle where the pieces didn't fit together properly and many of the most important pieces were missing altogether.

Brianna finally came to understand that there were two realities.

What Really Happened That Night. She was the only

one who had pieced that together and understood the raw truth of it.

And What Everybody Else Thought Happened That Night.

And that was sad, so sad. Poor Devastated Famous Baseball Player was crushed. Pictures of him and his wife at the funeral service, standing weeping beside the little casket. The whole team was there for support. The sports writers wrote stories about it, about oh, how sad it was. The players wore black armbands in Li'l J's honor for the final three games in that series.

Brianna sat quiet for a time, remembering, the pain almost taking her breath away.

Cade said nothing.

When she heard herself start talking again she was surprised her voice didn't even crack.

"That night I came back upstairs from the basement ... *staggered* back upstairs ... and when I passed by Li'l J's door, I thought ... see, I hadn't got to rock him to sleep. So I tiptoed into his room, probably sounded like an ox, and picked him up out of his crib. He was sound asleep, barely wiggled. I snuggled him, because I hadn't got to when he went to bed."

She stopped again, and when she spoke, her voice did crack. Just a little thing, a simple thing.

"His hair ... so soft ... it tickled my noise ... baby shampoo is the best smell in the world."

She drew in a shaky breath, felt herself begin to slide into the abyss.

"I put him back in his crib and went to bed. Elena's screams woke me up. She was running up and down the hall, wailing. *Shrieking.* I grabbed her and her eyes were wild. She said she went into Li'l J's room and he was lying there asleep. Still. *Too* still. She reached out ... just a tiny touch, felt his hand. She said, 'He was cold! He felt like a rubber doll.'"

"We both tried ... everything. CPR ... everything. I called 911."

Brianna had only said these words one other time in her life. She'd said them to Sarge.

... a searching and fearless moral inventory ... admitted to God, to ourselves and to another human being the exact nature of our wrongs.

"It was a SIDS death. He was asleep on his tummy." Cade didn't have kids, might not know what that meant. "You can't put a little baby on its belly! It's dangerous. They could suffocate. The single most significant cause of SIDS death is stomach sleeping — did you know that?"

She didn't think she was doing a very good job of explaining it, and it was important to her that Cade get it. Otherwise, he'd never understand.

"Doctors don't know why, they think maybe the pressure on the airways on the tummy is ... or they rebreathe their exhaled air with less oxygen in it ... Elena even had a slogan — 'back to sleep.'"

Her mind began to flit around — Elena was going to make a sampler with those words ... people used to fear babies might spit up and if they were on their backs they'd ... She recognized what she was doing. Her mind was yanking back like a finger from a fire.

But she had to hold her finger in the flame.

"He'd been on his back and then rolled over onto his belly, of course he did, that's what happened, everybody understood."

The flame *burned*, the heat was unbearable.

"But here's the thing — Li'l J didn't *know how!* Elena knew he'd never done it, but she didn't say anything. Jeff was never home, he didn't know. No one knew I'd been in his room after Elena put him to bed. And so nobody figured out ..."

The flames caught her whole soul on fire then.

"... that it was *my fault*. Nobody knew his drunk mother put him down into his crib on his stomach ..."

Her soul writhed in agony.

"... and he *died*."

In a tiny, crystalline moment of clarity, Brianna saw that Cade had a strange look on his face.

"Brianna—"

That's when they both heard it. The sound of an engine. A car was coming down the road toward them.

Chapter Forty-One

CADE LEANED out around the rock, searching for the approaching vehicle, saw it barreling down the road. *Fast.* Way faster than it was possible to go on a road like that. So maybe it was a local, somebody who knew the loops and turns.

The image grew. Black. A black car, small, maybe just a two-door.

It had to be somebody from Nowhere County because the car blew across the county line like the driver's pants were on fire. Had to have been doing fifty, fifty-five miles an hour. Then it weaved, crossed to the other side of the road, veered back, swerved back across the center line again. The tires squalled, smoke rose off lengthening black strips on the asphalt, the stench of burned rubber filled the air.

The car finally veered off onto the shoulder of the road and came to a halt in the wildflowers, dust hanging in the air all around it.

It was at least three hundred feet away, maybe more.

Not two first downs. He'd have to score the whole six points.

The driver's door flew open and a man leaned out and began to vomit violently. The man's shirt was black and his white hair caught the failing light coming over the mountain top to the west.

Cade leapt to his feet. *Foot.*

He jammed the crutch under his arm, and went windmilling — crutch-foot, crutch-foot, crutch-foot — across the stretch of roadside and out onto the asphalt. Then he took off down the road. It was three times as far as he'd thought he'd have to go. It looked like a mile.

The rubber tip came off his crutch before he even made mid-field. The bare wood slipped, skidded on the smooth asphalt, and then flew out from under him altogether. He fell forward, slamming violently into the pavement on his chest, on his broken/bruised ribs, couldn't stifle a cry. Then he slid forward, ripping his shirt and pants, skinning his knees and elbows in an agony of road rash.

When he finally came to a stop, he looked up and the man was still heaving, oblivious to the world.

Fingers closed around his arm and Brianna lifted him to his knees. He reached for his crutch and saw that one side of the hand grip hung at a skewed angle, missing the screw and wing nut that held it in place. It was useless.

Brianna pulled him the rest of the way up and he got his foot under him. She threw his arm around her shoulder.

"Come on!"

"What are you—?"

"Hop!"

The two of them lurched down the road together, her

half-dragging him, Cade leaping, hopping, lunging forward as fast as he could on his one functioning leg.

The man who was leaned out of the car vomiting lifted his head and saw them. Just saw them, knew they were coming at him, but unable to do anything but reflexively spew puke onto the dirt in front of the door.

Thirty feet.

Fifteen.

The man began to move then, to lurch backward. Still vomiting violently, he struggled to shove his upper body back into the car.

Cade and Brianna were only ten feet away now and he told her to stop.

She stopped dragging him, but stood beside him with his arm around her shoulder. Fighting for balance, he swayed, had to grab Brianna's shoulder tighter when he pulled the pistol out of the waistband at his back of his pants.

He could smell the vomit now, vile and pungent, could hear the gurgling sounds the man was making as he tried desperately to stop retching.

Then the world was still.

Gagging sounds.

Vomit stink.

The gun, extraordinarily heavy.

He lifted the barrel toward the man who had finally managed to pull most of his body back into the car and sat upright. He was still heaving, though, a reflex, jerking like he had the hiccups with nothing coming out his mouth.

The man lifted his eyes to Cade's.

An image flared as bright as the old-fashioned flash-bulbs, the kind that blinded you and then bubbled up and blistered from the heat.

. . .

THE VULTURE GRABS the arm of the man on his knees in the dirt, holds it out. The Butcher brings the chainsaw down, slicing noisily through it. Blood sprays up into both their faces.

The man shrieks.

The Butcher smiles.

The Vulture's eyes sparkle.

THE IMAGE VANISHED, but those same sparkling eyes were looking at him now.

Cade extended the gun out in front of him, couldn't manage a two-hand grip but the weapon was steady, pointed square at the man's heaving chest.

He didn't pull the trigger, though, stood there pointing the gun, but didn't fire.

Chapter Forty-Two

THE CAR DIDN'T STOP where they'd thought it would!

The man had been going way faster than Brianna believed possible on that road, had flown across the county line and then tried to stop and pull over. It weaved and swerved, veered to one side of the road and then the other. The tires squalled and smoke rose behind it as the car careened off the asphalt and finally came to rest in a cloud of dust.

Brianna felt Cade leap up and move. She sat frozen. She watched him hobble desperately forward, making his way across the grass and roadside dirt like some kind of sand crab with a broken claw.

She paused for a beat, stopped to consider. But only for a beat. The decision had already been made. Reaching down into the picnic basket, Brianna yanked out the Glock 17, jumped to her feet and ran after Cade.

She had just come up behind him when he fell. He was hurling himself forward, going as fast as he could down the center of the road when he slipped, his crutch skated away sideways and he fell heavily onto the asphalt and slid forward. The .357 Magnum was still jammed down in the waistband at the back of his pants.

She reached down, grabbed his upper arm with her free hand and yanked him to his knees.

"Come on!" she cried, draping his arm around her shoulders and dragging him forward. "Hop!"

The man leaning out of the dirty black car vomiting was the man who had chased her through the woods, the man with white hair who told her he would put out her eye, that he kept his knife sharp to cut off ears and noses.

Cade was grunting with each step but didn't know it, making a groaning pain/effort cry with each leap forward.

Thud.

Thud.

Thud.

His foot pounded on the asphalt, each impact and agony he didn't feel. The man looked up, saw them coming but was too sick to do anything but look. Uncontrollable vomiting shook his body. He was struggling, though, trying to check the reflex. Somehow, he managed to lurch upward, got part of the way back into the car — still heaving.

She hauled Cade along beside her, supporting as much of his weight as she could, working desperately to keep her balance so the two of them wouldn't face-plant on the road.

Closer.

She could smell the vomit, hear the man's retching, heaving sounds.

Closer.

Off the road and into the grass.

"Stop," Cade cried and Brianna took another step or two before she came to a halt.

The man had soiled the whole front of his black tee

shirt, was sitting almost upright in the seat, still heaving, his mouth open with nothing coming out.

He lifted his head, made eye contact with Cade.

Cade lifted the gun, pointed it squarely at the man's chest and Brianna tensed for the boom of a gunshot. But she heard only her own ragged breathing, and Cade's, and the man's heaving. She looked from Cade's face to the man's and back to Cade's, whose expression was unreadable.

He was holding the gun out, his hand steady. Any second now he would pull the trigger.

But he didn't.

One beat, two.

Words appeared in her mind as if they'd been whispered in her ear.

I TOLD YOU, I'm not a killer. You might be able to put a gun to somebody's head and blow them away, but I couldn't.

BRIANNA HAD TOLD the gunman that his partner was in the trunk of his own car, that she'd shot the man with a nail gun.

She'd told the *truth*.

Cade had *lied*, told the killer that Brianna hadn't killed his partner. But the rest of what he'd said was the truth, *Cade's* truth, shocked out of the core of his being as surely as the truth had been shocked out of hers.

Cade wasn't a killer. He couldn't just murder this man in cold blood.

He began to lower the gun and then everything happened at once. It was all a blur of confused motion that she would probably never be able to put together in sequential order in her mind.

The man leaned forward, made a jerking motion, reaching down his right leg toward his foot.

She saw the camo pants move upward on his calf.

Saw the ankle holster.

Saw him pull the pistol out of the holster and raise it.

Then the sounds of gunfire filled the air, the sounds she'd been cringing back from. One shot. Or two. Or a dozen.

Bam-Bam. Bam!

Blood spurted out the side of the man's chest and his body pitched sideways in the seat.

Then the side of his head was gone.

Silence.

She smelled vomit and blood and cordite.

She looked down at the pistol in her hand and let it fall to the ground from her limp fingers. She had no idea if she'd fired it. Cade dropped his pistol, too, almost flung it away.

Then he turned to her and put his arms around her.

Chapter Forty-Three

CADE DIDN'T KNOW how long they stood there. Brianna was crying soundlessly. Or maybe she was just shaking violently. He pivoted on his foot to turn them away from the horror of carnage, pushed her gently and she walked a couple of steps as he hopped along beside her.

He wasn't completely sure what'd happened. He had balked, then the man had gone for a gun and Cade had fired. Maybe several times. He thought Brianna had fired, too, and he hadn't even known she'd brought the gun along.

It was getting dark. Shadows puddled under the trees, the pools merged, the shroud of night settled around them.

When she finally stopped trembling, Cade asked her to go get the black Lincoln, and stood balanced on one foot until she came back. She pulled up close to him so he could reach out to the car for support, got out and came to stand wordlessly beside where he leaned against the hood. Finally she gestured at the dead man.

"What are we going to do with——?"

"Give me the key."

She opened the door and got it for him, then he hopped along beside the car to the back, pushed the button on the ignition key and the trunk lid released. Leaning forward, he raised it and stood looking into the interior. It took Brianna a moment to connect.

Then she gasped and her eyes grabbed his. She squeaked out a little cry and took a step back.

"He was going to ..." She was shaking her head in denial. "He brought ..."

Cade just nodded, staring at the chainsaw lying in the trunk beside the can of gasoline.

"We can use the gasoline."

While Brianna went to retrieve his crutch, Cade looked around in the Lincoln and found a ballpoint pen he could jab into the hole in the side of the crutch and through the handle to fix it temporarily.

Brianna doused the killer's car with gasoline, wouldn't let Cade light the fire, said he was too slow. They pulled the Lincoln fifty yards away, Brianna went back, tossed a lighted match into a puddle of gasoline by the door, then ran back. It caught immediately with a distinctive *whump* sound. Then Brianna drove to the bend in the road, stopped and they watched the flames envelop the vehicle. He was surprised by how long it took before the gasoline tank exploded, and it wasn't nearly as impressive as all the car explosions he'd seen on television. It was an old car, a junker. Might have been almost out of gas.

Then Brianna drove in silence down the winding mountain roads to Granny Haggarty's house on the side of Shagbark Mountain. They'd be safe there — for the time being. When the man Santiago had dispatched to do the job *per-son-al-ly* didn't show back up on schedule Wednesday ... but that was two days from now.

"I want to take a look at that gunshot wound—" Cade

began, when they got out of the car and started toward the motorhome, but Brianna stopped him before he could continue.

"You up to ... sleeping on that cot tonight?"

It was something of a non sequitur, though he'd been planning to demand a return to Granny's house ... a lifetime ago.

"Sure, I—"

"Then ... do. I ..." She didn't seem to know where to go from there.

"Need some space. Of course, you do. You sure you don't want me to help with—" He gestured to the wound where dried blood had caked in her hair, but she waved him off dismissively.

"Tomorrow. Morning. Coffee. Then ..." She lifted her head and looked at him direct. "We have to figure out the logistics of how ..." There might have been a pause. "... I'm going to deliver you to Louisville Wednesday to check in for the hearing on the twenty-second."

The words hit Cade like a blow to the belly and he might even have sucked in a breath from the impact.

They both stood there in the twilight.

She gestured toward the motorhome. "Do you ... need anything? Are you—?"

"No, I'm fine."

How did this get awkward? He suddenly felt like he was delivering his prom date home to her front porch.

"In the morning, then ..." She wasn't doing a whole lot better with the sudden weirdness than he was. "I'm sorry, but right now I just can't—"

"I totally get it," he said with far more resolution than he felt. "We'll talk tomorrow, get it all worked out then. You ... get some rest." Which was a monumentally stupid thing to say but it had leapt out his mouth and face-planted in front of him and he just left it lying there. He turned and hobbled away from the car toward Granny Haggarty's house, managed to make it all the way through the back door without saying anything else at all.

Chapter Forty-Four

CADE KNOCKED on the motorhome door and she called, "It's open," over her shoulder as she finished making the strong black coffee they were going to need.

He smelled like the Irish Spring soap she'd gotten for him at Walmart. He looked awful, which meant he looked a whole lot better than he'd looked a few days ago. He still had two shiners, but they were fading. His split lip had healed and his face was still bruised badly, but it wasn't swollen anymore. No, his nose was still swollen a little. Maybe it had been broken after all.

As he hobbled up to the table and sat down, she saw the dark circles under his eyes that seemed actually to be worse today than they'd been before. He looked like he hadn't gotten any sleep.

He was moving better, too. Either wasn't in as much pain as before from his broken/cracked ribs or had just gotten used to how bad it hurt. Yesterday must have been torture for all his injuries, particularly the gunshot wound in his leg, but she was sure he hadn't felt it at the time. She hadn't gotten a full dose of the ouchie the gunshot grazing her scalp had created until she stood in the shower last night with the water washing the caked blood out of her hair.

She imagined she wasn't a candidate to win any blue ribbons at the county fair either, unless it was in the drowned-rat or what-the-cat-dragged-in competitions. She would, indeed, have a sizable scar on her cheek, which maybe a plastic surgeon could make not so heinous someday if she cared, but she didn't.

She wondered how the federal marshals were going to react when this battered, beaten man with a gunshot wound in his leg showed up out of nowhere to put himself in their care the night before the hearing.

How could they do that? Cade wouldn't even remember how he got the injuries!

She'd puzzled those issues around in her head as she lay down last night, certain she would be puzzling over them throughout the whole sleepless night. But then she'd opened her eyes and it was morning. It was amazing what a sleep aid total physical and psychological exhaustion could be.

She sat a cup of steaming coffee in front of him — a little milk, no sugar, the way he liked it — sat down, started to paste a fake smile on her face, then thought better of it and didn't bother.

"We have a lot of planning to do," she said. "This is not going to be easy to pull off."

"No, it's not."

"But somehow we *have* to leave me out of this whole thing — like I drop you off at the corner and drive away or something, because I can't get involved—"

"Could we not start there?"

"Okay, where would you like to start? Like maybe ...

what I do with you sitting in the front seat beside me and suddenly you don't know who—"

"Not there, either. I want to talk about ..."

He took a breath.

"About your little boy, your baby, Li'l J."

She couldn't have been more surprised or stunned if Cade had suddenly sprouted yellow feathers, tweeted zip-a-dee-doo-dah, and fluttered out of the room. So many emotions boiled up inside her she couldn't possibly sort them out to feel any of them.

So she just went with outrage.

"What in the world ...?" She found herself sputtering. "What could you possibly want to know ... why—?"

"What you said doesn't make any sense, but I don't think you know it."

He had ripped the scab off the deepest wound in her soul and now he was pouring salt into it.

"*I* don't know it? Hey, I'm the only one who *does* know." She stood up, just stood up. "Why in the world did I ever tell you—?"

"You left your little girl because you didn't think she was *safe* with you ... because you'd ... killed your baby."

Don't. Oh dear God, please don't.

She sank back down into her chair because she could no longer stand up.

"Why are you doing this?"

"You have to listen to me." He reached out and took her hand but she snatched it away.

"No I don't! I don't want to talk about ... who do you think you are, demanding that I—"

"I get it that I'm dragging you into a place you never go. A place you walled off because the pain of it would drive you crazy. I get that. I have places like that, too. But please … *please* trust me that I have to do this and you have to let me."

There was such sincerity, such intensity in his plea that she felt the resistance drain out of her. She was left empty, could hear the wind blowing through the dark, lonely caverns of her soul, making a sound like sand across stone.

She wanted to cry, but she couldn't.

"What do you want?"

"Tell me again about the night the baby died."

If it'd been an actual physical blow, it couldn't have hurt any worse.

"Why?" She was begging now.

"Just do it!"

She didn't deserve this. After all she'd done for this man, she didn't deserve to be treated like this. But just as she had seen yesterday that he couldn't be talked out of ambushing the killer, he wasn't going to leave her alone until she did what he wanted.

"I will never forgive you for this."

"Fine, don't. You said you put your little girl to bed that night and the nanny put the baby down — right?"

"What are you suggesting, that Elena put him on his belly—?"

"I'm not—"

"I watched her from the doorway."

"And then you left. You went downstairs. You … drank."

"Yeah, drank. That's what drunks do. They drink. They feel sorry for themselves. Poor, pitiful, mistreated Brianna, abandoned by her famous husband, bless her heart. I could have filled PNC Park with my pity party guests and had a Yankee-Stadium full waiting outside for tickets."

"Then you started to go to bed, you passed by the door to the baby's room, and you stopped because ..."

"I didn't get to rock him that night!"

It was an anguished cry.

"Because he was fussy, had bumped his head."

"Don't go there. The bump on the head, the doctors said it had nothing—"

"I didn't say it did. So you went into his room because you hadn't gotten to rock him to sleep."

He was shoving her down into the memories, pushing her head under the dark water.

"I picked him up and cuddled him and put him back in his crib."

"Remember the day you were getting the splinter out of my finger — you told me about the memory you had, the beautiful memory of the baby ... you asked if my mind had ever taken a snapshot, a single still frame. You can pull it up and look at it, but it's just that one frame, nothing before or after."

A light blinked on in the darkness. The glow grew brighter and brighter.

"He had a bedside lamp his father brought from some-where, the globe was the floating part of a hot air balloon, and there were puppies in the basket. It cast a sweet, golden glow on his face."

The image reformed and took her breath away.

"He was so ... beautiful."

"With eyelash shadows on his cheeks and a little bruise on his forehead that looked like ashes from Ash Wednes-day. That's what you told me, right?"

She could only nod, her mind captured by the clarity and purity of the image.

"So you leaned over and kissed the bruise ... very softly."

"I didn't want to wake him up."

She felt hot tears coursing down her face and didn't bother to wipe them away.

"That memory's from the night he died, isn't it?"

She'd never considered the when.

"I don't know ... I guess."

"The little bruise on his forehead, it *had* to be that night, didn't it? Did he bruise his forehead any other time?"

"No. I suppose ... it must have been that night." She'd never tried to place the image in time or space. It just *was*. The memory faded away slowly and was gone. "So what's your point? Why are you doing this?"

"You don't see it?"

She looked at him, uncomprehending.

"You blew butterfly kisses to him from the doorway when the nanny put him to bed, didn't go into the room. Then you came upstairs, cuddled him and put him back to bed."

"Yes! What difference does it make—?"

"How did you kiss a bruise on his forehead if you laid him down in the crib on his belly?"

His words made absolutely no sense.

"What are you talking—?"

"Brianna, you went into his room, you picked him up and cuddled him, you put him back in his crib ... and you kissed the bruise on his forehead. How could you possibly *kiss a bruise in the middle of his forehead* if he was lying on his stomach?"

"Well I ... he ..."

Her mind began to spin out of control.

"Think about it. That's impossible."

He just kept talking.

"All this time you've been blaming yourself. You were

afraid you'd hurt your little girl, too — that she wasn't safe with you. All because you think Li'l J's crib death was your fault. But it *wasn't!*"

"What are you ... how ...?"

"He rolled over onto his belly *after* you put him in his crib."

"But he'd never done that—"

"Then he *figured out how to do it that night* because you put him to bed *on his back.* You leaned over him, saw eyelash shadows on *both his cheeks*, kissed his forehead. You left. And sometime *after that* the baby rolled over ... and died."

Cade's words finally found a home in her mind. The meaning of them registered. They made sense.

Her hand flew to her mouth. She uttered a little cry.

"I ... didn't. It wasn't ..."

"It wasn't your fault."

She put her head in her hands and sobbed.

Chapter Forty-Five

CADE HAD SEEN it as soon as she told him the story, while they sat together on the cold rock in the fading light, waiting to ... kill a man. Put it together with her memory of kissing the baby's bruised forehead, figured out events couldn't have happened the way she remembered them.

He'd have told her right then, pointed out the impossibility on the spot, but then the car had come and they ... got busy doing something else. He had spent half the night trying to figure out how he was going to bring it up now. Just cold, out of nowhere — *hey, how about we talk about the night your baby died.*

It had been heartbreaking to watch, but he had to free her from the prison of her own making.

He sat quietly, watching her cry, his mind now free to tackle the second impossible conversation of the morning. He was supposed to be in Louisville tomorrow to be taken into protective custody by the U.S. Marshals Service so he could be "kept safe" overnight for his testimony Thursday before the grand jury.

It was possible they'd cancelled the proceedings after

he bailed out, but not likely. He was one of a parade of witnesses on the docket — obviously the one who could deliver the knock-out punch, but not the only game piece on the board.

He got up, got a wash cloth from the bathroom, wet it under the cold water tap and handed it to Brianna. She took it, washed her face, sniffled, and then looked up at him, made eye contact. Something was profoundly different about her. You had to be there to see the shift to catch it, had to have seen the deadness back deep in her eyes only five minutes ago to realize how bright they shone now. There was a light now shining somewhere in the depths of her soul, a candle re-lit.

That look was worth the price of admission.

"I don't know how to—" she began, but he held up his hand like a traffic cop at an intersection.

"I'll tell you the same thing you told me when I tried to thank you for letting me stay — which, oh by the way, has turned out to be one of the most monumentally stupid decisions you ever made in your life."

The edges of her mouth twitched upward in an almost-smile.

"You remember what you said?"

"Something about not singing Kumbaya."

"Then you told me to go baste a duck."

"Oh yeah, that. All right, then, how about just 'thank you'? That much, okay?"

"Okay."

Silence.

How did he get from here to …? He could think of no transition from Impossible Conversation Number One to Impossible Conversation Number Two.

She barked out a laugh with no humor in it, pushed

her chair back and stood, then seemed to lose all her momentum.

"I told Sarge, my sponsor, that coming here to my grandmother's house in the mountains would be the perfect place to stay sober. You know, no stress. Butterflies and hummingbirds and There's No Place Like Home Samplers. Peaceful. She'll never believe a word of this."

"Neither will anybody else."

"Anybody else? How am I supposed to convince *myself* I didn't make it all up once you're not here to tell me I'm not crazy?"

She sat back down, started to pick up her coffee. Didn't.

"When I haul you across the county line tomorrow, you will forget the whole thing." Her velvet voice held equal parts wonder and horror. "You won't know how you got beat up and shot." She drew a breath. "You won't remember you ever met anyone named Brianna Haggarty."

"I'm not going to forget."

"Right. You're suddenly immune to the Jabberwock? How'd you manage that?"

He tried to think how to say it, couldn't, and just spit it out.

"I'm not going to forget because I'm not leaving tomorrow."

"It won't change anything to put it off. No matter when you go, the same thing—"

"Not today. Not tomorrow. Not … well, until the storm blows it all back out again."

"What are you talking about?"

But he thought she knew, because she got very still, and her breathy voice was an octave lower.

"I can't go. Correction, I *won't* go. I refuse …"

Then he went for broke.

"I refuse to forget I ever met a woman named Brianna Haggarty. Not happening. If leaving means I forget all about you, then I'm not leaving."

"That's crazy ..."

She said nothing else.

"Unless you *want me to leave*."

"How can you stay? What, become a prisoner here, trapped, never go anywhere, never see anybody ... Swiss Family McCade or something?"

"Do you want me to leave?"

Silence.

"Answer me, Brianna. Do you want me to leave?"

The word was a whisper on a breath.

"No."

He didn't realize he'd been holding himself rigid until the tension went out of him.

"No, I don't want you to leave, but how can you stay? Unless you testify, there'll be more of *them*" — she slathered the word in loathing — "looking for Hag-gar-ty."

"Yeah, we'll definitely have to fix that flat and crank up the motorhome, find a new campsite *ASAP*." He made a sweeping gesture. "I hear there's a lot of prime real estate around here you can have for a song and sing it yourself."

"You can't *hide* forever!"

"The Jabberwock can't *last* forever!" He didn't mean to shout, but Dawson McCade believed that with all his heart and soul. "A couple thousand people go poof and vanish, and all the rest of it. There's never been anything like it ... I absolutely do not believe, *will not* believe that it's permanent. Do you believe it is?"

They'd never talked about it, not after that first day.

. . .

IT'S SOME FREAK SOMETHING ... storm, sunspot, E.T.'s buddies — something caused it to happen and I think eventually it's going to 'un-happen.' Reset.

SHE DIDN'T SAY ANYTHING. He captured her gaze with his, held on.

"*Do* you?"

She shook her head.

"It'll ... go away ... eventually. One morning, we'll just wake up and it'll be gone."

We. She said *we.*

Cade didn't do anything foolish or sappy. Didn't leap up and grab her. He just sat very still and looked at her until she smiled a little and looked away.

"I won't leave here until—"

"—until when you come back later, you won't puke your guts up?"

"Yeah, something like that."

THE END

Do you want to know ALL THE SECRETS? Like what happened to Brianna's grandmother ... and everybody else who disappeared from Nowhere County? Are you wondering what the Jabberwock is? Nowhere U.S.A. is a seven book series that will answer all of your questions and keep you racing through the pages as you read these gripping tales of ordinary people struggling to survive, pitted against something utterly unexplainable.

What To Read Next

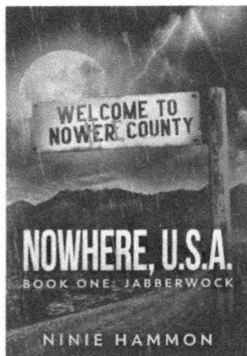

Want to find out what happened to everyone who was inside Nowhere USA when the Jabberwock stuck? Start reading the Nowhere USA series with *Book One: Jabberwock*.

Get Nowhere USA Book One: Jabberwock

A quick favor

Thank you for reading *Road To Nowhere*.

If you enjoyed this book, you please consider writing a review on your favorite bookselling site so other readers might enjoy it too. Just a couple of sentences would mean a lot to me.

Thank you!
Ninie Hammon

About the Author

Ninie Hammon (rhymes with shiny, not skinny) grew up in Muleshoe, Texas, got a BA in English and theatre from Texas Tech University and snagged a job as a newspaper reporter. She didn't know a thing about journalism, but her editor said if she could write he could teach her the rest of it and if she couldn't write the rest of it didn't matter. She hung in there for a 25-year career as a journalist. As soon as she figured out that making up the facts was a whole lot more fun than reporting them, she turned to fiction and never looked back.

Ninie now writes suspense--every flavor except pistachio: psychological suspense, inspirational suspense, suspense thrillers, paranormal suspense, suspense mysteries.

In every book she keeps this promise to her Loyal Reader: "I will tell you a story in a distinctive voice you'll always recognize, about people as ordinary as you are--people who have been slammed by something they didn't sign on for, and now they must fight for their lives. Then smack in the middle of their everyday worlds, those people encounter the unexplainable--and it's always the game-changer."

The Saved

The Unexplainable Collection

Five Days in May

Black Sunshine

The Based on True Stories Collection

Home Grown

Sudan

When Butterflies Cry

The Knowing Series

The Knowing

The Deceiving

The Reckoning

The Fault

Stand-alone Psychological Thrillers

The Memory Closet

The Last Safe Place

9 781629 551371